THE OYSTER QUAYS MURDERS

A gripping crime thriller full of twists

PAULINE ROWSON

The Solent Murder Mysteries Book 9

Originally published as *Undercurrent*

Revised edition 2022
Joffe Books, London
www.joffebooks.com

First published by Fathom in Great Britain
in 2014 as *Undercurrent*

This paperback edition was first published
in Great Britain in 2022

Cover art by Dee Dee Book Covers

ISBN: 978-1-80405-393-5

To Bob as always

AUTHOR'S NOTE

This novel is set in Portsmouth, Hampshire, on the south coast of England. Residents and visitors of Portsmouth must forgive the author for using her imagination and poetic licence in changing the names of places, streets and locations. This novel is entirely a work of fiction. The names, characters, businesses, locations and incidents portrayed in it are entirely the work of the author's imagination. Any resemblance to actual persons, living or dead, events or locations is entirely coincidental.

CHAPTER ONE

Monday

The wailing police siren sliced through the rain-washed night. Horton quickly checked the mirrors of his Harley and dropped his speed, but the police car sped past him on the motorway, heading towards Portsmouth city centre with its blue light pulsating like a homing beam for a lost alien. Swiftly he calculated the time. It had been 8 p.m. when he'd been ejected from the London School of Economics Reading Room because it was closing. And it had been just after nine thirty when he'd left the nearby pub after a meal and two Diet Cokes, which was an hour from London say. The roads were relatively traffic-free, so it must be some time between ten thirty and eleven p.m. at the latest. About right for the drunks to start rolling out of the pubs looking for trouble. It wasn't his concern. He was off duty until tomorrow morning when he'd probably return to find his desk in CID buckling under the weight of his six-day absence.

It hadn't been much of a holiday, he thought despondently, as he negotiated the roundabouts into the city centre. The one day he'd spent with his daughter had been the highlight of it, and even that had been tainted by the fact that

Catherine, his estranged wife, had promised him two, but had yet again found an excuse to whisk Emma away. God only knew when he'd get to see her again.

He pulled up at the traffic lights trying not to feel disgruntled and frustrated. He'd spent the day searching an archive file for a clue as to the identity of six men in a photograph that he believed were somehow connected with the disappearance of his mother just over thirty years ago, which hadn't helped to lighten his mood. His research had yielded nothing except stiff shoulders and bleary eyes. Maybe he was looking in the wrong place. He'd been convinced, however, that the date on the reverse of the picture, written in black ink — 13 March 1967 — was linked to the sit-in protest by students at the London School of Economics. There was nothing else significant about that day that he could find. But perhaps the date meant nothing. The photograph could have been taken anywhere. There was also nothing to indicate its location, no slogans, no buildings or scenery, just six men sitting on the floor, their arms linked around one another with a small group of people in the background. Even the clothes provided no clues as to the whereabouts and the occasion of the black and white snapshot, except that the men were wearing the fashions of the late 1960s and their haircuts and, in two cases, beards bore that out.

He squinted through the rain of his visor watching the police vehicle stop at the end of the road in front of the Hard. They'd probably been called to a fight at one of the pubs there. He should go home, but as the lights changed, he found himself swinging right instead of heading straight ahead, home to his boat. He must be mad; the days when he needed to restrain drunken fighting yobs were over, but he found himself rather relishing the prospect of getting stuck in. He needed a distraction from his maudlin thoughts, and he needed activity to release some of the frustration he felt over yet another day wasted in the search for the truth behind his mother's disappearance.

It was with a sense of disappointment then that he pulled in behind the police vehicle straddling the closed double wooden doors of the Historic Dockyard and silenced the Harley. There was no fight and no drunks; just PCs Bailey and Johnson talking to two security officers at the side gate. Removing his helmet Horton asked what was going on.

'Suspicious death, sir,' Johnson answered.

'Inside?' Horton asked, troubled as he dismounted.

The younger and stouter of the two security officers answered him. 'We think it's Dr Douglas Spalding. He gave a public lecture here tonight and he hasn't signed out.'

Horton caught the brief exchange of glances between him and his colleague, a man in his mid-fifties, lean with a haggard face and nervous manner. It didn't take a mind reader to see that someone had made a balls-up.

'He's in Number One Dock,' the younger of the two security officers continued.

That meant nothing to Horton, except that docks were very deep and sometimes full of water — or was that a basin? Perhaps they were one and the same thing. 'He's in the water?' he asked, suppressing a shiver as he visualized the body floating face down in a dark, icy pool of stagnant water. He'd wished for action but not this kind. He hadn't wanted anyone dead.

'No, it's a dry dock. The last one at the end of the Historic Dockyard before you hit Portsmouth Harbour.'

Horton wasn't sure that conjured up a better picture. 'You can confirm that he is dead?'

A worried expression crossed the security officer's round face. 'No, but I've seen enough dead men to know,' he said somewhat defensively.

'Ex-army?'

'Marines. And nobody falls from that height and gets up to tell the tale.' Horton cocked a quizzical eyebrow. The security officer added, 'The dock is nearly thirty feet deep.'

Then he was right; it was unlikely that Dr Spalding was still alive. He'd be a mess of blood and bone. But there was always a chance. 'Have you called the fire service and paramedics?'

'I've only just called you lot,' he answered somewhat tetchily.

Horton swiftly gave instructions for PC Bailey to do both. The emergency services would enter the Historic Dockyard via the gate at the naval-base entrance, which was nearer the city centre, and permanently manned with a security office. He told Bailey to stay with the police vehicle because they were already beginning to draw a crowd, despite the heavy rain, and Horton didn't fancy anyone making off with his Harley or a police car. The security officer introduced himself as Neil Gideon and the tall, older, worried-looking man as Matt Newton. As Horton gave instructions for Newton to remain at the gate with Bailey and for Johnson to accompany him and Gideon, a blue Ford drew up behind Horton's Harley and Sergeant Cantelli climbed out. His dark, lean-featured face registered surprise at seeing Horton.

'Thought you were on holiday,' he said, zapping the car locked.

'I am.'

'Yeah, can't think of anywhere I'd rather be on a wet August night in a perishing wind than looking at a dead body.'

Horton gave a brief smile, introduced Neil Gideon and refused a piece of chewing gum from the packet Cantelli offered him. Swiftly he relayed to Cantelli what Gideon had told him as they made their way down the wide and deserted thoroughfare of the Historic Dockyard. Raising his voice against the wind whistling between the ancient buildings and boathouses he said to Gideon, 'Apart from Dr Spalding not signing out, why do you think it's him?'

'Can't see who else it can be. Besides, the clothes match those Dr Spalding was wearing: navy jacket, khaki trousers.'

'You saw him earlier this evening then?'

'Yes. Before the lecture there was a drinks reception on board HMS *Victory* at seven.' Gideon jerked his head at the illuminated three-masted flagship to their right. Hard to believe that it had been in active service until 1812, which

4

included her most famous moment, the Battle of Trafalgar in 1805, thought Horton admiringly as Gideon continued. 'I walked Dr Spalding and his guests over to the National Museum of the Royal Navy at seven thirty.' He waved his torch at the long three-storey brick building on their left. 'That's where the lecture was held.'

'And it finished when?'

'Not sure of the exact time, you'll need to check that with Julie Preston, the event organizer, but she was the last to leave the museum at ten minutes past ten. I walked her to her car, which was parked in the street just before you get to HMS *Victory*, and she drove out by way of the naval-base exit at Unicorn Gate. It was only when I returned to the side gate at the Victory entrance that I checked the log and saw that one of the other guest's signatures had sprawled over two lines.'

'Who was on the gate when that happened?'

'Newton. He claimed he didn't notice it. I thought that either Spalding had slipped through without signing out—'

'Not very good security.'

'No, or that he was still on site. Newton couldn't remember seeing him but then he wasn't on duty when Dr Spalding arrived and neither was I, but as I said I walked his party across to the museum. I returned here and began to look around thinking that maybe Spalding had been taken ill. I found him in the dock.'

They drew up in front of a waist-high, yellow steel reinforced mesh fence that completely encircled the oblong gaping concrete hole. Peering down into the gloomy depths Horton saw a very old grey and white naval vessel well over 170 feet long.

'It's a Monitor,' Gideon explained. 'Built in 1915.'

That didn't mean a lot to Horton but he nodded knowingly. Quickly he surveyed the area. To his left the dock gave on to the narrow entrance into Portsmouth Harbour and beyond it he could see the lights in the tower blocks of Gosport blinking in the slanting rain. To his right and slightly behind them was HMS *Victory* and straight ahead, across the other side of the dock and an expanse of quayside, Portsmouth Harbour broadened out west towards Fareham.

The rain was barrelling off the sea.

Gideon said, 'He's lying at the port bow.'

Cantelli looked blank. Horton explained. 'The front of the ship on the left-hand side.' Which was why they couldn't see the body from where they were standing.

They headed towards it, walking around the dock. As they went Horton studied the strong yellow fence. 'Doesn't look as though it's been breached,' he said to Cantelli.

'And the gate's still intact.'

Horton noted that the bolt across the gate in the corner was secure. There was another gate in the corresponding corner of the dock with which they now drew level. That too hadn't been tampered with. Cantelli rattled it. 'Locked. Do you have a key?' he asked Gideon.

'No.'

Horton stared into the gloom. He could see why Gideon hadn't risked climbing down. With only the light of a torch the security officer might have fallen on the steep and slippery concrete steps and injured or possibly killed himself. Horton would have thought that Gideon, as a former marine, might have taken the risk, foolish though it might have been, if there was a slim chance of saving the man's life. Horton himself would have done so and he was no ex-marine. Perhaps Gideon considered it was more than his job's worth now that he was a civilian. The rain seemed colder and more vicious here, sweeping off the sea behind them. As if to echo his thoughts Cantelli stamped his feet and rammed his hands deeper into the pockets of his rain jacket. Gideon's torch picked out the recumbent figure. It was lying face down, sprawled out. Horton tensed at the grisly sight, but before he could comment the sound of vehicles approaching drew his attention and he looked up to see a fire engine followed by a yellow and green paramedic's car. Within minutes the fire fighters had the dock bathed in light and the lock on the gate had been cut.

'Fancy a trip?' one of them asked Horton.

He didn't; he hated confined spaces, and although the dock was large and there was no possibility of him being locked in, it was also very deep and the steep concrete walls would give it the illusion of being closed in. He steeled himself to keep a lid on the panic that usually accompanied his phobia. He had no choice. He wouldn't duck out of doing his job.

'Do you need me?' Gideon asked, clearly not keen himself — perhaps he also suffered from cleithrophobia.

'Not much point,' Horton answered, noting Gideon's relief. 'I doubt you'll be able to identify him from his face.' It was going to be a mess. Cantelli's increasingly active gum-chewing signalled to Horton that he was preparing himself to view the shattered and broken body, but he sensed no heightening of tension in the fireman or the paramedic. Horton knew they had their own way of dealing with this kind of thing and worse. Even before they reached the bottom it was clear to Horton that Gideon was right; the man was clearly dead. A pool of purple blood had seeped out from under the head. A bloodshot eye on the right-hand side of the face stared sightlessly up at them in a deathly grey face. Horton couldn't see the left-hand side of the face but he knew it would be a bruised and bloody mess. The body was intact though, with the right arm exposed and stretched out slightly to the side, the left arm crumpled under the body, and the legs straddled unevenly, with no bones protruding. The paramedic confirmed life extinct. Horton asked how long.

'A couple of hours, possibly less. Do you want to me check his pockets?'

That was a task Horton was only too willing to delegate. 'The ones that are exposed, yes.' He didn't want the body moved until after the police doctor had seen him and photographs had been taken.

The jacket pocket was empty, but the back trouser pocket revealed a wallet. Foolish place to keep it, thought

Horton, taking it from the paramedic. Ideal for pickpockets, but theft was clearly not a motive here. Inside he found a credit and debit card in the name of Dr Douglas Spalding, forty pounds, a driving licence and a pass for Portsmouth University. There was also a photograph of an attractive dark-haired woman of about thirty-five with two young children, a boy of about ten and a girl of about seven or eight, the same age as his own daughter, Emma. Horton's heart constricted at the memory of the day they'd spent together sailing. It had gone too quickly. He handed the picture to Cantelli, turning his thoughts to the dead man's two children who would never see their father again, thinking grimly that he hadn't even known his. Cantelli shook his head sadly, no doubt thinking of his wife, Charlotte, their five children and how they would feel if anything happened to him.

Horton thanked the paramedic and sent him on his way. His job was to help save the living, not linger over the dead. He instructed the fireman to cover the body with a tarpaulin and await further instructions. Glancing around the dock, he felt relieved that the area where they were standing was bathed in light. The dark shadows further to his right, however, seemed to be creeping closer as he glanced at them, sending his heart into overdrive and threatening to overpower him with memories of being locked in a dark, dank, decaying place in one of those God-awful children's homes. He snatched his head away and forced himself not to look up at the walls; instead, he scoured the area around the body, but couldn't see anything that looked as though it shouldn't be there, except the body, and certainly no murder weapon. Not that he thought this was homicide — or did he?

'Pushed, fell or jumped?' Cantelli said, voicing Horton's thoughts.

'If he jumped, he must have climbed onto that fence and then thrown himself off.'

'His lecture couldn't have gone that badly.'

Horton gave a brief smile. Black humour was all they often had to relieve the tension. Why would a successful man throw himself into a concrete dock? But then who knew what had been going through his mind at the time. He could have had problems of a personal, financial or professional nature, or all three. Enough to make him want to kill himself? Possibly. Strange though that he'd gone to the trouble of delivering a lecture and then committed suicide. He voiced his thoughts to Cantelli.

'Perhaps it was his swansong, his final gesture.'

'Maybe.'

'And he knew he'd be alone. No tourists at this time of night.'

Cantelli looked up and frowned. 'Could he have been thrown over?'

Horton didn't follow Cantelli's glance. It would remind him too powerfully that he was standing in a deep hole. Instead, he studied the body, frowning. 'He's well built; it would have taken some doing.'

'Maybe he was caught off guard. A powerful shove might have been enough to send him toppling over while he was peering down into the dock.'

Horton recoiled at the thought of what might have been going through the dead man's mind as he'd pitched forward. 'But why would he be peering down into the dock in the pouring rain at night?' Cantelli shrugged. Horton added, 'It looks like suicide, but we'll reserve judgement until we get more facts. Call Dr Price and the scene-of-crime officers. I'll report it to the Major Crime Team.'

'Superintendent Uckfield might be out celebrating. They've got the man who attacked that Asian shopkeeper in Southampton.'

Horton had heard on the news that the shopkeeper had died a day after the vicious assault. 'Then the celebration is well deserved. No signal,' he added, glancing at his phone.

'Me neither.'

'We'll try at the top.'

The climb was steep and the concrete wet, so they had to take their time. Horton tried to concentrate his mind on speculations about the dead man but soon found his thoughts veering back to that photograph burning a hole in his pocket. Why had it been left on his boat by a man called Edward Ballard? If he could have found Ballard, he'd have asked him, but Ballard had disappeared. In fact, he'd never existed, according to all the databases Horton had consulted. Ballard had given no indication that he knew him when Horton had gone to his aid following an alleged assault at the marina in early June, and neither had he mentioned the photograph when he'd come to thank Horton for his help. It had been only after Ballard had left that Horton had discovered it stashed under a seat cushion where the man in his mid-sixties had sat and sipped at a drink. So who was he? And why leave the photograph behind? Questions he'd asked a thousand times in the last six weeks since encountering Ballard and which he'd probably ask another thousand without getting the answers. There was, however, one small glimmer of hope, he thought, reaching the top of the dock: perhaps the professor who had pulled together the archive project on the student sit-in protest might remember seeing one of the men in another photograph, which hadn't been included in the archives. The librarian hadn't had a contact number for Professor Thurstan Madeley but Horton would be able to find that. The name struck a chord with him, but he couldn't place it.

Turning his mind back to the job he told Cantelli to ask Gideon if he'd alerted the Ministry of Defence and Navy police. 'I don't want them crashing in here with the heavy artillery thinking the Third World War's been declared.'

As Cantelli crossed to a worried-looking Gideon, Horton retrieved his phone and rang Steve Uckfield's mobile number.

'What?' bellowed Uckfield in his customary manner. Horton could hear glasses clinking and the sound of laughter and shouting in the background. Swiftly he relayed what had happened. Uckfield hesitated, and Horton knew what he was thinking: leave his nice warm jolly party to attend an incident that might not be a major crime, or stay on and send a subordinate? The answer was obvious. It was peeing down;

Uckfield was a detective superintendent. He didn't have to get wet. 'DI Dennings will be there in five minutes.'

And that was Horton's cue to leave. That great hulking oaf could get wet. It was bad enough having to put up with Dennings at the station, he didn't have to suffer the man when he was officially off duty. Horton knew his views were prejudiced because Dennings had secured the job on the Major Crime Team that Horton had wanted and which he'd been promised by Uckfield. It had been denied him because of an undercover operation where he'd been falsely accused of raping a girl. Although he'd been cleared, it had been too late to save his marriage or his career. That was hardly Dennings' fault, but it had been Dennings who had accompanied him on that fateful operation at Oyster Quays and who had come out smelling of roses while Horton's name had been smeared in the same manure that had helped Dennings to bloom. Besides, Dennings simply didn't have the mental capacity to be a good or an even mediocre detective. But that hadn't stopped Uckfield appointing him. When Horton had challenged his decision Uckfield had said he'd had no choice; the then chief constable, Uckfield's father-in-law, had ordered it. And Uckfield's ambition would always be bigger than his loyalty to old friends.

For Cantelli's sake, Horton hoped Dennings was sober. He didn't intend staying around to find out. He broke the news to Cantelli, whose opinion of Neanderthal man, as Dr Gaye Clayton, the pathologist, called Dennings, was identical to his. Cantelli grimaced before shrugging his shoulders. 'Saves me making decisions. I might even be able to go home.'

'Which is where I'm heading,' Horton replied, eyeing the rain, which if anything seemed to be heavier than when he'd arrived. 'Yeah, I know, ducking out,' he added, catching Cantelli's eye, 'but you did say I didn't need to be here.'

'Did I?' Cantelli teased. 'No, you go. I'll let you know what muscle man has to say about Dr Spalding's death in the morning.'

Horton headed for the exit with a twinge of guilt at leaving Cantelli to it, and for not doing more for the dead man. But what could he do for Douglas Spalding now? Nothing, it seemed. And it didn't need two DIs on the spot as well as a detective sergeant. He'd just reached the main gate as Dennings' car drew up. The bulky shaven headed man climbed out and eyed Horton malevolently.

'The body's straight ahead, Tony,' Horton said. 'In a dock. That's a deep concrete hole and inside it is a grey and white boat, which even you can't miss.' He didn't catch Dennings' reply, if he gave one.

Horton climbed on his Harley and headed for his yacht, thinking that in one way he'd be glad to return to work tomorrow. It would be a welcome distraction from his personal problems. But it would mean having less time to spend on the investigation into the disappearance of his mother. Maybe that was a good thing though. Perhaps he should just forget it, concentrate on getting his life back on track and on tackling Catherine over getting greater access to his daughter. As he let himself in and showered, he considered the option, but knew in his gut he couldn't let go. Not yet.

Lying on his bunk, listening to the rain drumming on the deck and waiting for sleep to come he found his thoughts wandering back to the body in the dock and the photograph of the dark-haired woman with the two children. Had Cantelli broken the news to the widow yet? Had she any idea why her husband had killed himself?

He conjured up that gaping concrete dock and the body lying in it. Something tugged at the back of his mind. What was it? Mentally he ran through what he'd seen and heard. There was something wrong, something didn't add up, but then it wouldn't yet. Maybe it never would. Suicide left a great big empty hole, bigger than any dock, and a whopping great question mark hanging over the lives of those left behind which could never be answered. It blighted their lives, much as his mother's disappearance had blighted his.

But *was* Douglas Spalding's death suicide? It had all the appearances of being so, and yet something told him otherwise. Why?

He closed his eyes and tried to think what it was that was bugging him, but it was no use. Perhaps it would come to him in his sleep. Either that or Cantelli might provide illumination in the morning. He hoped so.

CHAPTER TWO

Tuesday

'Suicide,' Cantelli said, hitting the bottom of the brown sauce bottle with the palm of his hand and splattering the contents over his bacon.

'So Dennings is a doctor now and a coroner,' Horton sneered, stabbing a sausage and conveying it to his mouth. He was hungry. He'd slept fitfully and been awake at dawn. He'd run ten miles along the seafront trying to clear his head of the nightmares that had plagued him in which his mother had turned into a laughing ugly hag like something out of Hansel and Gretel, and had ended up staring at him with sightless eyes, dead in the dock. He was also still no clearer on what had been troubling him about Spalding's body. Cantelli slapped a slice of white bread over the bacon and yawned.

Horton said, 'What time did you get home?'

'Just after three, and then I might just as well not have bothered. Couldn't sleep.' And Horton knew why.

He addressed the other man at the station canteen table. 'And what excuse have you got, DC Walters, for showing us your tonsils.'

'Sorry, Guv.' Walters quickly stifled his yawn by shovelling a fork of baked beans into his mouth. 'Late night too,' he mumbled.

'I gathered that, and it certainly wasn't working.'

'But I was on the job,' Walters said with a sly smile.

Horton eyed the fat, sloppily dressed detective constable in the crumpled pale blue shirt that stretched over a wobbling paunch and a tie that didn't quite do up around his fleshy neck. He couldn't imagine any woman fancying him, but then there was no accounting for taste. He didn't want to hear about Walters' love life; that would be enough to put him off his breakfast, lunch and dinner. Addressing Cantelli he said, 'What did Dr Price say?'

'Nothing. We got his stand in, Dr Freemantle.'

Horton didn't know him.

'Looked as though he should still be at school.'

'That's just you getting old.'

'Tell me about it!' Cantelli said vehemently. 'At least he was young, fit and sober. Price would never have managed that climb down into Number One Dock. Dennings didn't even bother.'

'Got X-ray eyes now, has he?' Horton muttered.

'No, he just waited for the fire service to hoist the body up strapped on their ladder thing and then he looked at it.'

'What about the scene-of-crime officers?' Horton asked. 'What did Phil Taylor have to say?'

'Nothing. They didn't come. Dennings told me to ring them and tell them not to bother. Too wet and not much point for a suicide.'

'What!' cried Horton incredulously. It was sloppy procedure, and the dead man and his family deserved better than this curt dismissal. He'd noticed that Dennings' car hadn't been in the station car park and neither had there been any sign of Uckfield's BMW. The doctor's opinion must have persuaded Dennings that the death wasn't suspicious, but for Horton, ending up in that dock in the dark was suspicious enough for him to have summoned the entire circus. As far as the Major Crime Team were concerned it was clearly the end of the story, but not for him and not for CID.

Cantelli added, 'I called Clarke though, and made sure we got some photos before the fire boys brought him up. Clarke's probably emailed them over by now.'

'Good. So what did Dr Freemantle have to say?' Horton mopped up his fried egg with a thick wedge of bread and butter. His arteries would have to take a chance on it.

'There was no evidence that Spalding had been stabbed, shot or strangled, although Freemantle said it was difficult to be one hundred per cent certain because of the conditions.'

'Hedging his bets?'

'Yeah, he said his job was to pronounce death and Spalding was clearly dead. Think he must have been taking lessons from Dr Price. He didn't seem to like getting wet either, just like Price. Freemantle said that the probable cause of death was severe trauma caused by the fall. And as there was no indication that the fence had been breached, Dennings concluded that Spalding had climbed onto or over it and thrown himself off the side of the dock.'

'And what did his wife say?'

Cantelli pushed away his empty plate and wrapped his hands around his mug of tea as though his fingers were cold, even though the morning was hot and sultry. The crowded canteen was stuffy despite the windows being open and the smell of sweat, probably emanating from Walters opposite him, mingled with that of fried food.

'She's a nice woman,' Cantelli said sorrowfully. 'Boy of ten, girl of eight. I saw their photographs in the living room. Poor kids.' He shook his head sadly, his fingers tightened on the mug. Taking a breath, he continued more crisply, 'She said that her husband had been looking forward to giving the lecture and there were no signs that he was depressed or ill. I asked her why she didn't go; she said that she never went to his talks. They were part of her husband's job, and he didn't need her there.'

'Or didn't want her there.' Horton said, finishing his breakfast and sitting back. His head felt a little clearer now, but the niggle that had tormented him last night about Spalding's death was still there. So far Cantelli's report hadn't provoked it into the daylight.

Cantelli said, 'I thought that perhaps she has to stay at home because of the children but her widowed father-in-law, Ronald Spalding, lives with them in an apartment in the basement. The house is one of those four-storey Victorian residences just off Southsea seafront, not far from the Canoe Lake. Mrs Spalding was more worried about how he was going to take the news of his son's death than concerned for herself.'

Walters looked up. 'Perhaps the old boy's doolally and she doesn't trust him to babysit the kids.'

'I didn't see him, so maybe he is. Mrs Spalding said she'd break the news to him. She said that her husband usually walked to work at the university unless it was raining and he walked there yesterday morning, leaving the house just after ten o'clock.'

'Nice hours for some,' mumbled Walters.

Cantelli said, 'It's the holidays; Spalding didn't need to go into the university, but Mrs Spalding said there was some paperwork he wanted to attend to. He told her he would go straight from there to his lecture, which was scheduled to start at seven o'clock with a drinks reception on board HMS *Victory*, just as Neil Gideon told us. He was going to get a taxi home. His house keys were zipped up in his inside jacket pocket along with a mobile phone but there wasn't much left of that.'

'Did he call her during the day?'

'No, and she says he didn't call his father either. They all went for a picnic in the New Forest.'

'Was it usual for him not to call her?' Horton swallowed some coffee.

'Yes. Apparently, when he was working on a research project, he would become so engrossed that he would often lose track of the time.'

'And he's currently working on some research.'

'According to Mrs Spalding he always is.'

Horton nodded. They would get Spalding's mobile telephone number and check his calls, texts and emails to see if there was a message explaining why he was ending it all, *if* he was, which Horton wasn't sure about. That uncomfortable feeling between his shoulder blades told him this was more than a suicide.

'So what was this lecture about?'

'Something to do with women serving in the Royal Navy, but more than that Mrs Spalding said she didn't know.'

And Horton couldn't see why it should have any bearing on Spalding's death. 'Did Dr Freemantle give any idea of time of death?'

'Only to say that it had probably occurred within the last two hours because there was no sign of rigor.'

Which bore out what the paramedic had said. 'Remind me what time the body was discovered?'

Cantelli reached for his notebook from the pocket of his jacket hanging on the back of his chair. Consulting it he said, 'Gideon found Dr Spalding's body at 10.35 p.m., which according to Dr Freemantle puts Spalding's death at 8.35 p.m. But Gideon says Spalding would only have just finished his lecture and must have been in the naval museum at that time, tucking into his prawn vol au vents and making polite conversation with members of the audience who had stayed for the refreshments.'

Walters belched loudly. 'Don't like that buffet food, it's neither here nor there.'

'No one's asking you to reconstruct the crime and sample it. Go on, Barney.'

'Gideon doesn't know what time Spalding left the museum — we need to check that with Julie Preston. But we can assume he left before she did, which was at ten minutes past ten, and she signed out of the naval-base gate at 10.14 p.m.' Cantelli took two pieces of paper from his pocket and spread them on the canteen table. 'This list is the one Newton gave me of those who signed out of the Victory

Gate, who left on foot or by bicycle. The other is from the security office at the naval-base entrance, Unicorn Gate, of those who left by car.'

Horton glanced down at the latter and saw Julie Preston's signature.

Cantelli continued. 'On Newton's list the last person who signed out at 9.30 p.m. is a man called Ivor Meadows and it's his signature that is sprawled over the row on which Spalding would have signed. So if Spalding left the museum after the last guest, Ivor Meadows, that puts his death between 9.30 and 10.35 p.m., when Gideon discovered the body.'

Horton considered this. 'So it seems more than likely that Spalding went immediately to the dock after leaving the museum and threw himself off.'

'He might have hung around a bit for a final fag,' Walters suggested, wiping his mouth with a paper napkin.

Cantelli replied. 'He didn't smoke. I asked Mrs Spalding.'

'Maybe he did but lied to her,' Walters answered. 'Or perhaps he needed a cigarette to steady his nerves before throwing himself into the dock.'

Horton said, 'And as SOCO haven't been down there we won't know if there are any cigarette butts lying around.'

But Cantelli was looking puzzled. 'No cigarette packet was found on the body, and I can't see Spalding flicking his fag into the dock. Surely being a naval historian, he'd have had more respect for a museum piece like that M33.'

'What's so special about it?' Walters asked.

'It's a monitor that was used for coastal bombardment. Built in 1915 it saw action at Gallipoli and was then used to help the White Russians in the White Sea in 1919.'

'Who?' asked Walters.

'The White Russians were an anti-Communist army and opponents of the Red Army,' Cantelli explained. 'They fought the Russian Civil War from 1917 until 1921. Britain was one of their supporters. I looked it up this morning,' he added at Horton's surprised glance. 'Well, I said I couldn't sleep.'

Walters looked none the wiser and Horton wasn't going to elaborate although he knew nothing about the conflict. They didn't have time for history lessons.

'What made Gideon look in Number One Dock for Spalding? It's not the sort of place you'd expect to find someone at that time of night.'

'Gideon says he was just checking everywhere around the museum and happened to shine his torch into the dock.'

Horton didn't much care for Gideon's answer, but it was probably true.

'He claims he didn't hear a cry or the sound of a body striking the concrete but then he wouldn't have done because, as we know, it was very wet and windy.'

'What time did Spalding arrive?'

'He signed in at 6 p.m. Mrs Spalding said he always liked to arrive early to give himself plenty of time to prepare for his lectures.'

Horton visualized Spalding getting ready to present his lecture, standing at the lectern, testing the microphone, shuffling his notes. Or perhaps setting up his presentation on a laptop computer. Of course! That's what had been bugging him. Swiftly he recalled the body in the dock and the area surrounding it. Where was Spalding's briefcase? Surely he must have had one. Could it be wedged under the Monitor? Or perhaps it had landed on that old ship as Spalding had fallen clasping it. He asked if Cantelli had seen one, knowing the answer must be negative otherwise he'd have mentioned it.

Cantelli confirmed this, adding, 'And I didn't think to ask Mrs Spalding whether her husband carried one. I'm taking her to the mortuary at nine thirty for a formal identification of her husband's body. I'll ask her on the way.'

Horton rose, picked up his helmet, draped his leather jacket over the same arm and, gripping his breakfast tray with his free hand, slid it into the trolley close by. Another thought struck him: perhaps Spalding hadn't had a briefcase anyway — maybe he'd simply put his presentation on a memory stick and the museum had provided a laptop to plug it into. No memory stick had been found in his possession but something so small could easily have fallen from Spalding's pocket as he'd crashed down into the dock. And that meant it could be anywhere.

Heading out of the canteen towards the CID office Horton addressed Cantelli. 'Get SOCO down to the dockyard and ask the fingerprint bureau to send someone. We might still get some prints from the fence where Spalding fell.'

Walters, waddling behind them, said, 'You think he was pushed, Guv?'

Did he? He wasn't sure but that itch between his shoulder blades continued to irritate him. 'Get some background on him. Also call the university and find out if there is anyone there that we can speak to about him.' To Cantelli he said, 'Let me have a copy of those signing-out logs. Did you get anything else on Spalding?'

'Only that he was forty-one and had been married fourteen years.'

'Happily?'

'Seems so.'

Cantelli's answer reminded Horton too painfully of his own marriage, which had been officially terminated four days ago. Only when the letter had arrived had it really sunk in that his twelve-year marriage was over and that he was once again single. Some men would have cracked open a bottle of champagne or gone out on the town. He'd gone sailing to Guernsey in search of the last known sighting of Edward Ballard. Apart from meeting up with an old friend, Inspector John Guilbert of the States of Guernsey Police, it had been a fruitless exercise. No one at the marina in St Peter Port had any idea where Ballard had gone or what he'd done while staying there. In fact, no one at St Peter Port marina even remembered him.

Leaving Cantelli and Walters to their tasks Horton crossed to his office and pushed open the door. His heart

21

sank at the state of his desk. Piled with paperwork and files, it appeared to have become the dumping ground for every investigation in the county of Hampshire. He reckoned he must have his boss DCI Lorraine Bliss's share of files too. Thankfully she was on a leadership course at Bramshill, hence his debrief in the canteen, of which she would have heartily disapproved. Tomorrow she'd be back though, no doubt spouting forth some management claptrap she'd learned on the course and making his life as difficult as possible. His view of policing was as far removed from hers as it could be for he'd never been a desk johnny, while Bliss positively cosseted hers. She'd made it clear that as soon as she could rid her team of him and Walters she would do so, but for now, government cutbacks and a promotion freeze had thwarted her ambitions to replace them. Cantelli was spared the chop because she needed some continuity, but Walters she deemed stupid and lazy, an opinion with which Horton, reluctantly, couldn't help but agree.

He threw his leather jacket and helmet on the floor and cleared a space on his desk by pushing all the files, messages and scraps of paper over to one side and, while waiting for his computer to fire up, he opened the window and let in the traffic noise and petrol fumes. There was still no sign of Uckfield's car. He wondered what he'd make of Dennings' report when he read it. Very little, he expected, because Dennings would have said very little.

Resuming his seat Horton picked up the phone and called the mortuary. Tom, the mortuary attendant, informed him that the autopsy on Douglas Spalding was scheduled for 10.30 a.m. but it wasn't Dr Clayton who was performing it. She was on holiday until tomorrow. Horton asked to be contacted as soon as they had the preliminary results. Ringing off he wondered where Gaye Clayton's holiday had taken her. He knew that she was a sailor, like him. He wouldn't mind going sailing with her.

There was a knock on his door and Cantelli entered. 'SOCO and the fingerprint officers will be at the dockyard within the next thirty minutes. Here's a copy of the signing-out logs. Walters says that Spalding is clean, no previous, not even a traffic offence. I told him not to be so disappointed. There's no one at the university offices yet. He'll try again in half an hour.'

Horton glanced up at the clock above his door; it was just on 8.30 a.m.

Cantelli continued. 'I'll be off in a moment to Mrs Spalding's. I've arranged for PC Kate Somerfield to come with me.'

'Good.' Horton eyed his laden desk.

'Sorry about that, Andy. I tried to handle what I could, but the stuff seemed to multiply quicker than rabbits.'

'And most of it is probably rubbish,' Horton said, dismissing Cantelli's apology. 'Let me know how it goes at the mortuary.' Cantelli said he would.

Horton cast a despairing glance over his desk, then at his computer. He dreaded to think how many emails he had — perhaps enough to crash the entire system, he thought hopefully. It would take days to clear this lot. He picked up a file labelled 'performance targets' and then another entitled 'telephone customer survey' and groaned. What the hell did that have to do with real policing? He should be out there trying to solve crime, not filling in pointless forms and acting as a telephone sales clerk so they could massage government figures. Bliss would disagree. But then Bliss wasn't here. And there was nothing to keep him chained to his desk. He found Clarke's email and the photographs of Spalding's body, printed them off, rose, stuffed the copies of the security logs in his pocket, picked up his leather jacket and helmet and went to ask Julie Preston what time Spalding had left the museum.

CHAPTER THREE

'It was about 9.40.' Julie Preston's concerned brown eyes studied Horton from behind her square-framed modern spectacles.

Her tanned, attractive face looked worried rather than upset, which suggested that she hadn't known Spalding that well. But then there was no reason why she should have known him. She was in her late twenties, dressed in tight-fitting navy-blue trousers and a pretty white, blue and pink flowered low-neck blouse that showed the outline of her white bra beneath it and a cleavage above it. They were sitting in her roomy, extremely untidy and cluttered office on the first floor of the naval museum that made Horton's look poky and positively tidy. In the small window behind her Horton caught a glimpse of the Gosport skyline on the other side of Portsmouth Harbour. According to her evidence that left just under an hour before Spalding's body had been found.

'Had everyone left by then?' he asked.

'Yes. The caterers left at 9.30.'

That tallied with the signing-out lists Horton had seen.

Julie Preston added, 'There was only me and Dr Spalding left. I didn't expect him to stay that long but then he had been collared by Mr Meadows and *he* didn't leave until the caterers did at 9.30.'

Again, that tied in with the signing-out log.

'I didn't think Mr Meadows was ever going to go, you know how insensitive some people are to time and hints. I tried to steer him away but eventually I had to be quite forceful and tell him we were closing. He must have bored Dr Spalding to death . . . Oh God, I didn't mean that.' She pushed a slender hand through her mahogany-highlighted and poker-straight long hair.

'What happened after Mr Meadows left?'

'We both breathed a sigh of relief.' She gave a small and sad smile as she obviously recollected the moment, before adding, 'Dr Spalding did look tired though and he was rubbing his forehead as though he had a headache, which wasn't surprising after the lecture and being pestered by Mr Meadows.'

Horton was getting a very distinct picture of Ivor Meadows. His suspicious mind wondered if there had been any friction between Meadows and Spalding that could have led to an altercation between them outside. But if it had then either the timing of them leaving the museum was wrong, or Meadows had fabricated his signing-out time on the log and Newton, the security guard, had missed it.

'You know Mr Meadows well?' he fished.

She gave a wry smile. 'He's often in the museum, telling us how we should organize the exhibits or giving the staff a history lecture, and he regularly visits the naval museum library. It's in the naval area of the dockyard just before you reach this building,' she explained.

It didn't take much for Horton to see that Meadows was a pain in the arse. 'Did Dr Spalding know him?'

'I don't know. He might have met him in the naval museum library, I guess.'

'So how well did you know Dr Spalding?'

'I didn't, not really. I obviously liaised with him over the arrangements for last night but that was all. I can't believe he could have killed himself.'

So that's what Gideon had told her. It was the logical assumption and might still be the right one.

'Perhaps I could see where the talk took place.'

'Of course.' She stood up.

As Horton followed her along the narrow corridor, he asked her about the arrangements for the previous night.

'There was a drinks reception on board HMS *Victory* from seven o'clock until seven thirty, which the caterers handled. Then Neil Gideon walked the guests over here. I met them at the entrance on the ground floor. We escorted them up to the first floor. Here.' She pushed open the door and they stepped into the wide landing with a wooden floor so ancient that it looked as though it had been lifted off one of Henry VIII's ships. 'A few people used the lift.' She indicated the glass-encased cubicle totally at odds with the historic brick building. 'The rest came up the stairs. They hung their coats up on the stand to the right of the lift and I showed them into the Princess Royal Gallery.'

As she'd been speaking, they'd crossed to a set of double doors just beyond the lift. Pushing them open Horton entered a spacious, carpeted and well-lit room, broken up by cream-coloured steel pillars. Chairs were laid out in rows, theatre style, with a wide aisle through the centre and at either side of the room. At the far end, opposite them, was a large projector screen, to its right a lectern with a microphone on it and next to that a small empty low table.

'Is this how it was set up last night?' he asked.

'Yes.'

'What equipment did Dr Spalding use?'

'The lectern and microphone, and one of our laptop computers.'

'So he didn't bring his own?'

'He might have done but he had his presentation on a memory stick, which I put into the computer.'

He asked if Spalding had been carrying a briefcase.

'Yes, a tan leather old-fashioned one. It looked very battered. Why do you ask?'

'He left carrying it?'

'Yes.'

So where was it? 'And you gave the memory stick back to him?'

'No. He must have taken it out of the computer himself.'

'Did you check?'

'Er no.' Her face flushed.

He asked her to do so now. She left the room and Horton gazed around it looking for some indication as to why, after giving his lecture here to an audience of forty-six people, Douglas Spalding had ended up dead in Number One Dock. He was none the wiser when she returned a few minutes later.

'It's not there.'

So he must have taken it. 'Tell me about the lecture?'

She shifted and ran a hand through her hair. 'It finished at eight thirty then there was ten minutes for questions and the buffet was served outside in the adjoining Woolfson Room, just behind the lift.'

That wasn't what Horton had asked but it was an easy misunderstanding. 'I meant the lecture itself.'

'Oh.' Her eyes darted away. She was clearly nervous. He was doing his best not to intimidate her, but he knew that questioning could make some people incredibly uneasy. 'It was about women in the Navy,' she said. 'I didn't hear all of it because I was in and out making sure everything was OK with the caterers. Marcus Felspur was there though; he's the naval museum's librarian. He can give you more details.'

Horton recalled seeing the name on the list. He asked to see the buffet area and followed Julie outside to where long thin tables covered with green cloths were stretched out behind a glass partition wall.

'The guests helped themselves to the buffet,' she indicated the tables, 'although the catering staff were here to assist and they served the drinks, then people milled about and spilled out onto the landing.'

'How did Dr Spalding appear to you last night when he was giving his lecture?'

'He seemed OK,' she answered uncertainly, clearly not sure what he wanted her to say. He'd noted earlier her remark about Spalding looking tired and rubbing his forehead and he was beginning to wonder if he'd been taken ill. Perhaps once outside Spalding had tried to make his way to the quayside to get some air, but instead he'd staggered against the railings of Number One Dock and had toppled over.

He said, 'What happened after everyone had left?'

'Lewis and I did a security sweep of the museum.'

'Lewis?' Horton swiftly tried to recall seeing the name on the list.

'Lewis Morden. He works for the front-of-house staff and was on duty in the CCTV control room last night until we closed.'

Horton's hopes rose. That meant they might actually have some footage of Spalding leaving. Did Cantelli know this? If he did, he would have said though. Had Gideon told Dennings about the cameras last night? Horton remembered seeing the name Morden on the signing-out log. His was the last entry for the Victory Gate, which meant he hadn't left by car.

'Can you show me the control room please?'

They descended to the ground floor where Julie pushed open a door leading into a narrow corridor, and then proceeded to knock on a door to her left before entering. Horton followed her into a small room with a bank of eight monitors, showing different areas of the naval museum, and two of the rear entrance. At the desk in front of the screens sat a large woman in her fifties who swiftly quashed Horton's hopes of a firm sighting of Dr Spalding outside the museum by telling him that none of the footage was recorded. He'd need to speak to Morden, who would be in shortly. But, Horton thought with disappointment, if Lewis Morden had been conducting his security sweep of the museum with Julie Preston, then he wouldn't have seen anything of Spalding on the CCTV cameras, and in all likelihood had probably switched them off by then.

As they left the control room, Horton asked her about the caterers.

'They parked at the rear entrance, two vans, and they brought the food up the back stairs and prepared it in the staff room, just along the corridor from my office,' she informed him.

Horton had glimpsed it earlier. He asked to be shown the rear entrance and Julie went ahead of him a short distance along the corridor where she pushed open one of two big white wooden doors. Horton stepped outside and surveyed the narrow road. To his left it ran between the museum and a two-storey red-brick building whose arched windows had been bricked up long ago for a reason he didn't know and didn't need to know. Opposite him was a bike shed with a plastic corrugated roof and three cycles, then another building to his right, this time single storey without windows. The road led towards Number One Dock, which he couldn't see from where they were standing because it was situated further to the right of a brick building, which faced onto the end of the short road. To the left of this Horton could see the top of a pale grey crane and part of a naval ship moored up on the dockside.

Julie said, 'The caterers unloaded the drinks and food from here and entered via the back door and stairs further along to our left.'

Horton could see them. 'You let them in?'

'Yes,' she answered, now looking very concerned about his line of questioning.

'We have to check everything,' he reassured her with a smile.

She returned it, but hesitantly. Turning back inside, Horton said, 'This security sweep of the museum — what does it involve?'

'There's a set procedure: we start at the top in the attics where various artefacts we haven't got space to exhibit are stored. Would you like to see it?'

Horton said he would, though he wasn't sure how it would help him discover what had happened to Dr Spalding.

He followed her through the museum shop and up two flights of stairs, admiring her figure and the sway of her hips in those tight-fitting trousers as he went, a pleasant distraction from his thoughts of the mangled body he'd seen in the dock last night.

At the top she turned left and pressed a switch on the wall. The room with its low sloping ceiling became flooded with light and revealed a wealth of naval artefacts: ship memorabilia, lifebelts, ancient rifles, a ship's bell, a model ship in a glass case — it seemed endless.

'We check that no one's here then I move across the landing to the other attic.'

He followed her. More ships in glass cases and here she told him was stored Captain Scott's skis, as well as fabric and jewellery from Lady Hamilton's dress.

'Valuable?' he asked.

'I guess so. There's a market for everything, isn't there?'

She was right about that. As he followed her down the stairs her mobile phone rang and, snatching it up with a worried frown, she said to Horton, 'It's my boss, David Kalmore.'

Horton left her to break the bad news to him and went in search of Lewis Morden. He found him in the museum shop. In his mid-thirties, he was what the medical profession would class as obese, though Horton doubted Morden thought of himself as that. The loose-fitting black museum T-shirt did little to disguise the huge paunch or the fat that hung around the top of his thighs. His face was clean shaven and podgy with no definable chin. Horton asked if he could have a word and they stepped outside. The white SOCO van was parked on the far side of Number One Dock and behind it a blue car. Horton could see two fingerprint officers working on the railings but there was no sign of Taylor or his colleague Beth Tremaine, which meant they were in the dock.

Morden lit up a cigarette and drew heavily on it. 'So it's true that Dr Spalding's dead,' he said, exhaling, his cockily confident blue eyes widening in his bland chubby face.

'Did you see him leaving the museum on one of the monitors?'

'Yes. It was about 9.40. Julie let him out of the front entrance and then came to tell me everyone had left. I shut down the monitors and joined her in a sweep of the museum.'

'And you left when?'

'Just before Julie, must have been about ten o'clock.'

'You signed out at the Victory Gate.'

'Yes. I come to work on my bicycle. I only live ten minutes away in Southsea.'

At least he got some exercise, Horton thought, though not nearly enough. 'So you left the museum by the rear entrance?' That was where Horton had seen the plastic-roofed bike shed.

'Yes.'

'In which direction did you cycle?'

Morden looked bewildered for a moment before cottoning on to Horton's meaning. Inhaling, he said, 'Not towards Number One Dock.' He nodded in its direction and, following his glance, Horton saw Neil Gideon heading towards it in the company of a worried, smartly dressed woman in her early forties. He was surprised to see Gideon still on duty.

Morden, letting the smoke trickle out of his nose, added, 'I went the opposite way, came out just at the end of the museum building, turned into the main drag and up to Victory Gate.'

Shame, thought Horton. 'Did you see or hear anything that struck you then or now that was unusual, or different?'

'No, but I didn't hang around because of the rain.'

It was the answer Horton had expected. He saw Gideon was gesturing towards him. The woman beside him followed his gesture and looked anxiously at her watch. Horton could guess the reason for her concern. He had little idea of the time, but he knew that the dockyard opened to the public at ten a.m. He had just a few more questions to put to Morden.

'When Dr Spalding left, was he carrying anything?'

'Only a briefcase.'

31

So that seemed definite. 'Did you see him while he was giving his lecture?'

'In the Princess Royal Gallery, yes.'

'How did he seem?'

'OK.' Morden exhaled and stubbed out his cigarette with his foot then bent down to retrieve the stub.

'And you were in the control room all evening?'

'Yes, from seven o'clock.'

'You didn't leave to go to the toilet?'

'No.'

Horton eyed him carefully, not sure whether he believed that, but Morden held his gaze and didn't appear to be lying. Even if he had popped out to relieve himself, Horton couldn't see that it mattered anyway with the audience ensconced in the Princess Royal Gallery.

'Are you always in the control room?'

'No. I generally work in the shop and occasionally take a party around the museum, but I usually volunteer to do the control room when there's an evening function because it gives me a bit of overtime, and with a wife and three kids to support I need all the money I can get.'

Horton thought of Spalding's two children.

Morden said, 'Is it true he threw himself into the dock?'

Horton made no reply but thanked Morden and headed for the SOCO van, grateful that at least the storm of the previous night had passed, leaving behind an overcast humid day with little wind. It would have taken Spalding less than two minutes to reach the place where he'd fallen.

A haggard looking Gideon swiftly introduced the woman with him as Karen James, the Communications Manager for the Historic Dockyard. 'Will we have to close any attractions?' she asked Horton anxiously.

'No, that won't be necessary.' Spalding hadn't been inside any of them except for the *Victory* and the museum and his briefcase hadn't been left there. It had to be either in the dock, or the surrounding area. But another thought suddenly occurred to Horton, which fitted with his earlier theory of Spalding having been taken ill and trying to get some air by heading for the quayside. Could Spalding have dropped the briefcase into the sea before staggering back here? He'd grabbed the railing around the dock to steady himself but had doubled over and fallen in.

'We hope to be finished here by the time you open,' he said.

She looked understandably relieved. 'Do the press know?'

'We haven't informed them, Ms James, but they sometimes have a way of getting hold of this sort of information.'

'Then I'd better prepare a statement. It would help if I could have a brief comment from you, Inspector.'

He gave her one saying that the deceased was Dr Douglas Spalding and they were currently investigating the circumstances surrounding his death. Let the media ferret out more if they were so inclined, and he knew they would be. He hoped he'd be gone by the time they arrived, but he'd call Cantelli to tell him to warn Mrs Spalding that the press might be on to her.

As Karen James hurried off, Horton turned to Gideon. 'Julie Preston says that Dr Spalding had a briefcase with him. Did you see him carrying one when you walked him over from HMS *Victory* to the museum?'

'No. But he'd probably left it in the Princess Royal Gallery earlier.' Gideon dashed a puzzled glance at the dock. 'I didn't see a briefcase down there by the body.'

Neither had Horton. He said, 'Could your officers make a search of the dock, this area and around the outside of the museum? Oh, and we need to check the deck of the Monitor in case it landed there. Also, if there is any sign of a computer memory stick.'

'I'll get on to it now.'

Horton turned to the fingerprinting officers. He asked if they'd got any identifiable traceable prints. Not really was the answer, as he'd expected. He peered down into the dock and saw two white-suited figures at work close to the bow of

33

the Monitor. He surveyed the area and the steep stone steps. There was no sign of a briefcase, and neither could he see one on the deck of the old Monitor.

One of the white-suited figures looked up. Taylor, seeing Horton, shook his head. Horton guessed there would be nothing to find except blood, skin and traces of bone fragments, and obviously no sign of a small computer memory stick. His phone rang. It was Cantelli.

'How did it go?'

'As you'd expect,' Cantelli said solemnly, his voice tinged with sadness. 'Mrs Spalding identified her husband's body, though there wasn't really any doubt it was him. Tom had done his best to make the face look half decent. Ronald Spalding was very distraught. I thought he was going to keel over. While he stepped outside to get a breath of air, she told me that Douglas was an only child and that Ronald lost his wife five years ago. He worshipped the ground his son walked on. Neither of them could think of any reason why Spalding would commit suicide, in fact Ronald was most adamant that his son would never consider it. He was very angry that I'd even suggested it. And Mrs Spalding said her husband was in very good health. Their GP is Dr Deacon, Southsea Medical Centre, and Mrs Spalding said she'd ask him to give us his full cooperation.'

'And the briefcase?'

'Tan leather, very well worn, like an old-fashioned school master's, and he left the house carrying it. She said he took his laptop computer with him.'

Horton relayed his theory about the missing briefcase possibly ending up in the sea and what Julie Preston had told him about Spalding looking as though he had a headache. 'It's looking more like an accidental death brought on by an illness. He could have suffered a heart attack, aneurysm or stroke.'

'Want me to check with the doctor?'

'No, I'll do that. See what Walters has got in the way of background and whether he's had any joy contacting anyone at the university.'

'Mrs Spalding said her husband's boss is a Dr Sandra Menchip. She might be away as it's the holidays, but I'll see if we can track her down. I've got Spalding's mobile phone number. Do you want to apply to access his account?'

Horton did. He rang off and checked the time. It was five minutes past ten and ahead he could see the first trickle of tourists beginning to drift in. He hailed Gideon who had emerged from behind the naval museum with a shake of his head.

'Nothing so far.'

'Call me after you've finished searching.' Horton relayed his number. 'Is Matt Newton still on duty?'

'No. He went home hours ago. I can give you his address if you'd like it.'

Horton said he would. He followed Gideon to the security office situated halfway down the main thorough-fare where the security officer jotted down Newton's address. Handing the piece of paper to Horton he said, 'His wife's very ill — cancer.'

'OK, but we'll still need to interview him.'

'He'll be on duty tonight and so will I if you need anything more. Otherwise, you can reach me at home or on my mobile.' Gideon gave his address which was, like Newton's, in the north of the city.

Horton asked for the full contact details of all the guests and the caterers. Gideon extracted some papers from a file and ran them through the photocopier. Handing them over he said, 'We did a security check on all of them before the lecture as a matter of procedure. Nothing showed up and the caterers have been security cleared at a higher level, being regular visitors.'

Horton took his leave, checked the details of one address, then tucking the papers in his pocket headed for Ivor Meadows' apartment.

CHAPTER FOUR

'How did he die?' the little barrel of a man in his mid-sixties tossed over his shoulder as he led Horton through the small entrance hall of the fifth-floor flat in Old Portsmouth and into a spacious lounge. It had more navy memorabilia in it than Horton had seen in the naval museum, including in the attic rooms. Scores of photographs also covered the ochre-painted walls and judging by their composition it didn't need three guesses to know what Ivor Meadows had once done for a living. Clearly the Navy had been this man's life, and it was equally clear that he was reluctant to let go of it. This room had all the hallmarks of a shrine.

Horton gave his stock answer. 'It's too early to say. We're—'

'Of course,' Meadows interrupted. 'You have to wait for the post-mortem. And you can't give out that kind of information even if you knew it.'

Horton caught the smug gleam in the grey eyes that studied him. He had expected someone younger, though nothing in Julie Preston's remarks had hinted at that. 'We're trying to piece together the last moments leading up to Dr Spalding's death and I understand that you talked to him for some time last night.'

'I did. We had a most interesting conversation.' Meadows waved him into one of the three armchairs in the room.

Had Dr Spalding thought so? 'About?'

'The Royal Navy, of course,' Meadows announced promptly and proudly, easing his squat body into the seat opposite Horton. 'Joined as a boy sailor at seventeen. Could have retired with my pension at thirty-nine but I stayed on until I was fifty-five and then was asked to stay on as a security consultant until I was sixty. I was glad to. Only retired four years ago.'

And had never let go of the past, thought Horton, wondering if Meadows had really been asked to stay on until sixty. He found that hard to believe. Perhaps it was what he had hoped for and in his imagination, he had been attached to the navy, while in reality he'd been working for a private security company. Doing what? Horton wasn't going to ask. It wasn't relevant, and besides, Meadows was in full flow.

'I was Master at Arms, Warrant Officer, in charge of discipline and investigating crime when called upon to do so, like you. Liaised with you lot many times.' Meadows puffed out his chest. 'I did consider joining the police when I was thirty-nine, but it was not long after the Falklands conflict and we'd proved to the government we were still needed. We still are now, but this short-sighted bunch are no better than the last lot; they wouldn't see a conflict brewing if it was shoved under their noses. They'll call on us again, you'll see; there'll be another Falklands, Iraq, Gibraltar and when they need us, they'll have no ships and no men to respond.'

'If you could tell me—'

'I've worked through the Cold War, the Falklands, the Gulf War and the Kosovo conflict, and on several high-level investigations with Special Branch and others in British Intelligence,' he said conspiratorially and self-importantly. 'Can't speak about that, of course. Official Secrets Act.'

But Horton had the feeling that he was about to hear Meadows' service history from the moment he joined until he retired. No wonder Spalding had looked as though he'd had a headache. He'd only been listening to Meadows for five minutes and that was enough to bring on a migraine. Trying to be charitable, however, Horton told himself that Meadows was probably lonely — there seemed to be no evidence of a Mrs Meadows — but that didn't mean he had to suffer his reminiscences. Before the silver-haired man could launch on his trip down Memory Lane, Horton quickly said, 'Dr Spalding's lecture—'

'About the Women's Royal Navy. I told him what my views on that subject were after the lecture. I've seen what they do at first hand. Women were first allowed to serve on surface ships in 1990 and I saw their disruptive influence on the men. They're distracting, they cause unnecessary rivalry and jealousy, they're often manipulative and they use their sex to get what they want.'

Blimey, no wonder there wasn't a Mrs Meadows — she probably took off years ago. For a moment Horton had the desire to interview Meadows in front of DCI Bliss. He'd love to see her reaction. He also wondered what Spalding had made of Meadows' views. His phone vibrated in his pocket. He suspected it was Gideon calling him.

'Being at sea is no place for women,' Meadows declared with authority. 'Of course, I don't deny that women have a role to play in the services.'

'That's generous of you,' Horton said politely, knowing Meadows would miss the irony.

'They're good at the admin stuff,' Meadows acquiesced, 'but when it comes down to the rough and dangerous work, and the technical stuff, it has to be the men.'

Horton didn't waste his breath or energy highlighting the dangerous roles many women had undertaken in conflicts down the ages, and still did, or their technical capabilities; he recognized a bigot and chauvinist when he met one. Still, Meadows didn't have the monopoly on that. He wondered if Julie Preston had overheard any of the conversation. But even if she had she wouldn't have argued with him — not because she couldn't but because Meadows was a guest at the lecture, and it was best to smile politely and then wave him on his way. And that was probably what Horton should do now, but Meadows was still wittering on.

'Oh, Spalding said he'd been in the Navy, and he had, but not the real Navy,' Meadows dismissed with a snort.

'You mean he was in the Merchant Navy?'

'No, of course not. Dr Spalding got himself a degree at the Royal Naval Engineering College in 1994 and left the Navy in 2000. I doubt he ever went to sea.'

Had Meadows got Spalding's background from the man himself or had he checked naval records? Perhaps Walters had already ferreted out this information, not that it threw any light on his death.

'And I'm sorry to say his lecture was interesting but lightweight,' Meadows claimed dismissively.

'An hour isn't very long to go into much detail,' Horton suggested.

'I expected more, although I suppose he had to make it popular for the audience.' And by the sneer in Meadows' voice, he clearly considered himself above the other guests there.

Before Meadows could continue spouting his views Horton hastily broke in. 'Can you confirm what time you left last night, sir?'

'It'll be on the security log,' he replied abruptly before smiling knowingly. 'But I can see that you're testing my evidence. I'd do the same in your position. Now let me be precise, Inspector.' He steepled his fat fingers together and sat back in his chair. 'I said good night to Dr Spalding at 9.27 and was shown out by that young girl who'd been organizing the event at 9.30. I checked my watch. There was no one around. It was raining and blowing a gale. I hurried down the main drag to the gate where I signed out at 9.32. The security officer's mobile phone rang, while I was signing, and he turned away to answer it.' Which explained why Newton hadn't noticed Meadows' signature sprawling over two rows, thought Horton. Had Meadows done that deliberately? But why should he?

Meadows was saying, 'I then walked briskly home. I arrived here at 9.55.'

'You live alone?'

'Yes. So there's no one to corroborate that. But I can assure you I didn't kill Dr Spalding,' he said cockily and half-jokingly.

'I didn't say that he had been *killed*,' Horton re-joined sharply. But Meadows didn't take offence; he was too thick-skinned for that.

Leaning back in his seat and crossing his fat little arms over his pot belly he said, smiling smugly, 'No, but there must be something suspect about his death otherwise you wouldn't be here, Inspector. And I can't believe Spalding committed suicide. I would have noticed that something was troubling him.'

Horton very much doubted that. Meadows wouldn't have noticed anything short of Spalding collapsing in front of him. He was one of life's talkers, or pontificators, rather than an observer.

Meadows said, 'I'm presuming everyone checked out.'

'Did anything untoward or unusual happen during the evening, anything you felt perhaps a little strange? Was there any bad feeling, awkward questions, anyone causing a fuss?'

'No. It was all good-natured and Spalding seemed to be in good spirits. Bit excitable though, which I found surprising for an academic, but I suppose that's why the public liked his lectures.'

Horton noted that Meadows had slipped into using Spalding's surname, dropping his form of address. And clearly Meadows considered 'excitable' to be a negative quality. Horton wondered if 'animated' might have been a better description though he had nothing to confirm that Dr Spalding had been that.

'You've attended his lectures before?'

'Once. In May. But I've talked to him often in the library. I'm researching for a book I'm writing on crime and punishment in the Royal Navy in the twentieth century,'

Meadows proudly declared, waving an arm in the vague direction of the computer on a desk close to a door which Horton guessed led into the kitchen. 'There are over twenty thousand manuscripts held at the museum, including those of the Admiralty Library Manuscript Collection. My research has taken me—'

'What was Dr Spalding researching?'

'He said it was something to do with the Navy and prostitution.'

'You didn't believe him.'

Meadows sniffed. 'He got very touchy when I enquired about his source material. I told him his research might tie in with mine and that we could cooperate on it, but he dismissed the idea.'

I bet he did. Horton could just imagine an academic's response to that request and Meadows was one of those people on whom politeness was wasted. Spalding would have needed to be blunt.

Leaning forward Meadows said in a conspiratorial tone, 'If you ask me, I think he was looking into the death of Buster Crabb, the diver killed by the Russians just outside Portsmouth Harbour in 1956. Of course, the Navy said Crabb was taking part in trials of underwater apparatus, but we all know he was laying a mine on that Russian warship anchored off Stokes Bay, which was carrying the future Soviet president, Nikita Khrushchev.'

Horton knew the story well, and the number of rumours that the headless and handless corpse found in the harbour had inspired over the years. Crabb's life and exploits were even said to be partly the inspiration behind Ian Fleming's James Bond novels. Horton had no idea what had made Meadows think that Spalding was researching Crabb's mysterious death, but he didn't think there was any truth in it. And if Spalding had hinted at it then he'd probably done so in an attempt to get Meadows off his back.

'So apart from Dr Spalding being "excitable", did you notice anything else about his manner?'

'He didn't drink, if that's what you mean. Well certainly not alcohol, so he wasn't drunk. He stuck to the orange juice at the reception on HMS *Victory* and then water at the buffet, knocking it back a bit too.'

'Did he talk to any one person more than another?' Apart from you, Horton added to himself.

'Only one of the waitresses, long legs, black girl. I think she was one of his students. They seemed to know one another.' Interesting, thought Horton.

'Apart from that,' Meadows added, 'Spalding circulated amongst the audience, many my age, a few younger, a pretty mixed bag, though mostly men.'

'Anyone you know?'

'Only Marcus Felspur, the librarian at the naval museum. He left just before me, about 9.20. Where was Spalding's body found?'

Horton felt reluctant to tell him, not because it was confidential — far from it; it would probably be emblazoned over tomorrow's newspaper — but because he didn't care for the man. That aside, he had a job to do and he saw no need to keep the information from Meadows out of spite. Besides, his reaction might be interesting. 'In Number One Dock.'

Meadows seemed to reel back a little at the news. His little eyes widened. 'Where the M33 is. How could he have fallen down there? The area's fenced off.'

'You know it then?'

'Of course I do,' Meadows said dismissively, then his eyes narrowed as he considered this new piece of information. 'If he wasn't killed, and it can't have been suicide, then I think you'll find he died of a heart attack, Inspector. Must have been taken ill the moment he stepped outside the museum, staggered about, lost his way and went over into Number One Dock, although he must have been leaning some way over that railing, unless one of the gates wasn't properly secured.'

It was the same theory that Horton had considered earlier, and it now seemed more likely. He didn't think

Meadows could tell him anything more whereas Spalding's GP might be able to. Horton managed to extricate himself before Meadows could give him a guided tour of the Navy through the ages as witnessed in his numerous photographs. Outside he checked his phone and found a message from Neil Gideon saying that there was no sign of Spalding's briefcase, or any memory stick, and that he had gone home if Horton needed him further. Then it had to be in the sea. Horton called the marine unit mobile number and while he waited for it to be answered he wondered what Meadows would do next. Probably rush off to the Historic Dockyard to offer his expertise to the security officers. Gideon had had a lucky escape.

When Sergeant Elkins came on the line Horton told him what had occurred and asked him to be on the alert in case he came across a floating tan-coloured leather briefcase or it got washed up along the coast; although, the chances of that happening this side of the decade could be very remote. The tide could take it anywhere, and even if someone found it, it could be months, years later and they wouldn't realize the significance of it. Also, the laptop computer and anything else inside it would be pulp, damaged irrevocably. Elkins agreed that the chances of finding it were minimal. Perhaps that was why Spalding had ditched it in the sea, thought Horton, heading for the medical surgery only five minutes away. If he'd committed suicide then the briefcase could contain some incriminating evidence that had caused him to take such drastic action and that opened up a different line of enquiry.

He had to wait several minutes in a busy surgery with what seemed an unusually high proportion of people suffering from coughs and colds before being shown into Dr Deacon's modern consulting room. Deacon, in his mid-forties, casually but smartly dressed, gestured Horton into the seat facing him, saying that Mrs Spalding had telephoned and he was calling round to see her and her father-in-law, also his patient, as soon as surgery finished. The blue-grey eyes that studied Horton were both shrewd and sympathetic. Athletically built, Horton conjectured he was a runner and, judging by the strength of his arms, possibly a tennis player. He was too bronzed to be a squash player unless he'd just returned from holidaying abroad. The British summer hadn't been good enough to cultivate that kind of tan, especially for a GP who spent most of his time in the surgery.

'I won't keep you long,' Horton said, and indeed he'd be glad to get out of the germ-infested place. Doctors might build a resistance to them, but not policemen. Should have sent Walters. 'I need to know if Dr Spalding consulted you recently.'

Horton settled uneasily on the patient's chair. Doctors always made him feel uncomfortable. He didn't trust them, much as he didn't trust estate agents and car salesmen. But then being a copper, he didn't trust many people at all. A drawback of the job.

Deacon called up his computer screen. 'He did, six weeks ago, on the twenty-sixth of June, but it wasn't for anything significant. He was flying to the States the following week and needed something to help him. He was a terrified flyer, anxiety attacks, so I prescribed him a travel sickness medication and some antidepressants.'

'What type?' Horton asked with heightened interest.

'A mild relaxant, not enough to overdose on if that's what you're thinking.'

'Even if he took them all at once?'

'They would have made him drowsy, but that's all.'

'And if he'd taken them with alcohol?' But according to Meadows, Spalding had only drunk orange juice and water, although a lot of both. Had his drinks been laced with alcohol from his own supply, or perhaps given to him at his request by this black girl that Meadows had told him about? Julie Preston hadn't mentioned smelling alcohol on Spalding's breath though. Perhaps she didn't think anything of it or had been too nervous to mention it. But Meadows would have noticed it and commented on it.

44

Deacon said, 'He would have had to drink a copious amount.'

The autopsy would confirm if he had, but Horton thought it was unlikely based on the evidence he had obtained so far. He asked when Spalding had last been prescribed antidepressants and travel sickness pills.

Deacon consulted his computer. 'February last year.'

That was a long time to hoard drugs if he'd been contemplating suicide. 'Was his trip to the States a holiday or business?'

'Business. He told me he was to be a guest lecturer at a series of seminars at the summer school at Franklin Pierce University, New Hampshire. I remember it because my wife and I spent some time travelling around New Hampshire last year.' Deacon sat back and eyed Horton steadily and shrewdly. Horton had the feeling Deacon was a master at choosing a countenance to suit both patient and circumstance, a bit like coppers he thought. 'Douglas Spalding never consulted me for depression and there's no history of it on his record if that helps.'

But Horton knew that many people suffering from depression were often too afraid or too ashamed to admit it and didn't always consult a doctor. He hadn't when Catherine had thrown him out; instead, he'd sought relief in the bottle and refuge at sea, hoping that one or both would end his pain. It had been the sea and a particularly violent storm that had almost killed him, which had made him realize he didn't want to die but that he had to fight to clear his name of those rape charges. Had a similar thing happened to Spalding in that his wife had been threatening to leave him? But Cantelli would have noticed the tension.

Deacon was saying, 'Spalding was a very fit and healthy man. No signs of heart disease or high blood pressure, but that doesn't mean he couldn't have suffered a sudden attack just that he never came to me complaining of any symptoms.'

'Did he ever consult you about headaches?' asked Horton, thinking of Julie Preston's description of Spalding at the end of the lecture after he'd been talking to Meadows.

'No.'

So nothing specifically pointing to ill health. He asked, 'What was your impression of Douglas Spalding's personality?'

'From the rare occasions he consulted me I'd say he was confident and intelligent, an extrovert.'

'And his wife?'

'She is still my patient,' Deacon said a little stiffly.

'I just wondered if there could have been marital difficulties.'

'Not that I'm aware of. They seemed a happily married couple.'

'And the children? Are there any medical conditions that could have caused the parents anguish?' Horton obscurely probed.

'None,' Deacon replied firmly.

Horton guessed he'd read between the lines. He'd considered child abuse and the threat of being exposed could have driven Spalding to suicide.

Deacon glanced at his watch. Horton took the hint. Full medical records would be sent over to the pathologist anyway. And Deacon would probably be called to give evidence at the inquest.

Horton returned to the station mulling over what he'd learned. He still wasn't sure if they were looking at suicide or an accidental death caused by a sudden illness. It didn't appear to be homicide and yet Horton still felt uneasy. The sooner he had the preliminary results from the autopsy the better. He found both Cantelli and Walters in CID and gave them an update after dumping his gear in his office and trying not to look at his desk.

'Dr Sandra Menchip isn't back from her holiday until later today, but I managed to speak to a couple of people at the university who knew Dr Spalding,' Cantelli said. 'Suicide seems to be out of the question as far as they're concerned. And by all accounts he seemed in good health. I left a message on Dr Menchip's answer machine to contact me as soon as possible.'

'See if you can track down this long-legged black beauty that Spalding seemed to know.'

'Sounds promising.'

'You're a married man,' Horton replied, knowing that Cantelli would never be tempted away from the voluptuous Charlotte. He gave Cantelli the list of names and addresses that Gideon had provided. 'She works for the caterers.'

'Do you want me to check with Matt Newton — what time Meadows left the dockyard?'

Horton hesitated. He didn't see any reason for Meadows to have falsified the time of leaving or why he should have anything to do with Spalding's death, and he recalled that Gideon had told him Newton's wife was very ill, which obviously accounted for the haggard expression he'd seen on Newton's features last night. 'Leave it for now. He's probably asleep. We can check it after the autopsy results if we need to and when he's on duty tonight.' To Walters Horton said, 'What have you managed to get on Spalding?'

Walters put aside his packet of crisps and swallowed before saying, 'He's got a big mortgage, credit card debt, car finance and a few store cards which amount to over a quarter of a million pounds. Both kids go to private school and Jacqueline Spalding doesn't work.'

Cantelli whistled softly. 'He must be earning well.'

Horton said, 'Perhaps she's got an income.' He'd like to know how much was going into the Spalding's household. Could Spalding have killed himself because he was in debt? 'And?'

'He's been at Portsmouth University since April as a visiting lecturer, and before that he was at the Maritime Historical Studies Centre at the University of Hull for three years.'

'And that's as far as you've got?'

'There's only been me here, Guv, and I've had to answer the phones.' As though on cue one started ringing. Walters eyed him as though to say, 'see what I mean'.

'Well answer it,' Horton said crisply before heading for his office. He'd write up his reports and then try and make a dent in his paperwork. He wondered if he should update Uckfield; he certainly wasn't going to waste his breath reporting to Dennings. But peering out of the window he saw that Uckfield's car had gone. Perhaps he was meeting someone for lunch? Horton wondered who she was. He had no idea who Uckfield's latest conquest was but there was bound to be one. And as neither Uckfield nor Dennings had come pounding on his door asking to know what was happening about Spalding's death Horton decided not to bother informing anyone in the Major Crime Team. There was little more he could do on the Spalding investigation anyway except wait on the results of the autopsy and for the second time that day he wished Dr Clayton had been performing it. By now she would have given him some indication of how Spalding had died. Or he'd have headed for the mortuary to ask her for her views.

He finished his reports and was about to start on the paperwork that had accrued while he'd been away when his mobile phone rang. It was a number he didn't instantly recognize. Then it registered that it was Carl Ashton. He hadn't heard from him in over a year. Not since before his suspension when Ashton had dropped him quicker than hot coal. Before then Horton had often crewed for him on one of his company's corporate yachts.

'I need your help,' Ashton announced abruptly.

He might have guessed. Ashton was probably short of skippers to help for the forthcoming Cowes Week.

'I'm working—'

'It's nothing to do with sailing,' Ashton replied impatiently. 'I can't discuss it over the phone. I'll buy you lunch.'

'I've got a very heavy workload.'

'You get a lunch break though.' Rarely, thought Horton, as Ashton continued. 'I'll be at the Bridge Tavern at the Camber. I'll see you in ten minutes.' He rang off.

Horton stared at his phone, feeling annoyed. He didn't have time to take lunch breaks, and even if he did, he certainly didn't want to spend them with Carl Ashton. But Ashton asking for help was tantamount to admitting weakness and that was something that didn't exist in Ashton's book. So what was troubling him? And why did he need the help of a police officer? Horton was under no illusions that Ashton had called him as a friend. He looked at the clock above his door. It was just after one and he was hungry. He was also curious. Picking up his helmet and jacket he headed back into CID and told Cantelli where he was going and why. He asked to be contacted if there was any news on Spalding's death, then he made for the Camber.

CHAPTER FIVE

There was no sign of Ashton when Horton swung into the car park. That was typical. Ashton's ten minutes often meant twice that, and Horton's irritation increased as he headed for the quayside and the Bridge Tavern. Stifling it as best he could he turned his thoughts to Spalding's death. But the strong smell from the fish market and from a fishing boat coming in on the tide, mingling with the smell of beer and food from the pub behind him, transported him back to another time when this area had looked very different. Then the pub had been a workman's rough spit and sawdust place, and instead of the expensive town houses and apartments surrounding the Camber, there had been an engineering works and sail maker. As the seagulls screeched overhead against the backdrop of clanking crane barges, the diesel engines of the tugs and the Wightlink car ferry behind him, Horton remembered sitting on the quayside as a boy, with his legs dangling over the side. He'd been eating an ice cream while his mother sat behind him on a wooden bench talking to a man in a suit who had brought them here in a big car. Had it been one of the men in the photograph which Ballard had left on his boat?

A couple vacated the wooden bench nearest him. Horton sat down there and retrieved the photograph from his jacket pocket. He studied the six men, two with beards and untidy long hair touching the collar of their patterned open-necked shirts, and four clean shaven with short Beatle-style haircuts. He couldn't say if the man he remembered with his mother here was one of them. Ten years after this picture had been taken, they would have looked very different, and Horton couldn't rely on his memory. He scrutinized the figures standing behind the six men. He'd already scanned the photograph onto his computer and enhanced it but the faces of the group in the background remained fuzzy. Yet it was clear enough for him to see that none of the women was Jennifer. He'd only had one photograph of his mother and that had been given to him by his foster father, Bernard, just after Horton had witnessed the man he now knew as Ballard handing Bernard a small tin. That picture had been destroyed in a fire on his previous yacht.

In 1967 his mother would have been seventeen and too young to be a student at the London School of Economics, but she could have worked there and been the girlfriend of one of these men. And that meant that one or more of them knew something about her. There was no one he could ask. His foster parents were dead, and he doubted they'd been told anything about Jennifer anyway. His maternal grandparents were also dead. There was nothing on his social services files because there were no files. And the owner of the casino where Jennifer had worked at the time of her disappearance, the woman she had worked closely with and the police constable who had cursorily investigated her disappearance, were also dead. These men might be too. If only Ballard had given him some indication of the picture's significance and the identities of the men. But that would have been too easy. Why the mystery and subterfuge? What had Ballard been afraid of? But Horton knew that whatever had happened to his mother it was enough for people to lie and cover it up for years.

Was one of these men Zeus, the code name of the criminal that Detective Superintendent Sawyer of the Intelligence

Directorate was keen to find? He believed that Jennifer had run off with him. Zeus had never been caught and Sawyer was eager to use Horton as bait. So far, he'd refused, but perhaps it was a quicker route to the truth. Unless Zeus got to him first, which Sawyer had intimated was possible. Then it might be a quicker route to the cemetery.

He didn't get any further with his speculations because he looked up to see Carl Ashton climb out of a new silver Mercedes. Horton stuffed the photograph back in his pocket. He still needed to contact Professor Thurstan Madeley, who might be able to provide some information on the student sit-in protest.

'Drink?' Ashton enquired, shaking Horton's hand and removing his sunglasses to reveal tired pale blue eyes in a sun-tanned rugged face. Horton thought he had aged since he'd last seen him; maybe Ashton was thinking the same of him.

'Diet Coke. And I'll have the fish and chips.' Well, Ashton had promised to buy him lunch and now that he was here, he might as well eat. A flicker of surprise, or was it irritation, crossed Ashton's face but he nodded and disappeared inside the pub, leaving Horton to study the occupants of the two cars that had pulled in behind Ashton. Two bulky men in dark trousers, white shirts and patterned ties had got out of the four-wheel-drive vehicle and were heading for the pub while a couple in their thirties had alighted from the saloon car and were now on the quayside taking photographs of the boats. DCS Sawyer and his words of warning about Zeus had made Horton more conscious of the people around him and more watchful, which wasn't necessarily a bad thing, but if it also made him feel jumpy and insecure then it was.

Ashton returned with the drinks and slipped onto the bench seat facing Horton and the Camber. Horton watched him swallow a large mouthful of ice-cold lager.

'Heard about your divorce. Catherine told me.'

Horton said nothing. He certainly wasn't here to discuss his private life.

'Fiona and I have split up,' Ashton continued, frowning. His fair hair, bleached by the sun, had grown sparser since Horton had last seen him a year ago and there were more lines on the square-jawed face. 'We stuck together over Christmas for the kids though it was hell on earth. Called it a day in January. Divorce is going through.'

Horton was amazed that Ashton's marriage had lasted as long as it had, which he reckoned was fifteen, maybe sixteen years, because Ashton, like Steve Uckfield, hadn't exactly lived up to his marital vows of fidelity. But that was none of his business and he was beginning to wonder what was, and when Ashton was going to reveal what was bothering him.

As though reading his thoughts, Ashton suddenly announced, 'I'm being threatened.' He glared at Horton as though he was personally responsible for the threats, but Horton knew the anger was directed at whoever was doing the threatening. It occurred to him that it could be someone connected with Ashton's marital spilt.

'In what way?' Horton asked, thinking if Fiona Ashton wanted to get even with her philandering husband, then that was her business and Ashton's, not his or CID's.

Ashton scowled and took another pull at his lager before replying. 'Letters, silent phone calls, a tyre slashed on the Mercedes.'

This sounded more than personal animosity on the part of Ashton's estranged wife, though that was still possible.

'You've reported this?'

'I'm reporting it now.'

'Officially I mean.'

Ashton looked uncomfortable. 'No. I thought it best to have a quiet word with you, as one friend to another.'

Oh yeah, thought Horton, where were you when I needed a friend? He drank his Coke hoping that his unspoken thought would resonate with Ashton but if it did Ashton certainly didn't look guilty. He did look troubled though.

'So you'd like to make a report and get it investigated.'

'No!' Ashton cried, alarmed. 'I want you to look into it for me.'

'I'm not a private investigator.'

'But you are a copper.'

'Yes, and unless you report it, I can't act as a copper.' Horton knew that wouldn't normally stop him. It hadn't in the case of Edward Ballard, where he'd bent the rules considerably by getting Ballard's fingerprints and DNA analysed with negative results on both counts. But he didn't see why he should put himself out for someone who hadn't given a toss about him.

Ashton ran a hand through his hair and looked concerned. 'If I report it, I'll have police at my flat and my place of work. It's bad for business. I need to keep this quiet, you know what people are like, if they get a scent of trouble, they make more for you.'

'Yes. I know,' Horton replied with feeling, eyeing Ashton coldly. It must have penetrated because he squirmed.

'Yeah, well . . .' But he was spared an apology by the arrival of the food. Horton wondered if he would have given one anyway. Once the waitress had left Ashton resumed.

'I think it must be someone I sacked. You know, out for revenge. I just want you to check them out.'

'Them?'

'You know how it is in my business, Andy, they come and they go,' he answered, tucking into his food. 'You've got to have the right personality to teach people to sail or take them out on corporate events, on stag and hen parties, and be cooped up with them on a yacht for days.'

'When did it start?'

'So you'll look into it for me?'

'No, I asked when it started.'

Ashton looked cross but obviously remembered that he needed Horton's help. 'Three weeks ago. I found a letter on the doormat.'

'Which is where?' Horton stabbed a chip and conveyed it to his mouth knowing he shouldn't ask questions because that showed interest and therefore a commitment to do something, but the police officer in him couldn't help it. Besides, he told himself, he could get the details and then tell Ashton he could only get involved if it was officially logged.

'Cowes. I'm renting an apartment at the marina there, until the divorce is finalized. It's handy for the office too. Fiona and the kids will get the house at Alverstoke. It's got to be either an ex-employee or a competitor.'

'Or Fiona.'

But Ashton was shaking his head. 'She might hate me, but she wouldn't do this.'

'Jealous husband or boyfriend then?'

'I'm not seeing anyone at the moment.'

Horton wasn't sure that was the truth, and even if it was it might be a boyfriend or husband connected with one of Ashton's previous girlfriends. 'Did you keep the letter?'

'Of course not. I thought it was just some tosser who'd read about me in the local newspaper and got his kicks from slagging off successful businessmen.' When Horton looked blank Ashton added, 'There was a profile on me and the company in the local rag. You know how people in this country hate success.'

'What did the letter say?'

Ashton waved his fork about. '"Think you're successful? Well, you might be now but enjoy it while it lasts because it won't be for long. By the time I'm finished with you you'll be lucky to have a canoe let alone a fleet of expensive yachts." That sort of drivel.'

'Written or computer generated?'

'The latter, on ordinary plain paper.'

'Posted or hand-delivered?'

'Posted. And I didn't save the envelope either, but it was a Portsmouth and Isle of Wight postmark.'

That narrows it down, thought Horton cynically, given there were over two hundred thousand people living in Portsmouth and a hundred and forty thousand on the Island, not to mention all the visitors and tourists. The culprit could live anywhere though and posted the letter locally. He could have read the article while staying in one of the marinas, or hotels on the Island. But the article wouldn't have mentioned Ashton's address and Horton doubted the newspaper would have given it out. His business address would have been easily accessible to anyone, but this letter had been sent to where Ashton was temporarily staying and that smacked of someone closer to home who knew Ashton.

The man and woman from the saloon car had finished their photographs of the Camber and were walking along the quayside in the direction of their car.

Ashton polished off his food and pushed away the plate. 'Next was the tyre, three days after the letter. I was in Oyster Quays talking to one of my skippers on one of the yachts moored up there. I parked the car in Old Portsmouth around the back of the Cathedral and walked through the Wightlink ferry terminal to the marina, and when I got back the tyre was flat. When I changed it there was a ruddy great rip in it as though someone had slashed it with a knife. Then I found a scratch on the Mercedes two days later outside the office in Cowes. This bastard's following me, Andy.' Ashton glared around the quayside. Horton followed his gaze. Nobody looked remotely interested in them.

'Then I got another letter a week ago, which I didn't keep either. It said "How does it feel to have your precious possessions scarred? That's just a start."'

'You should have brought it to us,' Horton said, finishing his meal.

'Well, I didn't. I ripped the bloody thing up I was so furious. And you wouldn't have done anything about it anyway, not unless I'd been physically threatened or probably dying, which is why there's no point in me reporting it officially. I know how the police work. I've had enough of them sailing on my yachts. It's got to be someone I sacked. I've brought a list. I thought you could run them through your computer and see if any of them look likely.' He reached into his trouser pocket.

'Not unless I log the incident and give it a crime number,' Horton said stubbornly, not because he wasn't interested or reluctant to follow it up but because he wanted to test Ashton's reaction to see just how desperate he was.

'For heaven's sake, Andy, I'm asking you to do a favour for an old friend.' But Horton knew that favours could be dangerous for coppers. 'Look, if one of the buggers on that list looks likely then you can log the crime,' Ashton capitulated. 'If they all come out whiter than Persil I'll hire a private detective, *if* you can recommend any that are any good.'

Horton knew a couple. Former DCI Mike Danby was the best, but he specialized in security for the rich and famous and for peers of the realm like Agent Ames's father, Lord Ames. He'd worked with Agent Ames recently on a case when she'd been sent over from Europol to assist. He wouldn't mind working with her again, he thought, stretching out a hand to take the list with the feeling he was making a mistake. He compensated though by telling himself that he'd definitely make it official if one of these names flashed up on the database as a criminal, and therefore, a possible suspect. He glanced down at it; there were three men and one woman. 'Who's Sabina Jennings?' he asked. Knowing Ashton's track record, it could very well be a case of hell hath no fury if Ashton had ditched her.

'She was one of my skippers. Didn't work out. Couldn't handle the clientele, company directors, salesmen, bankers, not like the one I've got now, Melanie Jacobs. She's good.'

'And the three men?'

'Two skippers, James Saunders and Paul Brading, and Kevin Wallace who worked in the office in Cowes, marketing.'

'This list only covers the last two months.'

'It can't be anyone from before then,' Ashton replied confidently, glancing impatiently at his watch.

Can't it? thought Horton. He knew that people could bear grudges a very long time and take revenge years after an event, but he didn't say. 'What about casual labour?'

'I can't see any of them doing this.'

'Why not?'

'Not worth their trouble.'

'But there have been a few who have been dismissed.'

'Let go rather than formerly dismissed,' Ashton corrected. 'I took some students on. Some were a waste of space and I got rid of them within a few days.'

They could also be suspects but Horton didn't say so. He didn't want to volunteer for more unofficial work. But if none of the four names on the list seemed likely then either Ashton would have to make his complaint official, or Horton would give him the name of a private investigator. He folded the sheet away, tossed back the remainder of his Coke and rose.

'How soon can you do it?' Ashton asked eagerly, following suit.

'As soon as I have a moment. I'm investigating a man's death in the dockyard last night and working on a million other things.'

Ashton looked about to protest then forced a smile from his lips and said, 'Yeah, of course. I appreciate your help. We'll go out for a sail after Cowes Week on one of the new fleet.'

Business must be good. 'Let me know if there are any further incidents. And if you receive any more letters don't rip them up.'

Ashton promised he wouldn't. Horton watched him drive away. There wasn't anyone following him. Turning back and surveying the dock, the man and woman with the camera were climbing into their car and there was no sign of the men in white shirts. Horton made for the station checking his mirrors. It didn't appear that anyone was following him either.

He was concerned about what Ashton had told him. Threats weren't to be taken lightly and whoever was doing it had to be stopped before it escalated. Horton certainly didn't want that, so the sooner he ran those names through the police national computer and the sooner he could make this official, the better.

Cantelli greeted him in CID with the news that Uckfield wanted to see him the moment he came in. Horton assumed the summons meant that Uckfield had heard from the pathologist. He'd specifically asked to be informed of the preliminary results but perhaps the pathologist had sent his report to Dennings because of his involvement in the case last night. If Dr Clayton had been conducting the autopsy, she would certainly have rung him and copied him in. But maybe there was an email or message waiting for him. He didn't stop to check but tossed the piece of paper Ashton had given him onto Walters' desk and asked him to run the names through the database, briefly telling him and Cantelli that Ashton was being threatened.

He found Sergeant Trueman alone in the incident suite which meant that whatever Uckfield had been told, Spalding's death was not suspicious. A fact that was confirmed after he had knocked and been granted entry into Uckfield's office where Dennings was sprawled in the chair opposite the Super, looking so smug that Horton would have given a lot to wipe the grin off his fat face.

Uckfield gestured Horton into the seat beside Dennings and announced, 'Spalding's death was caused by injuries sustained from the fall.' He glanced down at the paper on his desk and read, 'The tissue covering the bony orbital rims, and the skin covering the cheekbones and the lower jaw are torn and cut. There are injuries to the liver, the thorax, abdominal and pelvic viscera, which are all consistent with a fall occurring from a considerable height.'

'Any evidence that he was suffering from an illness?' Horton asked, recalling what Julie Preston had told him.

'No. Heart and arteries were sound, no sign of cardiac arrest, no evidence of a stroke, brain clot, brain haemorrhage or aneurysm. Spalding jumped into the dock. Suicide.'

'From the few people we've spoken to, including Spalding's wife, there's no testimonial evidence to suggest he killed himself and no note has been found.'

'Not everyone leaves one.'

I know that. But Horton wondered if Spalding had, perhaps in his study at home. 'How did he fall?'

'Eh?'

Horton elaborated. 'Lots of suicides jump feet first. What does the pathologist say about that?'

Uckfield gave a sniff of irritation and again consulted the report. 'No injuries to the bones of the feet and ankle, or signs of trauma passing up the spine to the base of the skull. He jumped pitching forward.'

'So he could have been pushed,' Horton persisted.

'He wasn't,' Dennings declared.

'How do you know that?' Horton rounded on him.

'Because there was no one around to push him,' Dennings said, exasperated.

Except Neil Gideon and Matt Newton, thought Horton, and possibly Julie Preston and Lewis Morden, who could have done so before leaving the dockyard, but why would they?

'Would he have ended up in the position he did?'

'Yes,' Uckfield snapped. 'Now if—'

But Horton hadn't finished yet. 'Any sign of alcohol in his system?'

'No.'

'Or drugs?'

'Waiting on the toxicology tests.'

And if drugs were found in Spalding's system that would clearly add weight to the suicide verdict.

'And the missing briefcase?' he asked.

'What briefcase?' Uckfield threw a glance at Dennings who shifted and glared at Horton. Swiftly Horton told them about it.

'In the sea,' Uckfield pronounced, coming, not unexpectedly, to the same conclusion as Horton had earlier. 'DI Dennings was correct in his assessment last night at the scene. Suicide is the most probable cause. It's not our case, and unless you have nothing else to do, I don't think it's yours. Everything will go before the coroner.'

Clearly Uckfield was not in the mood to discuss it further. Someone had upset him, which wasn't difficult. Perhaps his lunch date hadn't gone well. But despite Uckfield's customary foul temper it wasn't like him to shrug off an investigation without further probing. And if Uckfield's love life wasn't the cause of his short temper, then it was probably the result of ACC Dean leaning on him for a quick result to make the performance figures look good. And from all the evidence it did look as though Dennings was right, even though Horton hated to admit it. Spalding had committed suicide. And yet, he still wasn't convinced. No one had searched Spalding's house for a suicide note or evidence that could point to murder. There was the chance that Jacqueline Spalding had by now found a note from her husband. And if she had, would she have called them? There was only thing for it. He needed to speak to Mrs Spalding.

CHAPTER SIX

Jacqueline Spalding glanced down at the slender, well-manicured hands clasped in her lap. Horton's heart went out to her. He could see why Cantelli had warmed to the elegant, quietly spoken woman sitting opposite them in the tastefully decorated lounge of the immaculate semi-detached Victorian villa. Dressed smartly in tailored grey trousers and a white blouse she looked tired and bewildered. Understandably so. She'd told them her father-in-law, Ronald, had been given a sedative by Dr Deacon and was sleeping and that the children were still at a friend's house. Soon, Horton thought, she would be facing the ordeal of handling their incomprehension and sorrow. His eyes alighted on the framed photograph on the desk in the bay window of Douglas and Jacqueline Spalding with their children at a ski resort. The children had dark looks like their parents, but the little girl resembled her father more than her mother. Beside the picture was a computer screen. Perhaps Douglas Spalding had used that computer and had left an explanation on it as to why he'd decided to throw himself in the dock? He would ask her about that, first though he asked if her husband had a study.

'Yes. It's at the top of the house. I haven't been able to enter it since . . .'

'We'd like to take a look around it with your permission,' he said. 'It might help us to understand more about your husband and why he'd want to take his own life.'

She flinched as though he'd physically assaulted her. Her head came up sharply and her pain-racked eyes locked with his. Cantelli had already broken the news to her about the results of the autopsy, saying that her husband's death had been caused by the fall. He hadn't mentioned the word 'suicide' as they'd agreed between them on the way here. Horton hadn't wanted to sound so cruel, but he needed to be blunt to provoke a reaction and he got one.

'You're wrong. Douglas would never kill himself,' she declared with a flash of anger, repeating what she'd previously told Cantelli.

'Why are you so sure about that?' Horton asked gently. He knew her denial was a natural reaction, but he wanted to see if her conviction was based on something more solid than instinct and disbelief.

'He was a very determined man, clever, confident. He was also very successful and had so much to live for.'

'Perhaps behind his confidence there was something bothering him.'

'No,' she said firmly. 'I would have known if there were. He wasn't worried or depressed, quite the opposite. He was very happy.'

Horton didn't know how much store he could set by that. Spalding could easily have disguised his true feelings from his wife. 'Did he talk to you about his work?'

'His research you mean?'

Not necessarily, Horton thought. Spalding also taught, but then perhaps research was his primary work activity. He nodded.

'No. He made it a rule never to speak about it. He didn't want to bore me, not that I would have been bored, but he said that talking about it took away the pleasure and the thrill of ferreting out the facts.'

'Was he troubled about anything at work? At the university?'

'No, everything was fine.'

He saw her fingers tighten in her lap and her body stiffen. She was desperately trying to keep hold of her emotions. The woman police officer with them, PC Kerry Fry, sitting next to Cantelli on the large leather sofa, threw her a sympathetic look.

'Had your husband's behaviour changed in recent days?' he asked gently.

She turned her sorrowful soft brown eyes on him. 'No. He seemed fine, his usual self. He simply wouldn't do that to me and the children. He had so much to live for. It must have been a terrible accident.'

But it wasn't, because the fence was secure and the gates to the dock hadn't been tampered with. And Spalding had been in good health.

'Did your husband use that computer?' he asked, indicating the one on the desk in the window.

'No, that's mine. Douglas only ever used his laptop.'

'Knowing that is your computer, is it possible he could have left you a message on it?' he asked as gently as he could but no matter how considerately he spoke he knew the words would hurt.

Her skin paled. She looked frightened. Horton left a silence. He didn't need to ask her to check it because now that he had sewn a seed of doubt, she would have to anyway. He said, 'Would you mind if we had a look at his study?'

'I'll show you where it is.' She half rose but Horton forestalled her.

'It's OK, we can find it ourselves.'

Gratefully she sank down into the chair. With a silent gesture Horton indicated for PC Kerry Fry to stay with Mrs Spalding. He heard her ask Mrs Spalding if she would like a cup of tea as they left the room.

They climbed the stairs to the top floor in silence. Horton sensed Cantelli's sadness and knew his thoughts were for the children being raised without their father. But at least they had a mother, thought Horton with a flash of anger, glimpsing into what was clearly the main bedroom, again well decorated and extremely tidy. And they had a grandfather. He'd had no one.

He stepped into a large attic room, pushing his personal feelings to the back of his mind. The room was light, airy and spacious and had clearly once been two smaller rooms now knocked into one. It was neutrally decorated and, like the other rooms he'd seen, it was very orderly and clean. It was also kitted out with modern furniture, a large sofa, coffee table, wide-screen television on a stand, and expensive hi-fi with headphones. Neat bookshelves lined the wall opposite the door and there was a desk in front of two sash windows, which Cantelli crossed to. Horton turned his attention to the bookshelves where there were several silver-framed photographs of the children and Jacqueline Spalding, as well as one of Douglas Spalding in naval uniform. Horton picked it up. Spalding looked an intelligent, friendly man with a broad smile, good teeth and laughing eyes, well-built and fit. Horton guessed women would have found him handsome in a young Sean Connery kind of way. By the braiding on his uniform, he had reached the rank of Lieutenant. The photograph had been taken on board a naval ship and judging by the fact that Spalding was wearing summer uniform and the sky was azure blue, it had been taken overseas. Meadows' comment about Spalding never having been to sea was just sour grapes. The little man had probably been angry at being snubbed by Spalding. Horton turned his attention to the books. There were several on the Navy, a great many biographies including those on explorers, sportsmen and politicians, and other factual books on various countries.

'Not much in here,' Cantelli said, indicating the open drawers. 'Just bits of stationery. No letters or household bills. And no suicide note.'

There was nowhere else in the room where Spalding could have left a note and nothing more they could glean from it.

Overall, Horton came away with the impression of an organized, tidy man, who was self-assured and comfortable with himself. Nothing in that or what he'd seen and heard so far equated with a man so distraught and depressed that he'd end it all by pitching himself thirty feet into that dark concrete hole.

Returning to the drawing room they found Jacqueline Spalding standing by the window staring out. She spun round as they entered; her face drawn. Anxiously she scoured their expressions. The computer beside her was on.

'Did you find anything?' she asked, her voice trembling with apprehension.

Cantelli shook his head. 'No.'

Relief flooded her face. 'Neither did I.' Horton knew that she would never accept her husband had killed himself. As Cantelli explained that PC Fry would keep her informed and that the coroner's office would liaise with her about the inquest, Horton studied the photograph on the desk. He recalled what Dr Deacon had told him about Spalding being a terrified flyer, but he'd flown somewhere recently, hence the travel sickness pills and antidepressants. He'd also obviously flown to wherever that picture had been taken, judging by the scenery. He made to turn away when something, he didn't know what, prompted him to say, 'A recent holiday?'

She looked at the picture with a bemused air as though it couldn't possibly be of her and her late husband. 'No. That was taken the February before last and the last time I managed to get Douglas on an aeroplane.'

Horton's nape hairs prickled. He resisted throwing Cantelli a glance. 'Your husband didn't like flying then,' he asked, not betraying that he'd already been told this by Deacon.

'He was terrified of it. We used to travel everywhere by train and boat.' Her voice faltered, as clearly, she thought *not any more*.

Horton had just a couple more questions. 'Had your husband been away recently?'

'Only to a conference in Birmingham at the beginning of July.'

And that tied in with when he had visited Dr Deacon at the end of June. 'How did he travel there?'

'By train. He preferred that to driving, said he could work on a train.'

'How long was he away?'

'Three days.'

'Have you got the dates?'

'Somewhere,' she said vaguely.

Horton was reluctant to press her, but he felt this was significant. He had to know. 'Could you check?' He glanced at Cantelli and could see he was thinking along the same lines. PC Fry was looking at them curiously.

Jacqueline Spalding opened one of the desk drawers and lifted out a diary. Flicking through it she came to the page and looked up. 'It was July the fourth, fifth and sixth.'

'Do you know who organized this conference?' Horton asked lightly, hoping she wouldn't ask him why he wanted the information.

She didn't. She was still in a state of shock. 'It was something to do with his old college, that is I should say university, Kings College London.'

Horton didn't see the need to probe any deeper at this stage. When they were in the car, he told Cantelli to head for the seafront. Cantelli didn't need to ask why. They'd known each other long enough to understand how each worked and Horton wanted time outside the station to think over what they'd just learned.

After a few minutes Cantelli pulled into one of the diagonal bays near to a cafe that bore the Cantelli name. 'Good choice,' Horton said, climbing out, heading towards it. 'At least we're guaranteed proper Italian coffee.'

The tables in the courtyard facing onto the pebbled beach were crowded and the beach was dotted with some late-afternoon bathers, but inside the cool interior there were several empty tables. While Cantelli went to find his sister Isabella in the kitchen, Horton took up position at one of the tables that overlooked the Solent. He gazed out at the yachts sailing in the breeze which had strengthened as the day had worn on. Beyond the white and coloured sails, he could pick out the steep streets of Ryde on the Isle of Wight and the rolling hills beyond it. It was so clear he felt he could almost touch it, which didn't bode well for the weather forecast, as local lore had it that the clearer the Island was, the worse the forthcoming weather. The sea was flecked with white spray and large rollers were crashing onto the beach. He could hear the squeals of the children as they jumped the waves. Bulky white masses of clouds were rapidly sweeping across the sky constantly changing the sea from a shimmering blue into a muddy, murky green.

'Andy, you're looking well.'

Horton turned to see the dark-haired, slender Isabella beside Cantelli. He rose, returned the compliment, which he meant, and greeted her warmly planting a kiss on each cheek. 'How's Johnnie?' He'd helped pluck her son from trouble some years ago and put him on the right path by introducing him to sailing.

'He's very well, though I don't see as much of him as I'd like. He's still skippering for Andreadis, that Greek millionaire. He'll be here for Cowes Week for the yacht racing.'

'Taking his uncle out on the sea,' Horton teased. Cantelli looked green at the thought.

She laughed and fetched their coffees, after both had refused something to eat. Then she left them in peace. Cantelli spoke first.

'So who did Spalding lie to, his wife or his doctor?'

'If he lied to his doctor about flying to America then it bears out the theory that he could have wanted the travel sickness tablets and antidepressants to help him commit suicide. They wouldn't have killed him but could have made it easier for him to leap into that dock.'

'You'd have thought he would have drunk alcohol though, at the reception, to make it even easier but he didn't.'

'No. And if he lied to his wife about attending a conference in Birmingham and he did fly off somewhere, hence needing the tablets, then why and where did he go? Three days is not really long enough for a long-haul trip, so I don't think he went to the States like he told Dr Deacon.'

'I hope to God there's not another woman,' Cantelli said with feeling. 'I'd hate for her to discover that.'

Horton swallowed some coffee. 'If he did travel by plane then we should be able to find out where he went, or at least which airport he flew from and to.'

'Do we need to?'

'No, but you know me.'

'Yeah, loose ends don't come into it.'

'If he was seeing another woman and took her away for an illicit weekend of lust then why didn't he travel by train or boat?'

'Perhaps she gets seasick, like me.'

'OK, let's say she does. And let's say Spalding is having an affair. She wants more, threatens to tell his wife and destroy his career unless he leaves his wife for her. He says buggered if I will and calls off the affair. Now she has nothing to lose, she starts threatening him, following him. She says she's going to drag his name through the mud, ruin him. He can't cope with the shame of it and kills himself after throwing the briefcase in the sea, which contains his laptop and has evidence of emails between them as well as anything else they might have got up to. His phone is smashed so maybe he thought that meant we wouldn't be able to trace his calls.'

'He was cleverer than that.'

'You're right, Barney. But maybe he knew we wouldn't bother checking the telephone company records if it was suicide.' Horton thought for a moment before continuing. 'But his death wouldn't have stopped this woman from bringing out the truth; it might even encourage her if she's that vindictive. She'd want to rub Jacqueline Spalding's nose in it and show the university that Spalding wasn't quite the blue-eyed boy they thought he was, *if* they thought that. And I can't see Spalding letting her do that. Everything we've learned about him so far says he'd be able to handle this, and his study is so neat that I can't believe he'd leave a loose cannon of a thwarted woman behind him.'

'Maybe there's more to this affair.'

Maybe. 'I'd like to know where he went for those three days in July. His passport. Do we know where it is?'

'It wasn't in his desk. We could ask Jacqueline Spalding.'

Horton hesitated. He didn't want to disturb her again 'No. She might get curious this time and I don't want to explain our doubts over her husband's death and worry her unnecessarily. Besides if he was only away for three days and two nights, as we've already said, it's unlikely he flew long haul. My bet is we're looking at a domestic flight or somewhere within Europe.'

'He'd still have taken his passport. It could have been in his briefcase.'

Horton acknowledged this, adding, 'We know he caught the train.'

'Do we?'

'No, you're right, Barney. His lover could have picked him up and driven them to an airport. If they flew to a destination within the UK or Europe there's a chance they flew from Southampton.'

'I could make some inquiries. And I could also talk to Alvita Baarda, the black girl Spalding seemed to be friendly with at the lecture. There's a possibility she could be Spalding's bit on the side. Perhaps she said something to him yesterday evening that caused him to panic and end it all. An affair with a student would certainly put the kibosh on his career and damage his reputation.'

Horton considered this. 'OK.' He finished his coffee and rose. 'Do it tomorrow and see if you can have a word with Dr Sandra Menchip, Spalding's boss. Get Walters to contact Kings College to find out if there really was a conference in Birmingham on July the fourth. Drop me back at the station and then get off home.'

There was no sight, sound or smell of Walters or his food in CID and his jacket had vanished from the back of his chair, which meant he'd sneaked off home. It was thirty minutes past Walters' usual clocking-off time and there was no major investigation to make him linger longer than he possibly had to.

Horton opened his office window admitting the sound of the rush-hour traffic and eyed his desk with a heavy heart. He could have sworn the pile had grown two inches deeper in his absence. He found a note from Walters on top of Ashton's list of names. Walters had scrawled, 'All clean, nothing known.' Horton called Ashton.

'What is it, Andy? I'm rather busy at the moment.'

Horton gritted his teeth. 'I can ring tomorrow. It's nothing important. Only about those names you gave me,' he said with heavy sarcasm.

'Oh that, yeah. And?'

'There's nothing on any of them. Do you want me to log the crime?'

'No. No, leave it. Forget I mentioned it.' Ashton rang off.

Horton stared at his mobile seething. 'With pleasure,' he said, throwing the phone down on his desk. Well at least he'd got lunch out of the selfish, inconsiderate bastard.

For the next two hours he turned his attention to his paperwork and emails, grabbing some sandwiches from the canteen and coffee from the machine outside CID to keep him going. But all the while Spalding's death niggled at the back of his mind and in particular those three days at the beginning of July. He could *feel* it was significant.

Then there was Jennifer's disappearance to pursue and the identity of those men in that photograph, which made him remember he still needed to track down Professor Thurstan Madeley. The name was still bugging him. It wasn't as if it was a common one either. He was convinced he knew it from somewhere. He pushed it aside for another hour and then just after nine thirty he called it a day, but before logging off his computer, he keyed in Madeley's name, sat back and swore softly. No wonder the name had seemed familiar. Madeley was not only often a guest lecturer at the police training college, Bramshill, but he also acted as a consultant to various police forces around the country, lecturing and advising on issues such as crime culture, crime and the social classes and crime and the urban environment. God, he was dense not to recognize it earlier. He must have seen it in emails and memos or in articles in the force magazine. He'd probably even heard it mentioned so why hadn't he made the connection sooner? Probably because he couldn't believe that the man who might hold the key to some vital information about his mother's disappearance could be so close.

He logged off. Madeley's connections with the police made approaching him difficult. He didn't have to tell Madeley that he was a police officer, but he was certain Madeley would ask him what he did for a living and why he wanted to know about the archive project. If he lied or managed to dodge both questions, which was doubtful given Madeley's background and obviously high intellect, and Madeley subsequently discovered that he was a cop, Madeley could make things awkward for him. It could raise the issue of him using police resources for his own private use. And DCS Sawyer was bound to find out. But perhaps that didn't matter, thought Horton, switching off the lights, and heading out, because Sawyer knew he was researching the past, and maybe the next time Sawyer approached him he'd accept the offer of secondment to the Intelligence Directorate.

Horton made his way home thinking it over. By the time he parked the Harley in the marina car park he knew that he had no choice in the matter. He had to be straight with Madeley. As he headed down the pontoon the sound of a powerful motorbike caught his attention. There wasn't usually a lot of traffic, especially at this time of night, because the road didn't lead anywhere except to Langstone Harbour, but there was the sailing and diving club as well as the Lifeboat Station. He caught sight of the motorbike as it sped towards the harbour and following it was a dark saloon car. Neither came back immediately nor seemed interested in him and he hadn't noticed either following him, but then his thoughts had been distracted, and it was dark.

Shrugging, he unlocked the hatch and climbed below, thinking of Zeus, and again wondering if he was one of the men in the photograph. The breeze had stiffened, and it had begun to rain. He remembered the train journey to Portsmouth with his mother when he must have been about five. She'd been edgy and silent and after a while he had watched her, worried and fearful. He felt cold now as he sensed her fear. He recalled the small shabby rooms, an old woman, men, a new school with children who treated him with mistrust, fights, his mother's temper, and finally the flat in the tower block. He would stare out of the window at the ships in the Solent wishing he was on one of them and that he could make his mother happy again. Then it had changed. She changed. She was relaxed and happy. Had someone come into her life to make her happy? Had that man been Zeus?

He sat drinking a coffee, listening to the wind whistling through the halyards and the rain hitting the deck. He needed to remember more about his time with his mother. Vague snatches were coming back, but he didn't know how much of it he could trust, for a child's memory was often distorted. The sound of his mobile made him start. He glanced at the clock wondering who it could be at ten forty-six. Probably work, he thought, because he rarely got personal calls. But why should anyone call him? He wasn't duty CID. He was surprised and annoyed to see it was Carl Ashton. He was tempted not to answer it. He was under no illusion that Ashton was calling to apologize for his ingratitude; he obviously wanted something. But answer it he did.

'I need you here now. I'm on the boat at Oyster Quays and for God's sake hurry.'

Horton heard the panic and fear in Ashton's voice. 'What is it? Has the boat been trashed? Are you hurt?' he asked, sitting up.

'Worse.'

What could be worse, Horton thought, but before he could ask, Ashton said, 'He's dead. Stone bloody cold dead. For God's sake get here.' He rang off.

CHAPTER SEVEN

The body was lying sprawled face down in the cockpit of Ashton's yacht, partially under cover of the awning by the hatch. Horton had checked for signs of life knowing instantly that he wouldn't find any. And he'd checked for any obvious cause of death; no knife wound in the back and no gunshot wound either. The back of the dark-haired head was intact and there wasn't a speck of blood emanating from under the lean figure. The dead man's neck showed no signs of strangulation either, from the back view at least. From what Horton could see of the face, which wasn't much, he judged the deceased to be somewhere in his forties. The right hand and arm were pushed under the body, while the left hand and arm were exposed. The fingers were slender, there was no ring, but resting half over the arm and half on the deck was a navy-blue lightweight rucksack, which looked as though it contained very little.

'Who is he?' Horton asked Ashton, who was standing at the helm behind him, hunched over the wheel as though for support.

'I've no idea,' he cried, running a hand through his wet hair, his feverish anxious eyes skittering around the yacht and the pontoon as though searching for an escape.

On the way here it had crossed Horton's mind that the dead man might have been mistaken for Carl Ashton and the threats had escalated into murder, but now seeing the corpse Horton was inclined to dismiss that idea. The dead man was leaner and darker. His clothes — faded jeans, stout and worn trainers, and a lightweight navy walking jacket — were also completely unlike Ashton's smart chinos, deck shoes, and Henri Lloyd sailing jacket.

Ashton said, 'Look, can we go somewhere? Do I have to keep staring at him?'

Horton had no intention of negotiating their way around the dead man to the cabin below. There was nowhere else to go except on to the pontoon.

'Let's get off the boat.'

Ashton hastily climbed off and stood moodily on the pontoon, shoulders hunched against the steady rain, collar of his sailing jacket enveloping his petulant jaw.

Horton said, 'Tell me what happened.'

Taking a deep breath, Ashton said, 'I came here shortly before six thirty, had a chat with the clients — we've had two on board today, along with Melanie Jacobs, my skipper, and Steve Drummond, crew. We all went up to a restaurant on the boardwalk. I left there just after ten thirty, came back here and found . . . him.' Ashton jerked his head at the body. 'I called you. You arrived ten minutes later. Longest ten minutes of my life. Can't you call an ambulance and move him?'

'Not as simple as that, Carl,' Horton replied, wondering why Ashton hadn't done that immediately himself. It's what many would have done unless they'd felt for a pulse and, realizing there wasn't one, called the police. Ashton had called him. Horton didn't think Ashton had checked for a pulse though. And even if he had called an ambulance, it would have been no use to this poor man. He said, 'This is a suspicious death, which means I've got to call it in.'

Ashton rounded his angry and troubled eyes on Horton. 'You mean police, scene-of-crime and all that bollocks?'

Horton nodded.

'But the poor bugger probably died of a heart attack!'

Horton stepped a short distance away from Ashton and, reaching for his phone, thought of another poor bugger who had been found lying at the bottom of a dock not very far away. He'd once considered that death as a possible heart attack and now it had been deemed suicide. But this man couldn't have killed himself — and if he did, why would he do so on one of Ashton's corporate yachts? Horton toyed with the idea that he'd been killed and planted here as part of this hate campaign against Ashton in an attempt to frame him and ruin him. That seemed a bit extreme though, and although people did weird things, he didn't think it was a workable theory. Could the dead man have been threatening Ashton? He'd come here intent on causing damage to one of Ashton's yachts, only Ashton had caught him as he was about to break in. They'd quarrelled, Ashton had struck out, the man had suffered a heart attack and died. It was possible, he guessed. So until he had clear evidence that this man had died of natural causes, he was treating this as a crime scene, which was why he'd wait before going through the corpse's pockets to check for identification.

Horton requested uniform assistance, the police doctor, and SOCO. He also asked that the Oyster Quays security team be alerted. The marina office at the top of the bridgehead was closed at this time of night but Horton relayed the touch-pad security number giving access to the pontoons, which Ashton had given him earlier. Taylor and the patrol unit would need it. He could call Cantelli, who was still duty CID officer, and go home, but he didn't see any need to disturb the sergeant's night. And, for now at least, he also saw no need to call Uckfield. He'd wait to see what the doctor had to say.

Ringing off he surveyed the area through the rain sweeping off the sea. There were several boats in the marina but only two moored up on this short pontoon, which was based the furthest away from the marina office, Ashton's yacht and another large sleek one behind it. There were no signs of life on board, but the ensign flying at the rear meant that someone was on board, only judging by the lack of signs of life, they were in fact ashore. He didn't think the dead man had come from that yacht, but he could be wrong.

The pontoon turned sharp right where two yachts and one small motor boat were moored, but again there were no signs of life on board. It was possible that one of the craft could belong to the dead man, although he wasn't dressed for boating. But that didn't mean much. Opposite these was a pale blue, unusually shaped motor boat, which Horton knew from reading the sign on the boardwalk above it many times that it was a motor gun boat built in 1942, an MGB 81, and used to protect the coast during World War Two. If he remembered correctly, they had been nicknamed the 'Spitfires of the Seas' and inspired by the PT boats of the United States Navy. Another touch of history he thought, recalling the dock and the Monitor lying in it along with Spalding's body. But then history seeped out of almost every orifice in the city. There was nothing sinister in that.

Returning to Ashton he said, 'Why did you come back to the yacht?'

'Because Melanie was going to debrief me on how the day went.'

Horton glanced at his watch. It was just after eleven. 'Bit late for a debrief,' he said archly, wondering if Ashton and Melanie had the physical kind of debriefing in mind.

'I don't keep office hours and neither do my staff,' Ashton snapped.

'Is Melanie coming here as you instructed?'

'No. I rang and told her not to. I didn't mention the body.'

Horton wondered how she'd taken that if their meeting had been a romantic assignation. 'Is she still in the restaurant?'

'She and Steve were just leaving when I called her. The other two had already left.'

'Where do Steve and Melanie live?'

'Why do you want to know that?' Ashton eyed him suspiciously.

'Because we'll need to interview them and your clients.'

'You can't be serious!'

'Perfectly.'

'Great, that will lose me business.'

'I don't see why it should if none of them knew the dead man.'

'Of course they didn't know him!'

'We'll still need to check.'

After a moment Ashton answered tersely, 'Steve lives in Gosport and Melanie in Southsea. Simon Watson lives at Prinsted.' Horton knew that to be a very small hamlet along the coast east of Portsmouth. It was expensive and bordered a quiet natural harbour. 'He works for Longman Biomedical; they're good clients of mine. I don't know where Nigel Denton lives but he's a director of an agricultural company, who I'm hoping to get as clients,' Ashton said pointedly.

They'd get the addresses tomorrow and they could probably interview Steve Drummond and Melanie Jacobs here in the morning, because SOCO would have finished with the yacht by then. Horton was sure they'd be sailing it back to its base in Cowes, unless Ashton had another group of clients on board tomorrow. If he had though, he'd have been bleating about it.

He said, 'Did you touch the body?'

'You must be joking. I could see he was dead.'

'So you didn't turn him over or look at his face to see if you recognized him?'

'No.' Ashton eyed him incredulously. And that meant it could still be someone he knew.

Horton looked up to see PCs Johnson and Bailey climb out of the police vehicle, as another drew up behind it. The activity was bound to attract the ghouls from the restaurants and bars along the waterfront and Horton for once was glad it was raining. It would keep them at bay.

Ashton, who was looking more haggard by the minute, said tetchily, 'I called you because I thought we could avoid all this unnecessary fuss.'

'Then you thought wrong,' Horton brusquely replied. With instructions for Ashton to remain where he was and touch nothing, which drew a cynical look, Horton set off up the pontoon, swiftly glancing into the three moored craft opposite the MGB 81. No signs of life and no red ensign on the aft to show that anyone was on board. Turning right onto the lengthy pontoon that led up to the marina office he glanced across the small stretch of water to see Ashton's huddled figure pacing the pontoon on the far side. Could he be involved in this death? For now, Horton was keeping an open mind.

He gave Johnson instructions to ensure that neither Ashton nor any unauthorized personnel went on board the yacht and posted Bailey outside the marina office. PCs Allen and Barnes headed down the pontoon after Johnson with the canvas awning which they'd erect over the cockpit of Ashton's boat in readiness for the doctor and SOCO. It would help to protect them from the worst of the rain driving off the harbour.

Horton met the security officer by the marina office. Flashing his warrant card, he quickly explained what had happened, adding that they would need to view footage from their security cameras.

'I'll go back to the control room and let them know.'

Horton returned to the pontoon and had just reached Ashton's yacht when he saw the white SOCO van pull up and behind it photographer Jim Clarke's estate car.

'Can I go now?' Ashton addressed Horton irritably.

'Not until the doctor turns the body over. I want to be certain you don't recognize him. It would be a great help, Carl,' Horton quickly added, seeing that Ashton was about to protest. 'And the quicker we get this cleared up the better,' he added for good measure.

'Then can I have a fag?'

'Only if you move further down the pontoon.'

Ashton trundled off, clearly unhappy and very wet, as Horton was. At least the cockpit was now fully covered, and unauthorized personnel were being kept at bay by Barnes and Allen up the boardwalk.

He watched while Clarke took pictures and a video of the deceased before a movement on the pontoon caught his attention. Looking up he saw heading towards him a man and a woman. The reprimand that formed in Horton's mind to Bailey for allowing them into the marina was quickly replaced with shock as he recognized the slender yet shapely figure of Agent Ames from Europol. What was she doing here? Was she on duty? Did this dead man have anything to do with a European investigation? Thoughts flashed through his mind as he watched her walk towards him with a hesitant smile on her lips. Dressed in a sailing jacket and jeans with her blonde hair getting steadily wetter she looked even more beautiful than he remembered. He didn't know who the fair, suntanned athletic man beside her was but his instinct was automatically to dislike him because he was with Ames.

'Nice to see you again, sir,' she greeted Horton in that posh voice of hers which he'd recalled so many times over the last six weeks. It still had the same effect on him, of stirring his loins with desire while making him feel both hostile and defensive because it reminded him of how privileged and rich her life had been compared to his barren, empty one. With a father who was a peer of the realm she was clearly out of his league. And although she'd never given any indication of treating him as inferior, he knew that she made him feel that way and that made him angry, both with her but especially with himself.

'Although,' she added quietly, glancing at Ashton's yacht, 'the circumstances are not exactly happy. This is Rupert Crawford,' she introduced the man beside her. 'Inspector Horton.'

Crawford looked as though he was reluctant to shake hands with someone so low in the food chain but after a moment's hesitation he did so with an irritated frown.

'You're on holiday, Harry,' Crawford addressed Ames peevishly.

Harry? Short for Harriet or Henrietta? Horton hadn't discovered her first name when working with her previously and he'd not asked because there had seemed no point. So she wasn't on duty.

'You don't need to get involved.'

'I know I don't *need* to, Rupert,' she answered pleasantly but firmly, 'but I am a police officer and if I can help then I will. Why don't you go back to the yacht?'

Yes, why don't you? thought Horton.

'I'll join you in a moment,' she added. 'That's Rupert's yacht,' she indicated the expensive sleek craft behind Ashton's.

Horton's heart sank; clearly Rupert was her lover and Horton wasn't and never could be any part of Ames's life. He watched the disgruntled Rupert walk off, pausing before climbing on board to exchange words with Ashton. He couldn't hear what they were saying but after a few seconds Ashton with Rupert disappeared below decks.

'Does he know Carl Ashton?'

'I think his bank uses Sail Away for corporate hospitality and team racing events.'

'His bank?'

'Hamilton and Welland. Rupert's an investment banker.'

No wonder I don't like him. Horton didn't think she sounded that enamoured of Rupert Crawford herself — or was that just wishful thinking on his part? He asked her what time they'd arrived in the marina.

'Just after seven, sir,' she replied crisply, making him fully aware this was business. OK, if that was the way she wanted it. But then what other way could there be? She said, 'This yacht was moored up but there wasn't anyone on board.'

That tied in with what Ashton had told him.

She added, 'There wasn't anyone on the pontoons then or when we left for the boardwalk just after seven thirty. And I didn't see anyone on any of the craft moored here.'

So where had the dead man come from and what had he been doing here? Horton's attention was caught by the approach of a slim, auburn-haired man carrying a medical bag. Cantelli had been right when he'd said that Dr Freemantle looked barely out of medical school. But Horton wasn't concerned about his age, only his level of competence. Taylor issued the doctor with a scene suit. Clarke stepped away from the body to allow the doctor on board and smiled a greeting at Ames.

After a few moments Dr Freemantle straightened up. 'There's no sign of rigor, or of a violent struggle. I'd say he's been dead about two hours, four at the most.'

It was now eleven thirty-two so that put the death any-where between seven thirty and nine thirty.

'Cause of death?' Horton asked hopefully, while pre-paring himself for a sarcastic reply or at least a negative one. He wasn't disappointed. 'Can't say, Inspector. It's a bit too wet and dark to conduct an autopsy here. Want me to turn him over?'

Horton nodded. First Freemantle eased off the rucksack and handed it to Beth Tremaine. Standing under the awning she unzipped the main compartment. 'Empty, sir. And only tissues in the front compartment.'

So was theft the motive, *if* this was indeed murder? Horton watched Freemantle ease the body over. Horton thought the pale face and the staring dark eyes looked shocked rather than afraid. He gave instructions for Johnson to fetch Ashton. Clarke took some photographs as Freemantle stood back. When he'd finished Freemantle again examined the body.

'No signs of strangulation. No head wounds and no sign of bruising around the neck or face.' He made to reach into the man's jacket pockets when Horton forestalled him. He stood back and beckoned over Ashton. He smelt of alcohol, probably understandable in the circumstances.

'Have you ever seen him before?'

Ashton's face paled as he snatched a glance at the dead man. He shook his head and swallowed. Horton gestured for the doctor to empty the dead man's pockets. Reaching into the trousers he extracted a wallet, which he handed to Taylor. In the other pocket was a set of keys, which again

Dr Freemantle gave to Taylor who dropped them into an evidence bag.

Glancing at them Ames said, 'They're not boat keys. There's no float on them. House key and two smaller padlock keys.'

Which could be to the compartments on the rucksack. He asked Taylor to open the wallet.

'Credit card and bank debit card in the name of Daniel Redsall.'

That name sounded familiar to Horton. Why?

Taylor continued. 'No photographs, a card for a guest house in Southsea, and there's a pass for the University of Ulster.'

University . . . like Spalding. Turning to Ashton, Horton said, 'Do you know anyone called Redsall?'

'No.'

Was that a lie, wondered Horton? It didn't sound like one. Perhaps Ashton or one of his crew or clients had slipped away from the restaurant and met this man. But why? And as Freemantle had said there seemed no evidence of foul play.

'I need the keys to the yacht, Carl. We have to examine it,' he added.

Ashton handed them over grudgingly. 'I need that yacht back in Cowes tomorrow morning.'

'We should finish with it tonight if you want to wait.'

'You know where to find me,' Ashton growled before returning to Crawford's yacht. Horton watched him go before his attention was caught by voices at the bridgehead.

'That's the rest of the team,' Ames explained.

Team? Then she wasn't alone on that yacht with Crawford. Optimism rose for a moment to be quashed almost instantly as Horton followed her gaze to a man in his early fifties with a stunningly attractive long-legged blonde woman in her mid-twenties. They were a foursome.

'We've been practising for Cowes Week, the racing.'

He should have guessed Ames would return to England for one of the highlights of the social calendar.

'Can they come down, sir?' she asked.

He nodded. 'And tell Bailey he can let the undertakers on.' He watched her make her way up the pontoon, admiring her figure and wishing he didn't feel so attracted to her, then pulling himself up he dismissed her from his mind. He had a job to do. He turned his attention to the body. Daniel Redsall. The name struck a familiar note. Why? Could he be a criminal? But no, the university pass indicated otherwise. He thought of Douglas Spalding. He'd also had a university pass but for Portsmouth, not Ulster. And Spalding had also been found in an unusual place. Was it just coincidence or did the two men know one another?

My God! With a sudden rush of adrenalin Horton scrambled inside his pocket and pulled out the list of names and addresses Neil Gideon had given him earlier, which he'd forgotten to put in the file. And there it was. He let out a breath. Daniel Redsall. This man had attended Dr Douglas Spalding's lecture. And now both were dead. Now let Uckfield tell him there was nothing suspicious about it. He reached for his phone.

CHAPTER EIGHT

'Their deaths have to be linked,' Horton insisted twenty minutes later. The Super had arrived in his usual foul mood.

Horton had first called his home and awoken Alison Uckfield, who had told him her husband was on a late-night operation. Horton had then rung Uckfield's mobile. He'd eventually answered, very grumpily, which revealed to Horton that the kind of operation Uckfield was on had nothing to do with police work. Uckfield had arrived without giving any explanation of where he'd been. But then he didn't have to, and Horton certainly wasn't going to ask. It was none of his business.

Horton had insisted that the body remain until Uckfield had seen it. He'd told Ames to return to her friends who were now on Crawford's yacht. There was no point in her getting any wetter than she already was, and there was nothing she could do. She had at first insisted on staying but Horton had been firm. It wasn't her investigation. She couldn't help. She'd gone reluctantly after she'd introduced the two other crew members as Ben Otis and Keely Lambeth, the latter of whom had PC Johnson drooling like a baby. Keely Lambeth was stunning, Horton had to admit that, and Johnson, Clarke and even Phil Taylor, who was usually unaffected by anything and everything, looked as though they'd dash to her aid if she fainted at the sight of the body. If Uckfield had seen her, he'd probably have shoved his elbows in front of them to catch her first. But Keely Lambeth merely blinked her mesmerizing green eyes at the corpse, shook her long blonde hair and professed not to know or recognize him. Otis said the same. Crawford was fetched from his boat by Ames, and he too declared that he'd never seen the dead man in his life.

Uckfield sniffed, pulling up his collar. 'Just because this poor sod went to Spalding's lecture and worked at a university like him doesn't make his death suspicious. On the contrary, there's no evidence to suggest that. He probably fell ill, climbed on board hoping to find someone on the yacht, collapsed and died.'

They moved away from the yacht, finally allowing the undertakers on board. Taylor and Tremaine were working their way methodically through the cabins. They'd examine the cockpit again once the body had been removed but Horton wasn't sure they'd find much. The rain would have destroyed any evidence, if it existed, just as with Spalding's death.

Horton knew that Uckfield could be right, but as he'd waited for the Super to arrive, he'd formed another theory which he now voiced. 'We haven't had the results of the toxicology tests on Spalding yet. He could have been drugged after giving his lecture at the naval museum and Redsall could have witnessed it.'

'And I could be in a nice warm bed,' quipped Uckfield, making it perfectly clear what he thought of that idea.

Yeah, whose bed? thought Horton with irritation. He knew that Redsall couldn't have witnessed Spalding being pushed into the dock because according to the log he had signed out at 9.25, *if* the log was correct, and they would need to check that.

'Spalding committed suicide,' Uckfield said, stepping aside as the undertakers manoeuvred the body bag off the yacht, conveyed it onto the trolley and began to wheel it up the pontoon. 'There was nothing to witness.'

Horton was tempted to tell Uckfield about his visit to Spalding's house and the fact that there was a discrepancy between what Spalding had told his doctor and his wife about a possible trip abroad, but where would that get them? Nowhere. He needed the results of those toxicology tests and he needed more evidence. He might get the latter from viewing Redsall's room at the guest house.

He said, 'Redsall gave the Historic Dockyard security officers an address in Coleraine, Northern Ireland, so it's a fair guess he was staying at this guest house in Southsea.' Horton showed Uckfield the card retrieved from Redsall's wallet. 'He might not be alone.'

Uckfield consulted his watch. Horton knew what was running through his mind. It was a waste of time. Horton knew it was very late to be disturbing the owners of the guest house who must have thought their visitor had decided to stay out with friends all night. They could wait until the morning, but there *might* be someone waiting anxiously for Daniel Redsall.

He said, 'It's all right, Steve, you don't have to come. Go home or back to that operation Alison told me you were on tonight. I can handle this and brief you in the morning.'

Uckfield eyed him malevolently. After a moment he said tersely, 'I'll meet you outside in ten minutes.'

The implied threat worked. Not that Horton would have squealed to Alison Uckfield or anyone else, and he could have visited the guest house alone. But he wanted Uckfield along. He gave instructions for Taylor to drop the boat keys back to Ashton, who was still on Crawford's yacht, and then went to inform him. He didn't have to knock on the hatch; it opened as he stepped on board. Peering down into the cabin he caught Ames' enquiring look but there was nothing he could tell her in front of the others. Horton told Ashton that he would contact him tomorrow, which wasn't greeted very enthusiastically.

Ten minutes later Horton was pulling up behind Uckfield's BMW in a road of large semi-detached four-storey

Edwardian houses just off the seafront, and which he noted with interest was literally just around the corner from Douglas Spalding's residence, a fact he didn't mention to Uckfield because there wasn't time and it might mean nothing anyway.

It took a few stout knocks and a finger pressed on a bell before a stocky, bleary-eyed man with grizzled grey-black hair answered the door wearing a dark blue dressing gown over plain navy-blue pyjamas and an anxious frown which deepened into something akin to fright as he viewed them. Horton didn't blame him: two wet men standing on his doorstep, one wearing biker's clothing, was enough to worry anyone. He probably thought they were polite burglars who rang before breaking down the door. Swiftly Horton showed his warrant card. 'I apologize for the lateness of our visit, Mr Crossley, but we need to check if a Daniel Redsall is staying with you.'

'He is. Has he had an accident?' Crossley asked with a mixture of surprise and concern.

'I'm sorry to say he's dead.'

'Good God! Come in.'

They stepped into the hall. Horton swiftly took in the pale cream walls decorated with framed pictures of Portsmouth through the ages. There was an antique table to the right of the door and on it he noted the registration book, which was closed. Above it was a notice board with event posters pinned to it, one of which immediately caught Horton's attention. Beside the table was a rack of pamphlets detailing the local attractions.

'This is dreadful,' Crossley continued in hushed tones. 'Was he mugged?'

Sadly, Horton thought, that was a predictable assumption. 'It doesn't appear so,' he said somewhat non-committally, wiping his feet on the doormat and eyeing Uckfield pointedly, who reluctantly did the same. It was either that or removing footwear, and stocking feet always made Horton feel vulnerable and was to be avoided at all costs. He asked if

Redsall had been staying there alone and was relieved when the answer came that he was. The Northern Ireland police would probably have the unpleasant task of breaking the news to the next of kin.

'We'd like to see his room if that's possible,' Horton asked Crossley politely. He put him somewhere in his mid-sixties.

'Of course. I'll get the key for you.'

He hurried off to the rear of the building giving Horton the opportunity to open the registration book. Redsall had checked in on Sunday at three fifty-five p.m. His eyes flicked up to the poster on the notice board above the desk. 'Dr Spalding's lecture.'

'That probably confirms he went to it on the off-chance and his death has nothing to do with Spalding,' Uckfield said grouchily, glancing at it.

Maybe, thought Horton. But he wondered what had prompted him to attend a lecture on women in the Royal Navy. Redsall didn't look as though he was in the Navy, although he could be ex-Navy. And even if he hadn't known Spalding, it didn't rule out the fact that he could have witnessed something that had led to his death. There was no point repeating his theory, and anyway, coming towards them was Mr Crossley and behind him a woman at least a few inches taller than her husband, with long brown-grey hair pulled back from a cavernous face and large round brown eyes that looked excited instead of worried. She smiled, showing a wide mouth with large protruding teeth and pulled the cream towelling knee-length dressing gown tighter around her.

'Ted's told me about poor Mr Redsall,' she said in a hushed voice, clearly not wanting to disturb the other guests but Horton thought they couldn't have failed to have heard them banging on the door and ringing the bell, unless it only rang in the proprietor's quarters. 'I'm Brenda Crossley. How did he die?'

'We're not sure yet but he was found at the marina in Oyster Quays. Did he mention meeting anyone there?'

They both shook their heads. Ted Crossley offered to take their wet coats. Probably didn't want them dripping all over the stair carpet. He hung them up by the door and said, 'I'll take you up to his room. It's on the second floor, at the rear.'

'And I'll make some tea.' Brenda Crossley bustled off back down the corridor.

As they climbed the stairs, Horton said quietly, 'I see from your registration book that Mr Redsall signed in on Sunday at 3.55 p.m., did he go out again?'

'Yes, about 6.30 p.m., for something to eat I assume; we don't do dinners, just bed and breakfast. He came back about 9 p.m.'

'Has he stayed here before?'

'No. He booked over the Internet. I can let you have a copy of his booking form if it will help.'

'Thanks. How many guests do you have?'

'We're full. Eleven guests in three double rooms, one family room and one single, Mr Redsall's room, all en-suite and with free access to Wi-Fi,' Crossley said proudly but quietly, hoping not to disturb the other guests. 'This is Mr Redsall's room.'

He unlocked the door and stepped back to allow them in. Uckfield entered and Horton followed. Swiftly he registered the freshly painted cream walls displaying more local landscapes, the single bed, made up with a pale blue quilt, a large old-fashioned mahogany wardrobe and a matching chest of drawers on top of which was a tray containing a cup and saucer, tea and coffee-making facilities. A modern television set was mounted above it on the wall and to its left there was a door that led into the en-suite shower and toilet.

Turning back, he said, 'Did Mr Redsall have an accent?'

Crossley looked slightly taken aback by the question, and even Uckfield raised his eyebrows. 'No.'

Horton had wondered if Redsall was a native of Northern Ireland. He still could be but had got rid of his accent.

Crossley added, 'He was very well spoken though, educated kind of voice, quiet.'

Horton could see that Uckfield was impatient to get shot of Crossley and so was he. He said, 'Where can we find you when we've finished?' He hoped Crossley wasn't going to insist on staying. But he took the hint.

'Ground floor at the rear.'

Horton nodded and quietly closed the door.

Uckfield wrenched open the wardrobe door and peered inside. 'Nothing here. Looks as though he travelled light. Anything in the chest of drawers?'

'One cotton checked shirt, crumpled, three round-necked T-shirts, also worn, one with the University of Ulster logo on it, two pairs of socks and one pair of underpants. And this.' Horton held up a large brown leather wallet. As Uckfield crossed to him, he extracted the contents, relaying their details. 'Flight and railway ticket. Redsall flew from Belfast on Sunday arriving at Southampton at five past one and he was booked to return Thursday on the four o'clock flight from Southampton. The train ticket is for Coleraine to Belfast return, which matches with the address he gave the Historic Dockyard. There's another train ticket here for Portsmouth Harbour to Southampton Parkway. And here's a copy of his Internet booking form. There's a landline number but no mobile number.'

And Horton would like to know if Redsall had owned one, or an iPad or computer, because none of those items were here and they hadn't been in that rucksack.

In a bored manner Uckfield said, 'There's nothing here. Might as well go home. You can send a couple of plods around in the morning to take statements.'

But Horton had no intention of doing that. 'Let's see what the Crossleys have got to say first, especially as they've offered us a cup of tea.' He didn't leave time for Uckfield to protest but swept out of the room and down the stairs carrying Redsall's wallet.

Coffee was Horton's tipple, but he didn't tell Brenda Crossley that as she waved them onto the high bar stools across the breakfast bar from her and her husband in the spotlessly clean modern kitchen and poured them both mugs of tea.

Uckfield eyed the stool with distaste and grunted as he eased his short stout figure onto the stool while Horton climbed onto the one next to him with alacrity. Brenda Crossley pushed forward a plate of biscuits which Uckfield tackled with relish. Judging by the Crossleys' eager expressions and heightened colour, Horton could tell they had been speculating on the cause of Redsall's death and, if they weren't stupid, and Horton didn't think they were, also on why it had prompted the visit from such high-ranking officers instead of uniformed PCs or a detective constable at the most.

Horton opened the questioning. 'Did Mr Redsall say why he was here?'

Ted Crossley answered. 'I asked him, but he just said it was for a few days' break. He didn't elaborate and I didn't probe because I got the impression he didn't want to talk about it. You pick up on these things when you run a guest house. We get all sorts. Some will tell you their life story at the drop of a hat and you have a job shutting them up, others are tight-lipped and a bit stand-offish. I wouldn't have described Mr Redsall as that though, more shy, quiet, a bit nervy and nerdy like.'

'Ted! The poor man's dead.'

'Doesn't make my impression of him any different,' Ted quickly replied. Horton could see he was of the 'I speak as I find' type and bugger anyone's feelings, a bit like Ivor Meadows. Sometimes that was helpful, but often it was unreliable because those types could be blinkered by their own bigoted and narrow views.

'You said nervy?' Horton probed.

'Twitchy, on edge.'

'Worried?'

Ted thought for a moment. 'Possibly, but excited underneath it.'

Horton wasn't sure how much store he could set by that. Crossley could be fabricating it to add to the excitement and intrigue surrounding the death. 'Did you see him with a computer, or did he ask about your free Wi-Fi access?'

'No.'

'Did either of you see him with a mobile phone?'

Both Crossleys shook their heads.

'Was he carrying anything when he arrived?'

'Only his rucksack.'

'And you can confirm he was booked in until Thursday?'

Brenda Crossley pushed a piece of paper across the breakfast bar to Horton. 'Yes, I printed you off a copy.'

It was the same one Horton had found in the wallet, which was now in his pocket, but he didn't say. He smiled his thanks and took it asking if they knew what Daniel Redsall had done for a living.

Ted Crossley answered. 'He didn't say and I didn't ask. Like I said, he was quiet. Difficult to make conversation with. At breakfast I asked if he had a good night, and he said yes. We talked about the weather and that was about it. He didn't say what he was doing Monday or today, he just went out.'

'What time?' Uckfield asked with his mouth full of biscuit.

Ted Crossley answered, 'Almost straight after breakfast and he didn't come back until late afternoon on Monday, about 5 p.m., and then he went out again in the evening.'

And that was to Spalding's lecture. Horton said, 'And that was at?'

Brenda Crossley answered. '6.15 p.m. I was watering my tubs and window boxes in the front garden.'

Horton had seen the magnificent display when he'd drawn up.

'I said hello, he smiled and hurried off.'

'In which direction?'

'Towards the seafront and the Canoe Lake.'

The opposite direction to Spalding's house. But according to their evidence Spalding wasn't there anyway, but at the dockyard preparing for his talk.

Ted Crossley said, 'He returned about 10 p.m.'

And that fitted with the time he'd checked out of the dockyard at 9.25 p.m. Redsall had left ten minutes before Dr Spalding. And judging by the signature in the guest house registration book it looked as though it was the same as the one that appeared on the dockyard list and on the credit and debit cards.

'And yesterday, Tuesday?'

Before Ted Crossley could answer his wife jumped in. 'He went out early, before breakfast. I saw him leave. It must have been about 7 a.m. That was the last I saw of him. Did you see him yesterday?' She addressed her husband.

'No.'

Horton sipped his tea out of politeness and tried not to show he disliked the brew. 'How did he seem on his return on Monday?'

Ted Crossley answered. 'Fine. I asked if he'd had a good evening and he said "yes, thank you" and that was it.'

Uckfield slid off his seat, clearly believing there was nothing more to be gleaned here. Maybe he was right. And he'd finished the biscuits. Horton rose. He asked the Crossleys to leave Redsall's room as it was and added, 'We'd like to send someone round tomorrow to take fingerprints.'

'Of our guests?' Crossley said, alarmed.

Horton hesitated. There was nothing to say that any of the guests weren't connected with Redsall's death and he didn't think they'd mind their prints being taken, probably add a bit of spice to their holiday, but bearing in mind that Uckfield didn't believe there was a suspicious death to investigate and his glowering look, Horton said, 'Just the prints in Mr Redsall's room and yours and any other member of staff who went in there, so that we can eliminate them.'

'There's only us,' Brenda Crossley said.

'I'd also like a list of the guests who have been here during Redsall's stay. We can collect it tomorrow.'

Crossley nodded agreement and showed them out.

Outside Uckfield said, 'There's not one shred of evidence to say this is a suspicious death. We do nothing more until we get the results of the autopsy.'

Uckfield might not do anything but that wasn't going to stop Horton. He said, 'We need to trace the next of kin. It would help if Sergeant Trueman could do that.'

After a moment Uckfield nodded agreement. 'OK.'

At least Dr Clayton would be back to conduct the autopsy, thought Horton, as he watched Uckfield pull away, presumably heading home, although knowing Uckfield he could be returning to his lover, whoever she was.

Horton returned to his boat. He was tired but as he lay watching the minutes tick by into hours his whirling brain refused to be still. Uckfield was right — there was nothing to indicate that Spalding had been killed, and neither was there any evidence to indicate Daniel Redsall had been, but a whole swathe of questions kept spinning around his head like an endless merry-go-round. Why had Daniel Redsall attended Spalding's lecture? Why had he ended up dead the next day? Why had he been on Ashton's yacht? How did he get onto the pontoons at Oyster Quays? Would the security cameras reveal a sighting of him? Had Redsall signed in earlier at the marina office? And if he had signed in as a visitor then who had he been visiting? Someone on Ashton's yacht or someone on Agent Ames' yacht? Or someone else who had been in the marina?

It was pointless trying to answer these questions and useless considering them any further until they had more information, which he'd get despite Uckfield's lack of cooperation. He willed himself to relax and steeled himself not to look at his watch again. Instead, he focused on the sound of the sea lapping against the boat and the rhythm of its gentle movement, hoping that it would calm him. The rain had stopped and gradually he began to feel himself slipping into sleep. Infuriatingly though, just when he was on the edge one question sprang to mind and refused to budge. He knew it was critical. What had brought Redsall to Portsmouth from Northern Ireland?

CHAPTER NINE

An answer of sorts came to him the next morning. He looked up from his computer as Walters waddled into the CID office reading the *Daily Mirror*. Horton called out to him through his open door to come into his office, adding, 'You too, Cantelli.'

Cantelli, entering behind Walters, eyed Horton, concerned. 'Andy, you look knackered.'

He felt it. He'd had about three hours' sleep, and even that had been nothing more than a half waking kind of dose. Just before six a.m. he'd finally given up all attempts, taken a cold shower to shock himself into full wakefulness, was in the canteen by seven a.m. having breakfast and in his office by 7.30 a.m. in time to see from his window Bliss's sports car pull into the car park. He'd forgotten she was back from her course today, and wished they'd found her a role at Bramshill, which reminded him that he hadn't yet contacted Professor Thurstan Madeley. His telephone number wasn't on his website, but Horton knew someone at Bramshill who would give it to him. They'd have it on file there. He'd rung and asked for John Harrison, a police officer he'd served with over the years who on his promotion to inspector a year ago had taken up a post as training officer at the college. After a brief exchange of news Horton had told him he wanted to get in touch with Madeley.

'Thinking of asking his advice on policing?' Harrison had joked.

'Why not? He might have the magic answer to solving crime without having to fill in all this mountain of paperwork.'

'If he does, he's probably given it to DCI Bliss.'

'He knows her?' Horton had asked, amazed.

'He does now. He gave a lecture on her course.'

'About?'

'Understanding the social influences affecting today's criminals.'

Horton snorted. 'She needs to understand her staff first.'

'Well by all accounts Professor Madeley was most impressed with DCI Bliss, in fact we all were, and her governor will be too. She came top of the class.'

'I might have known.' Horton had got Madeley's mobile telephone number without having to explain why he needed it. He had sensed Harrison's curiosity, but Harrison knew that even if he'd asked Horton wouldn't have told him. He hadn't rung Madeley yet. It was too early, and he wanted to do it away from the station. He didn't want to risk anyone overhearing or crashing in on him as no doubt Bliss would soon, now that she must have seen Cantelli and Walters arrive.

'I had rather a late night,' Horton replied to Cantelli's enquiry, waving them into seats across his desk. He briefed them about Redsall's death. Cantelli looked shocked and then thoughtful. Walters simply looked bemused. Maybe this time he was right to be. 'I've found some information on Redsall that might suggest why he was in Portsmouth.' Horton indicated to his computer. 'According to the University of Ulster's website he was a marine archaeologist, interested in seafaring watercraft.'

'The M33?' suggested Cantelli.

'Possibly, and perhaps he consulted Spalding about it, him being a naval historian. And Redsall could have been on the pontoons at Oyster Quays because he was interested in the MGB 81, it's a 1942 motor gun boat,' he added for both their benefit. 'He's visiting lecturer at the Centre for Maritime Archaeology at Ulster, joined them last September and before that he worked just up the road here in Southampton at their Centre for Maritime Archaeology.'

That didn't answer the question why he was dead though. Horton had also read on the university's website that Redsall had been involved in a study of historic shipwrecks in Ireland. The Solent had enough shipwrecks to keep any marine archaeologist happy for decades, but it was a long way from Ireland. Horton wondered if Redsall had been researching a ship wrecked off Ireland which had set sail from Portsmouth. Perhaps that was where Spalding came into it. But neither theory meant either man's death was suspicious, as Uckfield would be quick to point out. But what did bother Horton was the fact that if Redsall had been engaged on research then where were his notes? Certainly not in his room or in his rucksack.

Addressing Cantelli he said, 'Ask Dr Menchip if she knows or recognizes Redsall and see what Alvita Baarda can tell us about him and Spalding. Did the two of them talk? Did they seem to know one another? You know the drill.' Horton handed Cantelli a photograph of Redsall which he'd printed off from the University of Ulster's website. It wasn't as grim as the ones Clarke had taken of the body.

'I'll re-interview Julie Preston. Walters, check if the control room at Oyster Quays has sent over the CCTV footage of the marina for last night, and if not chase them up. And call the marina office, ask them if Redsall signed in yesterday and get someone from the fingerprint bureau round to the Crossleys.'

The sound of footsteps in CID caught Horton's attention and he looked up to see Bliss striding across the deserted room with a scowl of welcome on her narrow face, her ponytail swinging high behind her head like a horse swishing its tail at irritating flies. Cantelli and Walters hastily rose as she entered his office, but Horton remained seated.

'Good course, Ma'am?' he asked, wondering how different she would look with a dash of lipstick and her hair down. Not that he really wanted to find out. She cast her cool green eyes over Cantelli and Walters. Walters shifted and looked as though he was going to belch but managed not to. With a nod of her head, she gave them a curt dismissal. They didn't need telling twice.

Plonking her narrow backside in the chair that Walters' fat one had vacated she asked him for an update on outstanding cases. Swiftly he gave her one, hoping she didn't ask too many questions because he'd hardly looked at the files. He ended with the news about Redsall's death but without saying that his officers were investigating it, which was just as well because she said, 'I understand that it isn't being treated as suspicious, so we don't spend time on it.' She was clearly singing from the same hymn sheet as Uckfield. Rising, she said, 'I expect your performance targets for July, which are seriously overdue, and your team's customer satisfaction survey results within the next couple of hours, Inspector.'

'Anything in particular you'd like us to ask the victims of crime?' Horton asked airily as she reached the door.

She spun round. Her eyes narrowed. 'You have the questions on the survey.'

'I wondered if you might have some new suggestions following your course. For example, perhaps we should ask the victims how they *feel* towards the criminal. Perhaps if they understood the social influences that made the scumbags beat up and rob innocent people, they might more readily forgive them, excuse them even.'

'Just get on with it.'

'Ma'am.'

With a brief smile, Horton rang Trueman and asked if the Northern Ireland police had any new information to report.

'They've been to Redsall's flat. It's rented and there's no personal correspondence in it or photographs. The other occupants in the building don't know anything about him. But the university have given them the details of the next of kin. It's a Beatrice Redsall and she lives at Three Laden Mansions, Craneswater, Southsea.'

'But that's local,' Horton said, surprised, not only because he hadn't expected that, but the address was just a stone's throw from Redsall's guest house. So why hadn't Redsall stayed with her? 'What relation is she to him?'

'Aunt. Daniel Redsall wasn't married and there are no kids.'

Horton supposed the aunt could be elderly and that was the reason Redsall hadn't stayed with her. Perhaps he didn't want to inconvenience her. Did she know her nephew was in Portsmouth? Had he visited her?

'Anyone told her yet?' he asked.

'No.'

'I'll do it.' And he'd better get going before the wicked witch in the wardrobe came out of it. 'Arrange for a uniformed woman police officer to meet me there in twenty minutes.'

Horton rang off. On his way out he told Walters where he was heading and that he was to keep quiet about what he was doing regarding the case if Bliss asked. Walters nodded. Heading for Southsea, Horton wondered who had briefed Bliss about Redsall's death. She didn't normally have early-morning meetings with Uckfield, but he guessed she might have had one this morning with ACC Dean following the glowing reports of her performance on the course and Uckfield must have reported the death to Dean.

Instead of heading straight for Laden Mansions Horton decided to call in at Spalding's house. He was reluctant to bother Mrs Spalding again, but he needed to check if she recognized Redsall's name or the man himself. There was a chance that Redsall had called on Spalding, he thought, pressing his finger on the bell. Or Spalding could have visited Redsall at the guest house although he felt sure if that were the case then the Crossleys would have mentioned it last night.

Mrs Spalding answered the door promptly, looking as elegant as she had the day before, only this time, she was wearing a patterned knee-length summer dress and sandals instead of the dark trousers and flat pumps. She'd again applied her make-up with precision, but it couldn't disguise the fatigue and pain etched on her oval face or the deep sorrow and shock in her dark brown eyes. If Spalding *had* been having an affair, then Horton, like Cantelli, hoped it wasn't the cause of his death, because he didn't want Jacqueline Spalding to discover it. She would though. Murder brought out all the dirty linen and hung it right in front of your nose. *If* this was murder, and Horton knew in his gut it was.

The house was silent. As though reading his thoughts she explained that her son, Julian, and Louise, her daughter, were in their rooms, either on their computers or watching television. Horton didn't ask how they were taking the news. How could they take it except with bewilderment, anger and sorrow once they realized the full impact of it? Ronald Spalding was in the kitchen. She invited him through and offered him a coffee, but he declined both. Standing in the small tiled outer hall he said, 'I won't keep you long. I just need to check a couple of things with you, Mrs Spalding. Have you ever seen this man before?' He showed her the photograph of Redsall and watched her reaction as she studied it carefully. After a moment she shook her head. 'His name is Daniel Redsall,' prompted Horton, 'does that mean anything to you?'

'No. Should it?' she asked, eyeing him, confused.

'He might have known your husband.'

'I never heard Douglas mention the name.'

Horton believed her. He said, 'Daniel Redsall was found dead last night. We don't know yet how he died but he was at your husband's lecture on Monday night.'

'I see.' But clearly, she didn't see and neither did Horton, yet.

'We're just examining all possible links,' he added.

'And you think this man's death,' she indicated the photograph, 'has something to do with Douglas'?'

'We don't know.' It was the truth.

She eyed him keenly. 'Do you think Douglas killed himself?'

'It's a possibility.'

'But you're still looking into it?' she asked hopefully.

'Yes.'

She took a breath then said, 'You'll tell me if you find anything?'

He promised he would. He again apologized for disturbing her and left feeling sorry for her and angry with Spalding if he had in some way brought this upon his family. But he didn't know that for certain. Spalding could be an innocent victim in this — only why had he lied to both his wife and doctor?

He wondered what she had done before she'd become Mrs Douglas Spalding. She was intelligent and had probably held down a good job. He also wondered how she'd met her husband. Could she have been in the Navy? Somehow, he couldn't see that. He indicated right and turned into Nettlecombe Avenue where he found Ted and Brenda Crossley. Again, he was offered coffee and again he refused.

'We thought you might be the fingerprint officer,' Ted Crossley said when they were in the kitchen. In the daylight Horton saw the room overlooked a well-tended garden with a neat square of lawn, a couple of trees provided shade for the tables and chairs positioned under them and a wide expanse of flowering shrubs bordered three sides.

'I wanted to ask you if Daniel Redsall mentioned his aunt while he was here. Beatrice Redsall, she lives in Laden Mansions.'

'But that's just around the corner,' Brenda Crossley answered, surprised. 'He never said anything to me about her.'

'Me neither.'

'Did he mention a Douglas Spalding?'

'No. Like I said last night he was a very private man. Didn't say much at all. Hang on, Spalding you say?' Ted Crossley paused, frowning. 'Isn't that the professor who gave that lecture on women in the Royal Navy?' He flashed a glance at his wife.

'Yes. Daniel Redsall attended it,' Horton replied, trying to interpret the meaning of the glance between them.

'Ah.' Again, Ted Crossley paused. Then said, 'Wasn't he . . . didn't he have an accident in the dockyard? I heard something about it on the news.'

'His body was found in Number One Dock.'

'Good God, where the old Monitor is?'

'You know it?'

'Of course. We've got leaflets on all the attractions in the Historic Dockyard for our guests and recommend a visit there. And Mr Redsall was at the lecture the same night Spalding had his accident?'

Horton didn't care for the way Crossley said 'accident' but he couldn't blame him for thinking it was more than that, which was certainly more than Uckfield thought.

He said, 'We have to explore connections even if they don't mean anything.' He could see that he wasn't fooling the Crossleys. They'd probably already fabricated a theory about why Redsall was dead and who had killed him, *if* he'd been killed, he silently added, along with how he had been killed. Maybe he should hand the case over to them. He withdrew a photograph of Douglas Spalding and asked if he had ever called upon Redsall here. They both agreed, with disappointment, thought Horton, that he hadn't.

As he was leaving, he remembered that look that had passed between them and the poster that had been exhibited above the registration desk, which he noted was no longer there. 'You advertised Dr Spalding's lecture, why?'

Again, that glance between them. It was Brenda who answered. 'We were both in the Navy. It's how we met. I intended to go to the lecture, but we had too much on with the guest house being full. It was a shame because I'd like to have heard what he had to say.'

'How did you find out about the lecture?'

'We're on the mailing list for all the dockyard events. We do our best to help promote them.'

Of course. That made sense. Horton was tempted to leave the Harley parked outside the Crossleys' guest house and walk the few hundred yards to Laden Mansions but decided against it. Soon he was pulling into the rear of the 1930s elegant three-storey building and drew to a halt to the right of a block of garages. His phone rang. It was Walters.

'Thought I'd better warn you, Guv, DCI Bliss wanted to know where you were. I said I wasn't sure, but I thought you'd gone to see an informant. Don't think it did much for her blood pressure.'

Or my chances of staying in CID. 'Did you tell her what you were working on?'

'She didn't ask but stormed off with a face like a fractured piston engine.'

Horton could well imagine. 'Have you got anything to report?'

'Oyster Quays are emailing over the CCTV footage. The marina manager says no one called Redsall signed in yesterday and I can't get hold of anyone at Kings College. I'll try again in half an hour, and so far, no joy with the airports. They're checking their passenger lists and said they'd get back to me.'

Horton rang off. As Redsall hadn't signed in that meant he'd either arrived after the marina office had closed at dusk or he'd come by boat with someone who had signed in or who kept his boat moored there. Horton hoped the CCTV cameras had picked him up.

Bliss would no doubt be calling him soon and demanding his return. But now that he was safely out of flapping ears at the station, and while he waited for the uniformed officer to show, he'd try getting hold of Bliss's new-found admirer, Professor Thurstan Madeley. He stabbed the number on his mobile that Harrison had relayed to him earlier and got Madeley's voicemail. Hesitating for only a moment he said crisply, 'Professor Madeley, this is Detective Inspector Horton. I'd like to speak to you about the thirteenth of March 1967. Can you call me please?'

OK, he thought with a slight quickening of heart, let's see what happens now. He was certain that Madeley would return his call, but would he tell anyone about it? DCS Sawyer of the Intelligence Directorate for example? But Horton had no evidence that Madeley was in league with Sawyer over the latter's ambition to track down Zeus. There was also no evidence that Madeley knew anything about the disappearance of Jennifer Horton — why should he? He was just a professor who had been in charge of that archive project on the student sit-in protest.

He pushed the thoughts aside, switched off his phone and went to break the news to Beatrice Redsall that her nephew was dead.

CHAPTER TEN

'As you are accompanied by a female police officer, Inspector, am I correct in assuming you are the bearer of bad news?' Beatrice Redsall said in a well-educated voice after Horton had introduced himself. He quickly assessed that this elegant woman in her mid-seventies, with short fine silver hair and dressed impeccably in camel-coloured trousers and a cream silk blouse was a no-nonsense sort of person. He doubted he'd need PC Louise Edmonds' assistance at his side.

Removing a copy of the photograph of Daniel Redsall, he said gently, 'Is this a relation of yours, Ms Redsall?'

'Miss,' she corrected, glancing at the photograph and then back up at Horton. 'Yes, it's Daniel, my nephew. He's the only child of my late brother, Jonathan, and his wife, Rosemary. Jonathan died eight years ago and Rosemary nineteen years ago.'

'I'm sorry to have to inform you that Daniel is dead.'

There was no reaction on her intelligent classically proportioned face or in the pale blue eyes. After a brief pause, she said, 'You'd better come in.'

She turned. Horton caught Edmonds' curious glance before following Beatrice Redsall into a wide airy lounge. It was tastefully and expensively decorated with high-quality, classically designed furniture, pastel-coloured Chinese rugs, and pale blue and grey curtains. From where he stood Horton could see the boating lake opposite the flats and beyond it the sea. There were a handful of paintings on the wall and various *objets d'art* dotted about the room.

She waved a slender arm at the armchairs, sat down and Horton followed suit, nodding at Edmonds to do the same.

'How did Daniel die?'

Still, she showed no emotion — was that because she didn't care? Perhaps she hadn't known her nephew that well or liked him even.

'We won't know until after the autopsy, but when his body was found on a yacht in Oyster Quays there were no visible signs of cause of death.'

'A boat? Daniel's?' she asked, raising beautifully shaped eyebrows.

'No. It belongs to a man called Carl Ashton.' The name seemed to mean nothing to her. Horton hadn't thought it would, but he wanted to check. 'Do you know him?'

'No.'

'Did your nephew know him or his company Sail Away Events?'

'I have no idea.'

Horton again left a short silence before saying, 'You seem surprised that Daniel might have owned a boat.' More than the fact that he was in Portsmouth, so perhaps he had visited his aunt.

'I'd be *very* surprised if he did. Daniel was not interested in material possessions.'

It was said as though it were a flaw in her nephew's character. He eyed her quizzically and said nothing, forcing her to add, 'He was never happier than when dressed in old clothes and grubbing around in the mud of ancient harbours or in a diving suit at the bottom of the sea searching for artefacts.'

Horton got the message loud and clear. Beatrice Redsall disapproved of her nephew's occupation. He wondered why.

'I understand he was very well respected in marine archaeological circles.' Horton had no idea if Redsall had been, but he said it to provoke a reaction and gain further insight into the dead man and his relationship with his aunt.

'He may have been, but it's not the career his father had chosen for him and it hardly makes a difference, does it?'

Horton quickly caught her meaning but decided to play dumb. 'A difference to what?'

'To society of course; to this insane world in which we live, Inspector, where greed and selfishness are the new gods, and sacrifice and duty are words that no longer exist.' It was said without bitterness. She added, 'The past can hardly matter to a generation obsessed with the here and now, the "me" culture.'

'An understanding of the past can give us an insight into the future.'

'Possibly, Inspector, but most of the time humanity chooses to ignore that insight and mankind continues to make the same mistakes. And that's why we need people whose jobs really matter, so that they can pick up the pieces. People like yourself and my brother.'

'He was a police officer?' Horton asked, stumped for a moment.

'Of course not,' she said dismissively. 'Jonathan was a Rear Admiral.'

That, clearly according to her philosophy, was way above being a cop. It probably ranked even higher than a chief constable. Swiftly reading the undertones he said, 'Your brother was disappointed then that his son didn't follow in his footsteps and join the Navy.'

A shadow crossed her eyes for the first time; he didn't think it was for her dead nephew but for her dead brother, whom she had obviously worshipped.

'Daniel had such a bright future ahead of him. He was clever. He had the best education money can buy, Salisbury Cathedral School, Winchester College. He never wanted for anything, including encouragement. He was due to join the

Navy after Winchester and had a place at the Britannia Royal Naval College, but he threw it all back in his father's face.'

'They rowed?'

'Of course not,' she said stiffly, although Horton wondered if that were the truth. 'But Jonathan could never understand why Daniel didn't want a naval career and neither could I. Our family has served in the Royal Navy for generations. We can trace our ancestry back to 1769 and Sir Thomas Masterman Hardy who served as flag captain to Admiral Lord Nelson and commanded HMS *Victory* at the Battle of Trafalgar,' she explained in case they didn't know their history. 'But Daniel decided to break with that tradition after centuries. He even went so far as to say he opposed acts of violence and was, as a principle, against wars. Principles are all very well, Inspector, but not very helpful when your country is being violated and your people terrorized and subjected to gross acts of humiliation. Bully boys thrive on people who are principled.'

Horton was growing ever more curious about Daniel Redsall's background and motivations. 'Did Daniel come to see you while he was in Portsmouth?'

'I haven't seen or heard from him since his father died. We didn't even exchange Christmas cards.'

It was clearly the truth. So there was no point in asking her if she knew what her nephew had been doing here. 'He named you as his next of kin.'

Again those perfect eyebrows rose and a frown knitted her brow. 'How extraordinary!' Then she paused and gave a slight lift of one shoulder. 'But perhaps not. Daniel was always a loner. He didn't make friends very easily and he obviously didn't marry, or if he did it didn't last.'

Horton was beginning to feel a little sorry for Daniel Redsall and he sensed that PC Edmonds was too. He got the impression of a lonely, sad child, desperate for his family's affection and approval and never getting it. It would have been easy for him to have enlisted in the Navy and pleased everyone. Everyone, that was, except for himself. So there had been a determined streak in Redsall that had made him defy his family's wishes, and that showed a quiet, hidden strength.

He said, 'Does the name Douglas Spalding mean anything to you?'

'No.'

He retrieved the photograph of Spalding. 'Have you ever seen this man?'

She glanced at it. 'No.'

'Daniel attended a lecture given by Dr Spalding at the National Museum of the Royal Navy here in Portsmouth the night before he died. And Dr Spalding died shortly after giving his lecture on Monday night.'

'I don't see how that can have anything to do with Daniel's death.'

Maybe, but Horton was convinced otherwise. 'The lecture was about women serving in the Royal Navy.' He watched her closely but there was no reaction. 'From what you've said I wouldn't have thought the subject would have been of interest to your nephew.'

'Neither would I.'

'You weren't in the Navy, Miss Redsall?'

'Certainly not,' she declared vehemently with distaste.

He was curious about her background. Fishing further he said, 'I wondered if Daniel's interest was because his mother or some other female in his family had been or was in the Navy.'

'No. My role was to assist my father in his career when my mother died, and Rosemary's was to further Jonathan's career. When she died, I took over and helped my brother. These views may be unfashionable now, WPC Edmonds,' she threw at the police officer by Horton's side whose expression must have betrayed her thoughts on that subject. 'But duty wasn't a dirty word then and it isn't now as far as I'm concerned, though I accept my views are in the minority. But if more women knew their duty, we wouldn't have so many broken marriages and delinquent children causing the police and society so many problems.'

PC Edmonds opened her mouth to reply but Horton hastily prevented her from saying something she might regret. 'We will need you to formally identify the body, if you feel up to it, Miss Redsall.' He knew his last statement would goad her and it did.

'Of course, I'm up to it, Inspector,' she tartly replied. 'When?'

'Later this afternoon about 4.30, if that's convenient?' The autopsy would have been completed by then.

'Quite convenient.'

'We'll send a car for you.'

'I am perfectly capable of driving to the mortuary, Inspector.' Horton thought the empire had been built on women like her.

'Where are Daniel's effects?' she asked, rising, indicating that she considered their interview at an end.

'We have the things he brought with him from Northern Ireland—'

'Northern Ireland?'

'Yes, why?' he asked, studying her with new interest as he stood up. PC Edmonds followed suit.

'Is that where he was living?'

'Yes. He worked at Ulster University as a visiting lecturer. You didn't know?'

She eyed him steadily. 'As I said we'd lost touch. I'd assumed he'd be living on the south coast.'

Why? Horton wondered. Because of his interest in marine archaeology, he guessed. But that could have taken him to the other side of the world. Redsall could have been living in Swaziland for all she knew of him.

'Four thirty then,' he said.

'I'll be there, Inspector,' she replied crisply.

Outside he turned to Edmonds. 'What did you make of her?'

'Cool, emotionless, buttoned up and didn't seem very fond of her nephew.'

'No law against that.'

'No, sir.'

He sent her on her way and checked his phone for messages.

There was nothing from Madeley. He felt disappointed but perhaps it was too soon for him to return the call. He could be in a meeting or giving a lecture. He'd expected Bliss to have been onto him, but all was silent on that front too, which was a blessing. He called Trueman and gave him the gist of what Beatrice Redsall had said, ending with the news that he'd arranged for her formally to identify the body of her nephew later that afternoon.

'Is Uckfield still insisting on doing nothing until after the results of the autopsy?' he asked.

'Yep.'

Horton rang off. He checked his mirrors and indicated out into the traffic. A Honda motorbike pulled out several cars behind him and behind that, easing into the traffic, was a black Ranger with tinted windows. As he rode along the sea-front, he again considered Redsall's body lying on Ashton's yacht. There had been no signs of foul play. It didn't *look* as though Redsall had been murdered. But then it hadn't *looked* as though Spalding had been murdered, and maybe neither had been. But that feeling in his waters told him differently. Then there was Spalding's missing briefcase and Redsall's empty rucksack. Perhaps Spalding had tossed his briefcase into the sea and Redsall had carried food and water in his rucksack, which he'd consumed. He'd been taken ill and died. No foul play, no suspicious circumstances. Just a question over how he'd got onto the pontoons at Oyster Quays, and what he'd been doing there. Perhaps being a marine archaeologist, he had obtained the security code in order to study the MGB 81.

Horton turned his mind to his interview with Beatrice Redsall. There was nothing in it to hint at why her nephew might have been unlawfully killed or why he might have killed himself. But again, Horton wondered why Redsall had attended Spalding's lecture.

He checked his mirrors. The Honda was still behind him and so was the Ranger. He dropped his speed. Any slower and he'd be pulled up for dangerous driving, but neither the Honda nor the Ranger seemed inclined to pass him. Perhaps they deemed it too unsafe to do so; the promenade was fairly crowded with holiday makers and sun seekers, who could step out into the road at any moment.

At Southsea Castle he pulled over into a parking space in front of the Castle Field but didn't switch off the engine. The Honda purred by. He was unable to see the driver's face because of the helmet and as the Ranger slid by, Horton again couldn't glimpse the driver because of the darkened windows. He watched it indicate right and turn into the tree-lined Avenue de Caen. The Honda continued on its journey along the seafront. It was too late to get either registration numbers, but Horton knew he'd recognize both again. He was probably being unnecessarily edgy — that was the wretched DCS Sawyer putting ideas in his head, he thought, pulling back out into the traffic and following in the direction of the Honda towards Clarence Pier.

His head felt heavy from lack of sleep and going round in circles with theories and questions. Facts were what he needed, not airy-fairy suppositions. And the sooner he got them the better. But instead of heading straight for the Historic Dockyard he diverted to Oyster Quays. He wanted to show the marina manager a photograph of Redsall. He wondered if Redsall might have signed in using a different name. He also wondered if Melanie Jacobs and Steve Drummond would recognize Daniel Redsall. But as he swung into the entrance to Oyster Quays, he knew there was another reason he wanted to visit there, and she was on a boat with a prat called Rupert.

CHAPTER ELEVEN

There had been no sign of Agent Ames or Crawford's yacht and the marina manager claimed he'd never seen Daniel Redsall in his life. Horton hadn't been able to ask Melanie Jacobs and Steve Drummond if they knew him because they'd already sailed Ashton's yacht back to Cowes. Horton had resumed his journey to the dockyard where he was informed that Julie Preston was on a day off. Irritatingly, so too was Lewis Morden. It was turning out to be a frustrating morning, Horton thought, making for the security office to enquire if the librarian, Marcus Felspur, was at work. He was surprised to find Neil Gideon there.

'I was just about to have a cuppa, care to join me, Inspector?' Gideon waved the kettle at Horton.

He accepted the offer of a coffee and followed Gideon through to the rear of the security office. 'I thought you were on nights?' he said, pleased this would save him a visit to Gideon's home.

'I was but the boss decided to switch me to days. Yeah, I guess he thought I couldn't be trusted to work in the dark any more,' Gideon added sourly at Horton's unvoiced comment. 'His shuffle around hasn't pleased everybody but I'm not complaining, never did like working nights much, and we're a man short, will be for some time. Newton is on compassionate leave.' Pouring hot water on the tea bag in one mug and on instant coffee in the other Gideon continued, 'His wife's been taken into the hospice. Milk?'

Horton shook his head. He didn't like to disturb Newton when clearly he already had a great deal on his plate and that, he suspected, was the reason why the security had slipped. He put this to Gideon as he took his mug of coffee.

Gideon wrapped his fingers around his mug and eyed Horton uneasily. 'I don't want to get Matt into trouble.'

'Just tell me what happened?'

Putting his mug down carefully on the table, Gideon gestured Horton into the seat across it. Taking up position opposite him, Gideon lowered his voice and said, 'He shouldn't have come into work at all on Monday night, with his wife being so ill, and he was in a state when he got here but he said he just had to get out of the house. He couldn't bear looking at her so ill. He'd left his daughter with Joanna, his wife. Poor Matt was at his wits' end. I didn't know just how bad he was, otherwise, I'd have insisted he go home,' Gideon quickly added.

Horton sipped his coffee as Gideon continued.

'Matt thought working might help him get some relief for a while but as soon as he arrived, he knew it wouldn't. He then felt guilty at having run away, or rather ducking out as he called it. He chastised himself for being a coward and selfish. All he could think of was how he had to get away from so much sickness and pain that he couldn't stand it any longer and there was his poor wife . . . His mind obviously wasn't on the job.' Gideon looked worried. 'Matt told me this morning on the phone that he rang his daughter a few times during the evening, to see how his wife was.'

'And during that time anyone could have slipped in or out or returned after signing.'

'No,' Gideon said vehemently, 'because Matt had to open and close the side door. No one could have walked in, and no one could have returned after signing out. He swears to me he physically opened the door as each of the guests left and he shut and locked it behind them until the next guest appeared. I don't think he's lying about that.'

Horton considered this. 'But he was on his phone when some of them left.'

Gideon nodded and sipped his tea.

Several thoughts ran through Horton's mind. Ivor Meadows had told Horton that Newton had been on the phone when he'd left, which was why he was able to sprawl his signature over two rows, one of which had Dr Spalding's name in it. So had Daniel Redsall really signed out, or had someone done it for him? Could Redsall have remained hidden near the museum, killed Spalding by pushing him over the railing and taken the briefcase? But why the devil would he want to do that? And if he did then it meant Redsall was in league with someone, and that person had signed him out of the dockyard. From what he'd learned of Redsall thus far, he just couldn't see him as a killer and there was no motive. So far there was also no connection between the two men.

He handed Gideon the photograph of Daniel Redsall, saying, 'Do you remember seeing this man?'

Gideon studied it carefully. 'Yes. But I didn't talk to him.'

'Did you notice him speaking to anyone?'

Gideon shook his head.

'Not even to Dr Spalding?'

'No. But I only escorted the group from the *Victory* to the museum.'

'Did you see him carrying anything?'

Gideon eyed him warily as he considered this. 'Yes, a rucksack. Why? Has that gone missing?' he added half-jokingly.

'No, but Daniel Redsall's body was discovered last night at Oyster Quays.'

Gideon reeled back, then took a deep breath. 'What the hell's going on?'

That's what Horton intended finding out. 'We will need to interview Matt Newton, but I'd prefer it if you'd say nothing to him about this for the moment.'

116

'I doubt he'd take it in anyway with everything else on his plate.'

Horton swallowed a mouthful of coffee. 'I'd like to see Marcus Felspur, is he in today?'

'Yes. I'll give you a pass. I'll call him and he can meet you at the naval museum library entrance.'

A few moments later Horton was sitting in Felspur's untidy office, which was sandwiched behind the library's public area and what Felspur had explained was the archive storage behind them.

'I take it you're here about Dr Spalding's death,' Felspur said, eyeing him keenly across a desk covered with papers, ring binders and books. Although there were three desks in the room none of the others were occupied. Felspur had left his assistant in the library where Horton had seen two men sitting at desks poring over books.

Horton would tell Felspur about Redsall's death shortly, but first he wanted to hear what he remembered about Spalding on the night of his death.

'His passing will be a great loss,' Felspur added sadly.

'You liked him?'

'I admired his work.'

Not quite the same thing, thought Horton, eyeing the pale-skinned, slight man with intelligent grey eyes, thinning brown hair and slender fidgeting hands.

'He had the gift of bringing the past to life, taking serious and complex subjects and turning them into a language that even the lay person could understand, which was why his talks were so popular. Monday night was no different and particularly interesting because of my own research.'

Horton looked blank, which wasn't difficult because he had no idea what Felspur's background was or why it would be relevant.

He gave a small and modest smile. 'I'm interested in how our interpretation of the past coincides with cultural, social and political interests. I know it sounds a bit weird,' he added at Horton's bemused expression. 'But take any part of history — the abolition of slavery for example. Just over two hundred years ago a Royal Navy squadron was established to patrol the seas of West Africa, searching and detaining slave ships, liberating some hundreds of thousands of enslaved Africans, and now that part of history forms the basis of an exhibition in the museum. It's become a cultural interest.'

'Doesn't most history in the end?'

'No. Some of it gets buried, or distorted, either to suit cultural or social needs or political interests. The archives and volumes here in the library can tell that truth but the interpretation people put on them, or their choice of the facts, can be selective to suit their own purposes.'

'And did Dr Spalding do that?'

Felspur again gave that smile but this time as if to say, 'that's not for me to comment'. Horton got the impression of a clever man and a slightly resentful one. Why? Because he'd never achieved what he thought he was capable of? But Felspur could give him more details about Spalding's lecture. So far he only had Ivor Meadows' bigoted view and Julie Preston's broad outline and it might be helpful to know more. It might throw more light on why Redsall had attended it.

'Tell me about his lecture?'

Felspur looked only too eager to do so. 'Dr Spalding talked about the cultural and social impact of women in the Royal Navy from 1917 when the Women's Royal Naval Service was first formed, although it was disbanded in 1919 and reformed in 1939 for the Second World War. We hold a comprehensive WRNS archive, which Dr Spalding drew upon as well as personal diaries and press reports. He also conducted research of his own outside the museum through the university and central library in Portsmouth and using local historical and naval organizations and personal accounts. His lecture examined the views of people across the generations from all classes and of both genders, their attitudes and their views of women in the Navy, focusing on whether the views expressed in 1917 were the same as they are today.'

'And are they?' Horton asked, interested.

'Mostly, and mostly negative.'

'Perhaps they were the only views he selected from his research.' Felspur eyed him curiously and, Horton thought, with a touch of surprise. Perhaps he hadn't expected him to be so astute. Or did he think he was being critical of Spalding?

'Dr Spalding was an historian; he wouldn't skew his findings or his presentation.'

Oh yeah? Horton thought, wondering if Felspur really believed that. 'Did he offer any of his own opinions?'

'He highlighted sections of the interviews and reports, social commentary and documentation and left the audience to draw their own conclusions. He posed questions.'

'Controversial ones?'

'Depends on your viewpoint, Inspector, but no one got annoyed or upset if that's what you mean.'

Perhaps they didn't display their true emotions, thought Horton, but he didn't think anyone would have pushed Spalding into the dock because of his lecture on women serving in the Royal Navy, and besides none of the guests had; they'd all left by then. And still Horton couldn't see why Daniel Redsall had been interested in this topic.

'How did Dr Spalding seem during the lecture?'

'Fine.'

Horton sensed a 'but'. He left a silence which Felspur eventually filled.

'He *was* a little on edge towards the end of it. Distracted, I'd say. He seemed to lose the thread of what he was saying once or twice, which was uncharacteristic. I've heard him speak a couple of times and he's always been very fluent. He also brought the lecture to a more rapid close than normal.'

The obvious explanation for that was that Spalding had begun to feel unwell.

'Did you speak to him afterwards?' Horton knew Felspur had from Ivor Meadows, but no harm in not letting on.

'Yes. I told him how much I enjoyed his talk and that I was particularly looking forward to hearing him present his paper to an academic audience at the university, and to reading his paper on the subject.'

'Why?'

'The paper would contain a great deal more detail and list his reference sources, which I was very keen to see. He was in here frequently conducting his research. And the academic lecture would have been more tightly argued. He'd also have voiced his real conclusions, or at least posed them, some of them might even have been controversial.' Horton considered this as Felspur added regretfully, 'And now that won't happen unless someone presents his paper.'

'Could they do that?'

'If all the material is available, yes, and I don't see why it shouldn't be, do you?'

Horton thought of that missing briefcase containing Spalding's laptop. Somewhere at the back of his mind something nudged at him, but it was gone before he could grasp it.

'Who would present it?' he asked.

'His Head of School or possibly a PhD student he worked closely with.'

'Would you know who the latter is?' Horton knew the first was Dr Sandra Menchip.

'No, but the Head of School should be able to tell you that.' A small frown puckered Felspur's slim forehead. 'I must say, looking back on it, Dr Spalding didn't seem his usual self. When I was talking to him, he seemed distracted, a little rude even; he kept looking away and he was rubbing his eyes and forehead. Clearly, he must have been taken ill. I thought at the time that he wasn't interested in talking to me. I moved off only to discover that Mr Meadows had taken my place.'

And judging by Felspur's tone he thought the same of Meadows as did Julie Preston. The little man was a pain in the backside. With a tight smile, Felspur added, 'Mr Meadows is a regular visitor to the library and can be a little overbearing. I'm amazed he's not in here today. He is most days.'

'Researching for his book on crime and punishment in the Navy.'

'Yes.'

'And Dr Spalding's current research?' Horton probed, recalling that Jacqueline Spalding had claimed not to know what that was. And there had been nothing in Spalding's study to indicate its subject matter.

Felspur answered promptly. 'The Navy's impact on Portsmouth society and the common people, the different attitudes towards it between 1945 and 1978.'

'He told you this?'

'Indeed.'

That wasn't what Ivor Meadows had said. He'd claimed that Spalding was working on something to do with the Navy and prostitution. Spalding had probably lied to Meadows to deflect him from his true research and to shut him up. He said, 'Why those years?'

'After 1978, or to be more precise in 1979, it was said that we entered the second Cold War with the Soviet War in Afghanistan. Perhaps he just thought it a suitable cut-off point.'

Perhaps. 'How long had Dr Spalding been researching the subject?'

'I don't know, only that he used to come in at least twice a week and had done since January.'

'Always on the same days?'

'Yes, Mondays and Wednesdays. I assumed that was when he wasn't engaged in lecturing.'

'And the last time he was here?'

Felspur thought for a moment although Horton got the impression he didn't really need to. 'Last Wednesday. Mr Meadows was in here too.'

There didn't seem anything more he could obtain from his questions about Spalding so Horton asked Felspur if he knew a Daniel Redsall.

'Redsall? No, I don't think so.'

'He was at the lecture on Monday night.'

'Was he?'

'This might help.' Horton showed Felspur the photograph of Redsall.

121

'Yes, I remember him, casually dressed, earnest face, carrying a rucksack, but I didn't know his name. We chatted very briefly for a few minutes about the lecture, but we didn't introduce ourselves to each other.'

'What did he say?'

'I can't remember exactly, it was just general chit chat, interesting subject, how good Dr Spalding was, that sort of thing.'

'Did he know Dr Spalding?'

Felspur looked puzzled by Horton's line of questioning. 'He didn't claim to and he gave no indication of knowing him, but I did see him speaking to Dr Spalding after the lecture. When I headed towards them, he broke off his conversation and moved away.'

'What were they talking about?'

'I don't know.'

'How had they seemed?'

'Seemed? Oh you mean the exchange between them. I didn't pay much attention but I wasn't aware of any animosity.'

'Did they appear or give any sign that they knew one another?'

'No.'

'Did he say what had made him attend the lecture?'

'No and I didn't ask.'

Shame. 'Did you see him talking to anyone else?'

'No. Why all the questions, Inspector?'

'Daniel Redsall was found dead last night at Oyster Quays.'

Felspur visibly started. 'My God, how terrible. An accident?'

'We don't know yet.' Horton rose. Felspur scrambled up. 'I'm sorry I can't be more helpful, Inspector.'

'Thanks. You've been a great help.'

He left the library mulling over what Felspur had told him. Had it been an innocent exchange between two scholars, he wondered, or had they known one another? Felspur's evidence seemed to confirm Julie Preston's though, in that

Spalding did appear to be distracted and possibly feeling unwell.

Horton turned left instead of right and made his way to Number One Dock considering this and reviewing the theory he'd put to Uckfield, which the Super had dismissed, that Redsall could have witnessed Spalding being drugged and because of that he'd had to die. And it was possible that Redsall too had been drugged. He wished to God they'd hurry up with the results of that toxicology test on Spalding.

He drew up at the railings and peered down into the dock at the grey and white Monitor and then beyond it to the harbour. Drugged and disorientated, Spalding could have made for the sea, lost his grip on the briefcase and then staggered back here and fallen over. And Redsall could have met someone in Oyster Quays marina, been drugged and staggered onto Ashton's yacht and died. 'Visiting the scene of the crime, Inspector?'

Horton spun round to find the stout little figure of Ivor Meadows eyeing him curiously. 'Have you got any further with the investigation?'

'Still making inquiries, sir.'

'Of course.' Meadows tapped the side of his bulbous nose and nodded knowingly.

Horton retrieved the photograph of Daniel Redsall from his pocket. At least this saved him a visit to Meadows' flat.

'Do you recognize this man, sir?'

Meadows took it, frowning. He studied it for some seconds before answering slowly. 'Don't think so.'

'He was at the lecture on Monday night.'

'Was he?'

'You might have seen him talking to Dr Spalding,' prompted Horton but Meadows was looking blankly at him.

'No, can't say I remember him.'

Horton took back the photograph. 'His name's Daniel Redsall.'

'Redsall?' Meadows said thoughtfully, his brow furrowing.

'You recognize the name?'

'No.'

But Horton thought it meant something to Meadows and judging by his expression he was trying to remember what.

'Why are you interested in him?' Meadows asked.

'His body was found last night on a boat in Oyster Quays.'

'My God! How did he die?'

'We're still conducting tests.' Horton wasn't going to reveal what they had, which was practically nothing anyway.

'Two men dead and both here at the lecture. Any theories, Inspector?'

If I had I certainly wouldn't tell you. 'It's early days yet, sir. Thank you for your help.'

Horton put the photograph away and walked off leaving Meadows with a slightly irritated expression on his round little face. He returned to the station where he found Cantelli polishing off the remains of a sandwich. There was no sign of Walters. He was probably in the canteen.

'Dr Sandra Menchip hated Spalding's guts,' Cantelli said. 'OK, so I exaggerate, but she did not like him one tiny little bit though she went through the motions, initially anyway, of expressing shock and horror. But when we got down to the real nitty-gritty, she said he was a self-opinionated arrogant man who fancied himself and anything female under the age of thirty.'

'Sounds a bit like Uckfield.'

'Yeah, and he's also married.' Cantelli wiped his hands on his handkerchief and then ran it over his lips. 'But her description of Spalding fits with the possibility of him having an affair. And Dr Menchip says that if Spalding hadn't died, she'd have been asking him to leave when the new term began.'

'Why?'

'Because if he didn't, she'd bring a case against him for sexual harassment. Not on herself but a woman called Erica

Leyton. She's a research fellow at the Institute of Marine Sciences.'

Horton knew it. It was situated just along the road eastwards from the marina where he lived, and close to the mouth of Langstone Harbour. Would such a charge and a smear on Spalding's character and reputation be enough to make him kill himself?

'Did this Erica Leyton want to press charges?' he asked.

'Dr Menchip says she's managed to mollify her, but Alvita Baarda disagrees about the sexual harassment. She says Spalding just fancied himself, and anyone who took him seriously needed their head examined. He was smarmy and old.'

'Forty-three isn't old,' Horton cried, dismayed.

'It is when you're twenty,' Cantelli replied. 'She said that at the lecture on Monday night, Spalding told her how lovely she looked in her catering uniform. She was wearing a short black skirt, black tights and a white shirt, which from how she described them didn't leave much to the imagination and she's got a cracker of a figure. Not that I noticed, of course. She thinks Spalding had a thing about women in uniform.'

'He wouldn't be the only one.'

'Didn't know you went in for that kind of thing.'

'Ha, ha. It's you who married a nurse.'

Cantelli smiled. 'Alvita says that Spalding kept winking at her. And I quote,' Cantelli consulted his notebook, '"The sad old git."'

'Not much shock and sorrow there then.'

'None. Probably thinks anyone over the age of forty-five ought to be put down,' he added, referring to his own age.

'Wait until she gets there.'

'By the time she does I hope to be getting my free bus pass and collecting my pension, though judging by the way this government is acting I'll probably have to wait until I'm eighty-five, *if* I live that long.'

'They're probably hoping we don't.'

Cantelli gave a brief smile before resuming. 'She said that Spalding asked if she was looking forward to returning to her studies; she's a second-year student doing a BA in English with History, and that was about it. If he said anything else I don't think she would have noticed or remembered. I got the impression that Spalding wasn't really worth listening to as far as she was concerned. She's the type that is bored with everyone and everything, unless it directly concerns her.' Horton had met them many times.

'I asked her how Dr Spalding seemed, but she shrugged and said "OK. He drank a lot though".'

'There's no report of alcohol being found in his system.'

'Mineral water. But Alvita Baarda thinks it was an excuse to keep talking to her and eyeing her up.'

'She would.'

'Apart from that she claims not to have noticed anything and was glad to leave as soon as she could. Dr Menchip claims not to know Daniel Redsall and Alvita Baarda vaguely remembered him at the lecture but wasn't sure. So not much help I'm afraid.'

'He was probably too old to register on Alvita's radar.'

'Who was?' Walters asked, waddling in. He looked well fed and as if to reinforce this emitted a loud belch.

'How did you get on at Kings College?' asked Horton, remembering that Walters was going to try them again.

'No one knows anything about a seminar in Birmingham at the beginning of July, or any seminar held anywhere at that time.'

Another lie then. He considered what Cantelli had discovered and what Marcus Felspur had told him about the snatched conversation between Spalding and Redsall. So where had Spalding gone for those three days in July? And had that been alone? Suddenly with astonishing clarity the answer came to him — not to the last question but certainly the first. 'Have you got anything from the airports?' he asked.

'Nothing yet.'

'Then try checking the flights from Southampton to Belfast and Southampton to Dublin around that time.'

Cantelli quickly caught on. 'You're thinking Spalding met up with Redsall in Northern Ireland.'

'It's possible but I've no idea why.' He told Walters to make a start looking through the security footage supplied by Oyster Quays as soon as he'd finished checking the flights, and to call him the moment he had anything on either. Then to Cantelli he said, 'Let's see if we can track down this Erica Leyton.'

CHAPTER TWELVE

'She's on the raft,' a stocky, olive-skinned man in his mid-forties with short-cropped dark hair informed them after some delay.

At the main gate to the complex of the Institute of Marine Sciences the intercom had finally been answered by a woman who said she had no idea where Erica Leyton was and didn't seem inclined to find out for them. Reluctantly, after some pressure, she'd agreed to ask around. Neither Horton nor Cantelli had much hope of a positive outcome but a few minutes later the buzzer had sounded to admit them and a man who introduced himself as Bradley Marshall had met them at the entrance to one of the larger of five buildings facing them. He explained that the raft was permanently moored in Langstone Harbour. 'It's where we conduct trials.'

Cantelli said, 'I can think of some villains I wouldn't mind putting on trial out there.'

Horton smiled. 'That would mean you'd have to give evidence on it.'

Cantelli gave an exaggerated shudder.

Horton explained. 'The sergeant gets sick just looking at the sea.'

Marshall smiled. 'Then I'd better ask Erica if she can meet you on shore.'

Cantelli looked relieved.

'What sort of trials do you carry out on it?' Horton asked as Marshall led them through the building to the rear. He recalled seeing the large oblong low structure when out sailing. He'd thought it was connected with the water treatment and sewage works at Bedhampton, at the northern end of the harbour. Now he knew differently.

'It's for paint manufacturers mainly,' Marshall tossed over his shoulder. 'Or rather I should say for those companies who manufacture anti-fouling paint for sea-going craft, and we do trials for companies using underwater cable coatings, and scuba diving cylinders.'

'Not for examining sea life then?'

'No. But we have five aquarium rooms for studying fish biology and non-native organisms; the latter is my area of specialism, the effects of the introduction of invasive and non-native species. Seaweeds and phytoplankton can come into the area on the current and once here can displace native organisms by preying on them or out-competing them for food, and space. It can lead to the elimination of indigenous species from certain areas. I'm sorry I'm boring you with my pet topic.' Marshall smiled and pushed opened the rear door. 'I find it fascinating, so I expect everyone else to. It's only when I see people's eyes glaze over that I realize the world doesn't revolve around marine biology, although it should, it has a major impact on many livelihoods, the economy and the food chain.'

Horton said, 'I didn't think you'd be working during the university holidays.'

'Organisms don't take vacations,' Marshall replied, reaching for his mobile as they walked down towards the shore. 'Our work continues throughout the year, commercial contracts to fulfil. I take it this is about Dr Spalding's death?'

'You knew him?' asked Horton.

'I recommended Erica to him, and I used to see him when he visited Erica here. It's tragic, such a waste. There she is.'

Across the small harbour Horton could see the figure of what appeared to be a youngish woman, probably in her twenties, dressed in loose-fitting blue overalls working alone on the raft. Surrounding the raft in the small harbour, although set some distance from it, were a variety of pleasure craft and small fishing boats. Horton watched the grey flat-bottomed Hayling ferry negotiating its way around a couple of boats northwards, which meant it was diverting from its usual course to pick up a couple of fishermen to bring them back to the shore at Portsmouth. He saw Erica Leyton reach for her phone in her overall pocket and look towards them and he heard Marshall ask her if she could return to shore where a couple of police officers would like to talk to her about Dr Spalding's death. She nodded, put her phone back in her pocket and climbed off the raft into a small motor boat.

Within a couple of minutes it was coming into shore. As she silenced the engine Marshall stepped forward and took the front of the boat. Erica Leyton jumped off.

'I'm really sorry to hear about Dr Spalding's death,' she announced, unzipping her overalls and stepping out of them, somewhat provocatively Horton thought, to reveal a good figure encased in tight denim shorts hugging a neat backside, long suntanned legs and a suntanned cleavage above the low-cut aquamarine T-shirt. She looked as though she kept herself fit. Not a runner though. He guessed she worked out in a gym and wouldn't mind an audience, especially a male one. Maybe he should find out which gym.

Marshall secured the boat. She threw him a smile which he returned before leaving them. Horton thought he glimpsed more than professional courtesy or friendship in their exchange. Pulling off her pink sailing cap she shook out her long light-brown curly hair.

Cantelli began the questioning. 'We understand from Dr Menchip that you made a formal complaint against Dr Spalding for sexual harassment.'

She gave an exasperated sigh. 'I did no such thing. That's Dr Menchip getting all het up. Really it was nothing. She asked me how I was getting on working with Dr Spalding. I was at the faculty that day meeting a friend for lunch. I said fine but I made a joke that he took working in close collaboration very literally. She didn't consider that to be "professional". She said she'd have a word with him. I told her not to. She took it completely the wrong way. I didn't want to jeopardize the project. I was enjoying working with him and it meant having my name on his paper.'

'When was this?'

She pushed a slender hand through her hair. 'At the beginning of June.'

'And did Dr Menchip speak to him?'

'If she did, he didn't let on.'

'When was the last time you saw him?'

'Two weeks ago on July the twenty-fifth. How did he die? Was it an accident?' Her eyes flicked to Horton's and stayed there. He saw anxiety in hers and maybe a touch of guilt, which was confirmed when she added, 'Only I wouldn't want to think that I . . . well you know.'

'We're still investigating his death,' he replied, thinking *well I am at least*. Her eyes studied his expression for a moment, seeking reassurance that her casual remarks hadn't pushed Spalding over the edge. Maybe she found it because she gave a little nod. He said, 'This project you were working on together, can you tell us something about it? Only I thought the Royal Navy and not marine sciences was Dr Spalding's area of specialization.'

'It was, Inspector, but this time the two coincided. Dr Spalding was researching the relationships between the crew and the scientists on board HMS *Challenger*.'

Spalding had been a very busy man, thought Horton curiously. This was yet another area of research totally different to that he'd told Ivor Meadows and Marcus Felspur.

Cantelli looked up from his notebook. Interpreting his glance she explained with a smile, 'The *Challenger* marked the birth of modern oceanography. It was a corvette class ship, a military vessel that travelled under sail but had auxiliary steam power. It was the first survey ship of its kind and left Portsmouth in January 1873. For three and a half years it circumnavigated the world with a crew of physicists, chemists, and biologists mapping the sea and discovering many new species. Dr Spalding was interested in life on board the *Challenger* not just for the officers and crew but for the scientists and he was particularly keen to research the relationships between them, how the crew reacted to the scientists, was there clear demarcation between them, were the scientists on the same level as the officers or did they consider themselves above them, that kind of thing. My PhD was about the *Challenger*'s survey, which was why Dr Marshall recommended me to Dr Spalding. I already had a great deal of information and reference sources. I compiled a list of the scientists on board, their professional backgrounds, and I have references to professional articles, journals and private diaries.'

Horton recalled what Beatrice Redsall had said about her family's naval pedigree. Was it possible that a Redsall had served on board HMS *Challenger* between 1873 and 1876 and had that been the connection between Spalding and Redsall? But even if it were, he couldn't see how it would result in both men being killed. He asked her if she'd come across anyone called Redsall serving on the *Challenger*.

'The name doesn't ring a bell. No, I'm sure there was no one of that name.'

'So Dr Spalding didn't ask you about him?'

She looked bewildered by his questions. 'No.'

He thought her reaction genuine, but he showed her the photograph of Redsall and asked if she recognized him. The answer was negative. There was possibly another connection. He said, 'What happened to HMS *Challenger*?'

'She was demoted to Coastguard watch ship at Harwich, then went into the reserves two years later. She was finally broken up at Chatham in 1921.'

So no wrecks there for a marine archaeologist to explore.

With a nod to Cantelli that they'd finished, Horton apologized for disturbing her experiments.

'That's OK. I needed a break anyway. If I can help in any way, please let me know. Would you like my phone number?'

Horton said he would, adding to himself *for work, though, not for pleasure*. He keyed it into his mobile phone, seeing by her eyes and her body language that she wouldn't mind the latter. She told them they could get back to the main entrance by way of a path around the side of the building and as they headed there Cantelli said, 'My money's on her leading Dr Spalding on rather than the other way around. I reckon she's a bit of a tease.'

Horton was inclined to agree. But how far had it gone? Erica Leyton had looked genuinely troubled by the fact that her remarks might have led to Spalding's death, but she wasn't distraught over it. Climbing into the car he said, 'Spalding might not have protested very strongly although Bradley Marshall might have done. He probably wished he'd never introduced them.'

'Perhaps he killed Spalding because he was jealous,' Cantelli said half-jokingly, 'And Redsall too. Maybe Erica was also having a fling with him.'

'She's been a busy girl, certainly if she was also at it with Spalding but then she is quite a looker.'

'So is Jacqueline Spalding,' Cantelli said somewhat defiantly.

He pointed the car in the direction of the station and as they negotiated the crowded city streets Horton considered this. Neither Bradley Marshall nor Erica Leyton had been at Spalding's lecture or on the pontoons at Oyster Quays and he didn't see that they could have any motive for wanting both men dead. After a moment he said, 'Could Sandra Menchip have been jealous that Spalding fancied Erica?'

'Possibly, she's divorced, and I didn't see any evidence of anyone living with her. Maybe when Erica made those remarks, or maybe taunted her with them, she decided that if she couldn't have him then she'd ruin him by smearing his name.'

'So if she threatened to bring a disciplinary charge against him, would that be enough to make him hurl himself into that dock?' Cantelli looked doubtful.

'No, I don't think so either.'

'Sandra Menchip could have threatened to tell Mrs Spalding because she was jealous.'

'I still can't see him killing himself because of it. And that doesn't fit with Redsall's death.'

Thoughts were tumbling through Horton's mind. He needed to get them into some kind of order, but the trilling of his mobile phone interjected before he could do so. He expected Bliss but it was Walters.

'Found him, Guv,' he cried excitedly. 'Spalding flew from Southampton to Belfast, Northern Ireland on the 8.35 a.m. flight on the fourth of July. He returned to Southampton on the 7.50 p.m. flight from Belfast arriving at Southampton at 9.15 p.m. on the sixth of July.' Horton felt a stab of triumph.

Walters continued, 'There was no one else booked under his name.'

That didn't mean he had travelled alone though. Spalding could still have gone to Belfast with a lover. With Erica Leyton?

'Find out if he hired a car, caught a taxi or bought a train ticket at Belfast.' Horton rang off and relayed the news to Cantelli, adding, 'My money's on him travelling to Coleraine to see Redsall, and if he did it rules out the theory of Redsall being an accidental victim because he saw someone drugging Spalding at the lecture.'

His mind rapidly replayed what he'd seen and learned over the last couple of days. Painstakingly he began to pull it together, not knowing where it would lead. 'We know that Spalding didn't want his wife or his GP knowing where he was really going, so lie number one, he told Deacon he was going to the States and his wife he was going to Birmingham when he did neither. He flew to Northern Ireland. So why did he fly when he was terrified of it? He could have driven or taken the train to Birkenhead and caught the ferry to Belfast.'

'Too slow.'

'So it was urgent that he went there.'

'Or perhaps he didn't want to be away for too long.'

There was that. Flying was quicker. Horton continued, 'OK, so lie number two, he told Ivor Meadows he was researching the Navy and prostitution; Meadows thought he was really researching the strange circumstances behind Buster Crabb's death, but I think that is just Meadow's imagination. However, Spalding told Felspur that he was researching into the Navy's impact on the people of Portsmouth between 1945 and 1978. And now we've just learned that Spalding told Erica Leyton he was researching into relationships between crew and scientists on the HMS *Challenger*. So which is it? Or are they all lies?'

'Perhaps he was researching all three.' Cantelli swung into the station car park.

'Would that be usual?'

Cantelli shrugged. 'No idea. Maybe it was for him.' Cantelli silenced the engine but neither he nor Horton made any attempt to alight. Cantelli said, 'Perhaps Spalding had identified the location of a shipwreck and had to keep others away from discovering that was what he was really working on. He needed Redsall's advice because he was an expert.'

Horton considered this. It sounded possible. 'I guess it would be quite a coup for a naval historian and a marine archaeologist if they'd discovered something that has eluded everyone else.'

'They might have been working on the project for years. They might even have been working together at the same university in the past; we haven't checked their backgrounds to see if they've been previously linked.'

'And Spalding told those lies to throw everyone off the scent.' Horton warmed to the theory. 'He lied to Meadows because he was a nosy bugger, and Felspur because he didn't want him to know the real reason he wanted access to the research material he requested. But why lie to Erica Leyton about the *Challenger*?'

'Because he fancied her.'

'But you said you thought she led *him* on.'

'Maybe she did and he fell for it. They just used the *Challenger* project idea as an excuse to keep seeing each other.'

But Horton had another idea. 'Or because whatever Spalding had discovered was linked to HMS *Challenger*. And who would be desperate enough for that information to kill, Barney?'

'Are you two going to sit in there all day?' Bliss's voice rang out making them both start. Horton had been so engrossed with their theorizing that he hadn't seen or heard her approach. She must have been watching them from her office window and had come charging down here as soon as they'd pulled in.

Horton opened the car door and made to speak but Bliss got there first.

'Detective Superintendent Uckfield has the results of the toxicology tests on Douglas Spalding and the autopsy report on Daniel Redsall. The major incident suite. Now. Both of you,' she commanded before turning and marching off.

'Better do as the boss says,' Horton remarked, watching her push open the rear door and brush a startled young, uniformed constable out of her path. As they followed in her wake, Horton considered what he was about to hear. Something that he sincerely hoped would step up both investigations.

CHAPTER THIRTEEN

'Spalding wasn't drugged,' Uckfield announced peremptorily and somewhat triumphantly, as soon as they entered the major incident suite.

Horton stifled his disappointment while his mind did a quick mental cartwheel. That didn't mean Spalding hadn't been killed. He could still have been pushed into that dock. But not because of the threat of sexual harassment charges. If Uckfield knew about that it would only convince him that Spalding *had* killed himself. Best not to mention it, his glance said to Cantelli, who understood perfectly.

'And the autopsy results on Redsall?'

Dennings answered, 'No signs of foul play and no alcohol in his system. Dr Clayton can find no evidence of heart disease or any other obvious cause of death. He died of sudden death syndrome.'

'That's Dr Clayton's view, is it?' Horton asked, thinking it was too pat.

'That's what I've just said,' Dennings reiterated as though speaking to a simple child.

Horton eyed him with contempt. Stiffly he said, 'But we haven't got the results of the toxicology tests yet. So how can

Dr Clayton establish that's how Redsall died? He could have been drugged and stumbled onto Ashton's yacht.'

'What is it with you?' Uckfield roared. 'Why can't you accept that one man committed suicide and the other one died of natural causes?'

'Because it's too damn neat,' Horton retorted, drawing a glare of disapproval from Bliss. Well sod that. He was certain he hadn't got it wrong. There had to be more to both men's deaths. 'And there are too many unanswered questions. For a start, why did Redsall come to Portsmouth?'

Dennings answered. 'To visit old friends.'

'Who?' Horton rounded on him. 'Have we found and spoken to them? No. He didn't even visit his aunt.'

'Maybe he didn't like her,' Bliss piped up, eyeing Horton beadily as though to say *you're out of order here and shut up*. Not on your life, thought Horton.

'Where did he go before ending up dead on Ashton's yacht?' Horton pressed. 'What did he do all day? Why was he at Douglas Spalding's lecture, and before you give some glib answer,' he said, holding up his hand as Uckfield opened his mouth to speak, Horton added, 'Walters has found evidence that Douglas Spalding travelled to Northern Ireland on the fourth of July. He's still checking exactly where he went after landing at Belfast, and who he was seeing, but I believe he was visiting Daniel Redsall in Coleraine.'

'No law against that,' quipped Uckfield.

'But it's a possible connection between the two dead men, which we *have* to explore,' insisted Horton, exasperated by Uckfield's blunt and blind refusal even to consider that the two deaths could be murder. Horton didn't expect Dennings to query his master's voice, or reason it out for himself because he was too thick, but why didn't Bliss see it? Why wasn't she questioning it? Too busy trying to suck up to the Super, Horton thought sourly, in order to secure a place on the Major Crime Team. Why was Uckfield being so obstructive?

'Possible is not enough,' Uckfield hissed, glaring at Horton.

'Then why don't we find *enough*,' retorted Horton, earning another black look from Bliss for daring to answer back and question a senior officer's reasoning.

'Because there is nothing to investigate,' bellowed Uckfield. Turning to Bliss he said sharply, 'Everything will go before the coroner and I expect your officers' reports by first thing tomorrow morning.' He stormed into his office, slamming the door behind him. Dennings threw Horton a conceited smile before heading for his office. Bliss turned to Horton with a face like thunder. 'I do not expect such appalling behaviour from a senior officer. Make your reports and do them now. No more excuses, Inspector.' She marched out.

Horton let out a breath and tried to release his tension. He glanced at Trueman who raised his heavy dark eyebrows before answering the phone that was ringing. Turning to Cantelli, Horton said, 'Beatrice Redsall is due to formally identify her nephew's body in half an hour. Meet her at the mortuary, Barney, and see what you can get out of her. She says she doesn't know Spalding and that she hasn't seen her nephew for years, but she could be lying. Also see if she recognizes Erica Leyton's name and ask her if any of her ancestors were on board HMS *Challenger*. I'm going to ask Uckfield why he's skimping over this investigation.'

Horton knocked perfunctorily and entered without being invited. He closed the door firmly behind him.

'The briefing is over, Inspector,' Uckfield snarled, looking up, but Horton could see the strain etched on his rugged face and the tension in his jaw. His suspicions were confirmed; someone had brought a lot of pressure to bear on Uckfield. Why? There was only one possible answer: to hush up both deaths, and that could only mean one thing. Somehow and somewhere along the line Redsall and Spalding were involved in something potentially big, which had nothing to do with sexual harassment, research into prostitution in Portsmouth, HMS *Challenger* or any other aspects of the Royal Naval history. No, he'd been wrong, and he knew it. It was written all over Uckfield's face and the case reeked of it. Why hadn't he seen it before? This had the stink of National Intelligence about it and the Northern Ireland connection between the two men flashed through Horton's mind. Could this possibly be connected with terrorism? He mustn't jump to conclusions. But why the hell not? There was no law against it, so he jumped. OK, so the general belief was that the threat of terrorism from Northern Ireland's Republican terrorist groups had ceased with the creation of a new power-sharing agreement between the Nationalist and Unionist political parties, but it hadn't. Some of the Republican terrorist groups rejected the political process and there had been cases on both sides of the Irish border recently of individuals being charged and convicted of offences relating to international terrorism. Horton recalled the emails he'd received telling him and his officers to be on the alert. He had no idea of Spalding's or Redsall's political or religious leanings. Perhaps he should find out, only he knew he wouldn't be allowed to.

Eyeing Uckfield steadily, Horton said, 'Since when have you done what you're told, Steve?'

Uckfield's eyes narrowed. 'Since I became a detective superintendent and since I decided I'd like to become a detective chief superintendent and an assistant chief constable. And if you want to remain a detective inspector then you'd better do as *you're* told. Now I've got work to do and so have you, so bloody well get on with it.'

Horton could see there was no point arguing. Uckfield had been warned off. He was, as he'd admitted, ambitious. And he had a trail of love affairs behind him, so the threat of exposing one to his wife and the new chief constable would be enough to ruin his marriage and career. Something Uckfield would be at great pains to avoid. It wouldn't cost much to make him toe the line. And Bliss? Did she know what was going on? Maybe. According to Horton's contact at Bramshill she was heading for dizzy heights. A big fat carrot of promotion would be enough to make her swear rubber was steel. It stank and he hated it. He was certain that

Dennings wasn't in on it. Too thick. But whatever was going on Trueman was attuned to it. The sergeant missed nothing.

Horton threw him a glance. 'Funny how anger makes me hungry,' he said on his way out. It was only as he stepped into the canteen that he realized he was. It seemed a lifetime ago that he'd eaten. He bought a coffee, packet of ham salad sandwiches and a banana and took them to a table where he could see the door. Four minutes later Trueman entered, bought a drink and sat down opposite him.

'Dean summoned the Super to his office half an hour before the briefing,' Trueman said, stirring his tea. 'He came back with a face like a cat's arse, told me to collate everything I had on both deaths and pass it over to him and to get on with my other work.'

'So who's leant on the ACC?'

'Your guess is as good as mine, Andy. Special Branch, MI5, MI6, National Intelligence, Interpol, Europol, take your pick.'

Horton swallowed his coffee. The mention of Europol made him think of Agent Ames and her timely arrival on the same pontoon where Redsall's body had been found. Could she be involved? He'd put it down to coincidence. OK, so as a copper he rarely trusted coincidences, but they happened. And in this instance? Now he wasn't so sure. He told Trueman his thoughts about a terrorist connection with Northern Ireland.

'Sounds possible,' Trueman ventured.

'Why not tell us though and then take us off the case?'

'Too risky.'

'Why?'

'Because the more people who know about it the more chance it has of going tits up if they're doing a whitewash job. They wouldn't want the truth to come out.'

'You mean someone ballsed up on the job?'

'Could have done.'

'Spalding?'

Trueman took a piece of paper from his trouser pocket. 'I did some digging.'

Horton smiled. He had guessed as much.

Trueman read, 'Spalding joined the Navy in 1989, attended the Royal Engineering College and got a BA Hons degree in Maritime Defence Technology just before the college closed and the Royal Navy's engineering officer training was transferred to the University of Southampton and the Navy's specialist establishments in Portsmouth. He left the Navy in 2000 and attended Kings College London where he gained an MA in War Studies. After which he worked for the Ministry of Defence for three years.'

'Doing what?'

'The files I've accessed just say "consultant".'

Horton was beginning to see what Trueman meant.

'And that covers a multitude of sins.'

Horton felt a shiver run up his spine.

Trueman continued. 'He returned to Kings College London in 2004 as a senior lecturer in the Department of War Studies, lecturing in early modern naval warfare, the social shaping of military technology, history of military strategy and strategic dimension of terrorism.'

Horton didn't like the sound of this. He could see that Trueman had already joined up the dots. There was the possibility that Spalding could have been working for the government. If so that meant Redsall could have been working for the other side, whoever they were, and it could be the IRA.

Trueman continued. 'Spalding was then awarded a three-year research fellowship with the Maritime Historical Studies Centre at the University of Hull for research into the Navy and its impact on Great Britain before he joined Portsmouth University as visiting lecturer last April.'

'Have you found any indication that Spalding and Redsall knew one another?'

'No. But I haven't had time to look.'

Horton sat back and considered what Trueman had said. If Spalding had been working for the government that could explain why Uckfield had been told to tread softly with the investigation into his death. Did that mean Redsall had been sent over to kill Spalding? Why?

'The briefcase!'

'Eh?'

'There was something in that briefcase that Redsall wanted or had been told to get.' Was it possible that it was some critical information about the Navy or naval shipping movements? Horton thought of that empty rucksack. 'After Redsall delivered it, he was killed.' Horton recalled the remark Beatrice Redsall had made about her nephew being principled. Principled about what, though?

Horton continued. 'Redsall must have waited for Spalding to come out of the naval museum and falsified his signing-out time, which wouldn't have been difficult given the state the security officer was in on Monday night. All Redsall had to do after pushing Spalding over the railings was transfer Spalding's laptop computer from his briefcase into his rucksack, ditch the briefcase and then hand over the laptop to his contact.'

'Would Redsall have had the strength to push Spalding into Number One Dock?'

'If Spalding had been drugged, yes.'

In the silence that fell between them they both knew that was possible despite the findings of the test results. Horton continued. 'The coroner will conclude that Spalding took his own life while the balance of his mind was disturbed and that Redsall died of natural causes, unless the toxicology test show drugs in his system in which case they'll say they were self-administered.'

'And they might have evidence to back up that theory.'

Horton eyed Trueman, surprised.

'Daniel Redsall suffered a complete nervous breakdown just after his eighteenth birthday.'

Horton groaned inwardly and swallowed his coffee. Beatrice Redsall hadn't mentioned that but then she was the type who wouldn't understand mental illness — to her it would have shown weakness, and perhaps Daniel's father had thought the same. The pressure to achieve, along with the expectation that Daniel would join the Navy and have a glittering career, had become too much for him, and he'd cracked up. Horton vowed silently never to put that kind of pressure on his daughter's young shoulders. It was the perfect excuse though to cover up Redsall's death as Trueman said. Redsall had succumbed to depression before it could happen again.

Trueman continued. 'Daniel Redsall was hospitalized for a year, before going to university where he obtained a BA in Archaeology, and then an MA in Maritime Archaeology and History at Bristol University. He's had several papers published, took a variety of lecturing posts and worked as a freelance maritime archaeologist. I get the impression he was something of a loner.'

'That'll be nice and convenient for the coroner,' Horton said acerbically.

'What are you going to do, Andy?'

'Write up my reports as the Super requested.'

Trueman eyed him knowingly. 'I'll let you know if anything else crops up.' He rose. 'I'd better go before Uckfield comes looking for me.'

Horton left the canteen a couple of minutes afterwards. He returned to his office where Walters informed him that he couldn't find any trace of Spalding having travelled from Belfast to Coleraine. 'He didn't hire a car and if he went by bus or train, he didn't pay by credit or debit card. Do you want me to ask the Northern Ireland police to make inquiries at Coleraine and at the train and bus stations and get them to show Spalding's photo around?'

Horton did but *he'd* ask them because if anyone was going to get bollocked it would be him. 'Is there any sighting of Redsall on the Oyster Quays pontoons last night?'

Walters shook his head. 'And only two boats arrived between six and ten thirty: Carl Ashton's yacht and another one. I could swear I saw Agent Ames get off it and walk up the pontoon with some poncey looking git, another man and the most gorgeous bit of stuff that—'

'You did. But we won't tell DCI Bliss that or she might get jealous.'

He relayed the outcome of Uckfield's briefing.

'So I can stop watching this screen?' Walters asked, clearly relieved.

'Yes.'

Horton closed his office door and rang through to the police in Coleraine. He asked them to make inquiries. Replacing his receiver, he wondered how long it would be before the intelligence services discovered that and put a stop to it. Next, he rang Dr Clayton from his mobile. When she came on the line he said, 'Superintendent Uckfield's told me the results of the autopsy on Daniel Redsall.'

'Yes, but I—'

'Fancy a drink?' he interjected.

There was a short pause before she said, 'OK.'

'The Bridge Tavern, at the Camber, seven thirty?'

'Perfect.'

And Horton knew by that one word she'd understood his purpose. He needed to know what she really thought of Daniel Redsall's death.

CHAPTER FOURTEEN

She was there before him. He'd been delayed at the station. Cantelli had returned to say that Beatrice Redsall had confirmed the body was that of her nephew. She hadn't batted an eyelid or shed a tear. Horton had known she wouldn't. It was the way she was made. She'd also confirmed that no Redsall had sailed on HMS *Challenger* and that she'd never heard of Erica Leyton or any research project connected with the *Challenger*.

As he swung into the car park Horton could see the red-haired diminutive figure of Gaye Clayton standing on the quay talking to a fisherman on his boat. Her boyish figure was dressed casually in jeans and a white T-shirt and she swung round on his approach with such a bright and welcoming smile on her freckled face that he felt a warm glow spread through him, as though he'd known her for years. He realized in that moment that she never made him feel inferior or defensive in the same way that many people did, even though he would never admit that, or perhaps he should say as Ames made him feel. He found himself attracted to Gaye but in a different way to Ames, how precisely though he didn't know and didn't care to analyse. On many occasions he'd been tempted to ask Gaye out, but his working relationship with her had prevented him, just as it prevented him getting closer to Ames. He wished he hadn't thought of Ames. His feelings for her were complicated — for Christ's sake he couldn't even think of her in terms of her first name — and those complications were now exacerbated by his feelings for Gaye Clayton. Best to avoid them both he guessed, in any emotional and sexual sense that was, as professionally he didn't have much choice. Besides, perhaps neither would touch him with a barge pole.

She dismissed his apology for being late, said a cheery goodbye to the fisherman and accompanied him inside the pub where he ordered their drinks. She refused an offer of food and they talked of her holiday, sailing in France. Horton felt a stab of jealousy when she spoke of the friends who had accompanied her, two male doctors and a female radiologist, an emotion that left him even more confused and frustrated and with a sense of loneliness. He hastily and angrily pushed this feeling aside while at the same time resenting his mother and feeling disappointed that Madeley hadn't returned his call. He turned his mind to Spalding and Redsall. Seated outside in the declining August sun he told her he wanted to discuss their deaths.

'And there's me thinking you wanted the pleasure of my company,' she joked.

'I do but I also want your expertise.' He returned her smile and as their eyes connected, he knew it wouldn't take much for him to take their relationship further. He said, 'Is there any indication on Redsall's medical records that he might have suffered sudden death syndrome?'

She picked up her glass and eyed him steadily and perhaps with a hint of disappointment, Horton thought. After taking a sip of her mineral water she said, 'No, but that's not unusual because he might not have had any symptoms. Let me explain. The conditions responsible for Sudden Arrhythmia Death Syndrome, to give it its proper name, causes a cardiac arrest by bringing on a "ventricular arrhythmia", a disturbance in the heart's rhythm, even though the person has no structural heart disease, and Redsall's heart was in perfect condition. There is a group of relatively rare diseases called ion channelopathies that affect the electrical functioning of the heart without affecting the heart's structure. This means that they can only be detected in life and not at post-mortem. It often affects mainly young people, but one form can affect middle-aged men, like Daniel Redsall; it's called Brugada syndrome and the patient may have no symptoms at all. Sudden death usually happens while the person is sleeping. It is a possible cause of death in Redsall's case, but I can see by your expression that you don't believe it.'

'Do you?'

'So your theory is?'

'Drugged or poisoned, whichever term you prefer, and deliberately so.'

'Homicide.' She considered this but made no comment.

'Yes, and I think the same method was used to kill Douglas Spalding.'

'Nothing showed up in the toxicology tests.'

'It wouldn't.'

She eyed him quizzically and he swiftly told her his theory that Redsall and Spalding could be mixed up in something that National Intelligence wanted suppressed, such as suspected terrorism, possibly connected with a cell operating in Northern Ireland. Even as he said it, he recognized that he had gone through several theories concerning their deaths and that perhaps he was just grasping at another to justify his intuition. Maybe he should give it up.

She said nothing for a few moments. 'I must admit they handled the tests on Spalding very quickly.'

'Too quickly?' he suggested, hopefully.

She shrugged. 'Of course, if you rush things mistakes *can* be made, although not often, and certainly not when I'm around.'

'Ah, but you weren't.'

'No.'

He smiled briefly before continuing. 'And you weren't there to examine Spalding's body for tiny pin pricks.' The theory of poison by injection fitted. It had been done before. Any sharp instrument could be used and easily concealed in a pocket until needed. And perhaps Daniel Redsall had done that while talking to Spalding after the lecture.

'But I did examine Redsall's body,' she said, 'and I didn't find anything like that. Perhaps I had better make a closer examination.' She took a sip of her drink. Horton could see the thoughts racing through her mind.

Sitting forward and lowering his voice he said, 'OK, so discounting the results of the toxicology tests, Spalding was last seen alive when Julie Preston let him out of the naval museum at 9.35 p.m. His body was discovered by Neil Gideon at just after 10.35 p.m., so he could have met someone outside the museum, who administered the drug and it took effect immediately. That person could have been Daniel Redsall who in turn was killed with the same drug on the pontoon at Oyster Quays last night.'

'And he died sometime between six and ten p.m.'

'No, Redsall died after seven p.m. because there are witnesses who said he wasn't on Ashton's yacht then.'

'Right.' She frowned as she considered this. 'So we're looking for something that acted quickly?'

That gave Horton three options as far as Redsall's death was concerned: someone in one of those boats moored up in Oyster Quays had administered the drug, and there was only Ashton and Rupert Crawford's party on the pontoons; someone dropped Daniel Redsall off in the marina after drugging him, except no boat was seen mooring up during that time; or the drug was administered by a person with access to the pontoons, someone who knew the security code and how to dodge the security cameras, who met him there. Why did he want to think of Rupert Crawford? Jealousy, he guessed. He said, 'Any idea what drug could work speedily?'

She blew out her cheeks and ran a hand through her spiky hair as she considered this. 'It could be something specially manufactured and unknown.'

Ashton's clients flashed into Horton's mind. Ashton had said that one of them had worked for a biomedical company. Simon Watson. Was it possible he was involved? He brought his mind back to Dr Clayton as she continued.

'Or it could be a good old-fashioned poison. Nicotine for example can be rapidly absorbed through the skin or gastrointestinal tract. It can be injected, and death can occur within minutes. It would have caused respiratory failure, which Spalding would certainly have had anyway after hitting a concrete slab. So that's a possibility. Cyanide is another possibility. However, with cyanide the face and lips of the victims would have been blue, and there would have been a cherry-red appearance in the blood. This wasn't picked up in Spalding's autopsy and it certainly wasn't present in Redsall's body. Then there's Aconite. If a large dose is taken it can kill almost immediately. It affects the central nervous system, paralysing the muscles. There would have been nausea and possibly vomiting.'

'Which could have been washed away by the rain in both instances.'

'Yes, but there would have been traces on the victims' clothes. I didn't find any traces of vomit on Redsall's clothes. Did the pathologist make any comment about vomit being found on Spalding's clothes?'

'I haven't read the autopsy report, only been told the results.' And if there was vomit then Uckfield might have been told to ignore it.

'I'll read it and send you over a copy. If Redsall and Spalding had been given massive doses they would have suffered burning and tingling in the mouth, numbness in the tongue, throat and face, and blurred vision.'

With heightened interest Horton picked up on this. 'Blurred vision could have caused Spalding to stagger about outside. He panics, struggles to breathe and doubles up over the railings surrounding Number One Dock then topples over as the pain grips him and his breathing slows.'

'Possible.'

'And Redsall doesn't know where he is or what he's doing, he staggers onto Ashton's boat, the poison takes effect, and he dies.'

She sat back looking concerned. 'I don't like the thought that I've missed something.'

'You haven't. You don't do the toxicology tests.'

'No, but maybe I should.'

'Look, this isn't official.'

'Didn't think it was for one moment.' She tossed back her drink. 'I've got work to do. I won't be able to take fresh samples for tests for either Spalding or Redsall until tomorrow morning, but I'd like to re-examine Redsall's body tonight. I'll let you know if I find anything. Thanks for the drink.' She rose.

'My pleasure,' he said, also rising. 'And thanks.' *Do something, say something, for Christ's sake, say that next time I'll buy you a drink and it won't have anything to do with work.* But he said nothing. He watched her stride across the car park and climb into her red Mini. Cursing himself as she drove away, he hoped that perhaps she'd wave or turn back, but she didn't even glance in his direction. He picked up his helmet then froze. A dark saloon car had pulled out and turned left. Nothing unusual in that — or was there? Only one way to find out. He hurried towards his Harley; he could easily catch them up, but before he reached it his phone rang. Damn. He could ignore it but glancing quickly at the number he knew he couldn't. It was the one call he'd been waiting for. Professor Thurstan Madeley. Cursing its timing but with a quickening heartbeat he answered it.

Madeley introduced himself and without preamble said, 'Why do you want to know about the thirteenth of March 1967, Inspector?'

'I'd like to meet up and talk to you about it. When would be convenient?'

'Is this police business?'

Horton took a silent deep breath. He'd anticipated the question and his answer. 'It concerns a current investigation.'

He wasn't sure whether Madeley was fooled by his evasive answer, probably not. Quickly Horton continued. 'I'm based in Portsmouth, but I can visit you.'

There was a moment's pause before Madeley replied. 'I'm going over to the Island tomorrow for Cowes Week. I could meet you at the Castle Hill Yacht Club in Cowes.'

Madeley moved in exalted circles: that was a very exclusive place.

'Would you be able to get away from your work?' Madeley asked.

Horton would. In fact, it fitted in with his work perfectly, *if* he could dodge Bliss's eagle eye, because there were a couple of people on the Island he wanted to interview, such as Melanie Jacobs and Steve Drummond. And he wanted to ask Carl Ashton about Simon Watson. He was under orders not to pursue the case but that wasn't going to stop him.

He made arrangements to meet with Madeley at three o'clock with the proviso that the time and date might have to change depending on his workload. Madeley seemed happy with that. Horton rang off letting out the breath he'd been holding. He'd become so accustomed to disappointment and dead ends that he didn't dare hope for an answer to even one of his questions, but if Madeley could recall the name of just one of those men in the photograph, or give him something that could lead to one of them, then it would be something.

Climbing on his Harley he wondered about Dr Clayton. Had that dark saloon car been following her? Would she be allowed to conduct her tests? But how could anyone stop her? They might have covered up the results of the tests on Spalding, but he didn't think they'd be able to do the same with Redsall — whoever *they* were. There was nothing more he could do for the moment.

He headed for the yacht. The lack of sleep was finally catching up on him and he hoped for once he'd be able to slip into oblivion for seven hours; six would do. He'd even settle for five if it was dreamless. But although exhausted he decided that he needed a run along the seafront to release his tension and clear his mind. Besides, physical exhaustion might also help him sleep more readily and peacefully.

By the time he'd reached South Parade Pier it was dark, and he was both exhausted and hungry. Time to head back. He turned right at the end of the esplanade by the swimming baths into Melville Road and past the caravan site, which seemed to be doing a brisk trade with disco music booming from the club house, accompanied by the laughter of children and adults. Soon though he was leaving it behind and running along a deserted and darkened road longing for a shower, food and sleep. His trainers pounded the tarmac in a rhythm that kept him going. Not far now.

The sound of a car engine behind him caught his attention. There was plenty of room for it to pass and the flashes on his running vest would be picked up by the vehicle's headlights. But the car didn't seem to want to pass, obviously a cautious driver. He could stop and let him go, but if he did, he didn't think he'd be able to start running again. He could walk the remaining few hundred yards but that was against his rules. The sweat was pouring off him. He wiped it from his face. The shore was on his left now and a narrow strip of grass to his right bordering the fenced-off ground of Fort Cumberland. The engine behind him revved up. Glancing over his shoulder the full beam of the headlights blinded him. Dazed, he almost stumbled but quickly rectified a faltering step. His heart leapt into his throat as a terrible feeling swamped him. He knew in his gut that the only way this driver was going to pass him was by running right over his body. Shit. He increased his pace, finding energy from reserves he didn't realize he had. The car's engine revved again. It was a four-wheel drive and it was coming straight for him. Christ! His eyes glanced wildly around. If he dived to the right the car would drive right over him, and to the left there were now large slabs of concrete bordering the shore, but he could leap over them. He might injure himself, but he'd still be alive.

He had seconds. The car would get him on the slight bend. He'd wished for oblivion. He was about to get it. His

heart was racing. His head was throbbing. His limbs scream-
ing in agony. The car behind him sped up. Then suddenly
out of the night came the throb of a motorbike and there
it was bearing down on him. If the car behind didn't get
him the motorbike ahead looked set to. It all happened in
a split second. The motorbike rider saw the car speeding
towards him, the car driver registered the bike; it swerved
to the left, the bike swung and swerved to the right. Horton
ran on. There was the squeal of brakes and the throb of the
motorbike as it revved up and sped away. Horton, his chest
heaving, craned his head back in time to see the four-wheel
drive career over a bank of grass to its left, almost topple over,
straighten up, reverse and then screech off down the road
away from the marina and away from Horton, leaving him
with only a glimpse of the colour, black, and nothing of the
registration number, which must have been hidden, and only
a vague impression of a man inside it.

CHAPTER FIFTEEN

Thursday

The shrieking of his phone startled Horton out of a troubled sleep. He woke in a sweat, his bones aching and his muscles burning. He felt as though he had been running all night. It had taken him hours to drift into sleep with his mind whirling through the events of the night. The same questions remained now as he surfaced into wakefulness. Had whoever tried to kill him been sent by Zeus to prevent him from finding out the truth about Jennifer's disappearance? Or was the incident connected with Spalding and Redsall? If the latter, was it someone from the intelligence service or a terrorist faction? He didn't know. Only that they'd try again.

He picked up his mobile. It was Cantelli.

'We've got a suspicious death, Andy. At the Round Tower at Old Portsmouth.'

Horton leapt out of bed and groaned.

'You alright?'

'Yes. Man or woman?'

'Man, about late sixties, Caucasian. It's a vicious attack.'

'I'll be there in twenty minutes.'

As he showered, shaved and dressed Horton thought of the Round Tower, a grey stone edifice built in 1420 to protect the harbour entrance from a French invasion during the Hundred Years War. It was now a popular viewing point for people watching the hundreds of ships and naval vessels coming in and out of Portsmouth every year. Its opposite number, the Square Tower, some few hundred yards to the east along a raised walkway above the small shingle beach, had been built later in 1494 before the dockyard had existed. In those days the King's ships had been moored in the Camber where he'd sat last night drinking with Dr Clayton. He wondered if she'd managed to re-examine Redsall's body. Had whoever tried to run him down seen him talking with Dr Clayton? His heart did a somersault. He should have called her to make sure she was OK. He rectified that now.

'I'm fine,' she said in answer to his concerned enquiry. 'Just having my breakfast, why?'

He didn't want to tell her about his dice with death. The saloon car that had pulled out behind her hadn't been the same one that had tried to flatten him into the tarmac last night, which he knew to be the same black Ranger with tinted windows that he'd seen following him from Beatrice Redsall's apartment. 'Just wondered if you'd had a chance to look over Redsall's body?' he dodged her question.

'I did and with the largest magnifying lens I could find, not a sign of a pin prick. I'll take some more tissue samples for tests, which I'll conduct myself this morning.'

'You might be delayed, as we've got another body.'

'Any connection with Redsall's death?'

'No, it sounds like a mugging gone wrong. I'm on my way there now.'

'Call me if you need me.'

He said he would and headed for Old Portsmouth, thinking of the body he was about to view. Had the victim tried to resist his attacker and got killed as a result? It must have happened some time after eleven when the pubs in the area had closed and when it was dark with fewer people around to come to the victim's rescue, because it was a popular area for locals and tourists.

Heading along the seafront he knew that he'd have to postpone his trip to the Isle of Wight and his meeting with Professor Madeley. He might also need to put on hold his investigation into the deaths of Spalding and Redsall. He was loathed to do both.

He indicated left at the junction between Pembroke Road and the High Street and headed towards the sea with the Cathedral on his right before swinging right and turning into Broad Street. On arrival he saw that Cantelli had already marshalled SOCO and there were two cars behind the white van; one he recognized as belonging to Dr Freemantle, the other was Jim Clarke's. The area had been cordoned off from the base of the Square Tower on Horton's left to the far end of the fortifications to the west, taking in the Round Tower and the wide pavement area which encompassed the Pioneer Statue erected in 2001 as a permanent legacy to those who had set sail to create a new home in America. The raised walkway on the fortifications had also been sealed off and he could see a uniformed police officer standing at the entrance to the Round Tower from the walkway.

They had already drawn a large audience and in the houses and apartments opposite many residents were standing at their doors watching them. Horton hoped that someone would remember seeing something that could lead them to a quick arrest. Soon the media would arrive with their cameras, microphones and Dictaphones.

'It's nasty,' Cantelli greeted him solemnly as Horton ducked under the tape. He noted the sergeant's dark sorrowful eyes and pale skin.

Horton steeled himself for the ordeal as they crossed to the stone steps where Beth Tremaine issued them with crime-scene suits. 'Who found him?' Horton asked.

'The woman over there talking to PC Kate Somerfield.' Cantelli jerked his head at a smartly dressed lady in her late fifties wearing a denim skirt and a floral blouse. 'Mrs

Smithson. She came to set up an art exhibition inside the Round Tower but went up to the top first to look across the Solent as it was such a lovely morning. She's a level-headed woman and called us immediately, although she's obviously distressed at what she's seen.'

They logged in at the inner cordon and with Tremaine behind them began to climb the steps. Pushing a fresh strip of chewing gum into his mouth, Cantelli continued. 'I couldn't see a murder weapon within the immediate vicinity of the body, but his killer could have thrown it into the sea.'

They reached the top where Taylor and Clarke nodded a greeting. Dr Freemantle, wearing a scene suit, straightened up. Horton saw the crumpled figure at the doctor's feet lying awkwardly in front of the seats that overlooked the narrow harbour entrance. His stomach clenched with tension and he controlled his breathing as he noted the silver hair, the crisp navy-blue trousers, the checked casual shirt and the bloody and battered head.

'Been dead about seven or eight hours,' Freemantle announced. 'Severe trauma to the skull. He was struck more than once, probably three or four times, but the pathologist can confirm that.'

Horton stepped nearer the body. There was something familiar about it. The man's face was turned to its right and Horton, looking more closely, started with surprise.

'My God! It's Ivor Meadows.'

Cantelli flashed him a look. 'The man at Dr Spalding's lecture?'

'Yes, and the last of the guests to leave.' He turned his troubled gaze on Cantelli. 'You know what this means?'

'He must have witnessed something.'

'Yes, and that means Spalding's death wasn't suicide and Redsall's death wasn't sudden death syndrome.' Now let Uckfield tell him the deaths weren't connected and weren't suspicious.

He stepped away and reached for his phone, leaving Cantelli to thank the police doctor and instruct Taylor,

Clarke and Tremaine. The seagulls dived overhead, squawking and squealing as Horton rapidly considered the implications of this latest murder while waiting impatiently for Uckfield to answer. Meadows dead. He was sickened by it and furious. He couldn't help thinking that if Uckfield had sacrificed his promotion chances for just two days and had continued to investigate Spalding's death, Ivor Meadows might still be alive.

When Uckfield at last came on the line Horton said brusquely, 'Ivor Meadows, the last of the guests to talk to Douglas Spalding before he walked out into the night and ended up dead in Number One Dock, has been brutally murdered and there's no sudden death syndrome or suicide about this one. He's been bludgeoned to death.'

There was a brief silence while Uckfield assimilated this. 'Any of his belongings missing?'

Horton in his eagerness hadn't checked. His gut tightened. 'Hold on.' He instructed Taylor to empty the dead man's pockets.

'Only a handkerchief, sir.'

With a silent groan Horton said into his mobile. 'There's no wallet or house keys. I've no idea if he had a mobile phone.'

'Sounds like a mugging to me.'

Yes, it damn well would, thought Horton angrily. Oh, this was clever. With difficulty he bit back his anger. 'But it has to be linked with Spalding and Redsall's death,' he insisted. 'It can't be another coincidence. Come on, Steve, we've got to at least look into the possibility.'

Abruptly Uckfield said, 'We treat it as a violent assault until we know differently. I'll get a unit over to Meadows' apartment and send Dennings to the crime scene.' He rang off.

Horton took a deep breath, trying to control his fury. His blood was pumping fast. Turning to Cantelli he said, tight-lipped, 'You got the gist of that?'

Cantelli nodded. 'He could be right.'

'Yeah, and I could be Tinkerbell. Whoever is doing this is clever, evil and powerful. And I intend to get the bastard.' *Unless they get you first.* Horton looked down on the crumpled bloody face of the man who had so proudly told him that he'd fought for his country in so many conflicts. He didn't care how dangerous pursuing this might be. He'd get whoever was responsible. He would just have to be more careful, or, he thought grimly, take more risks and flush them out. If the intelligence services had decided they needed to hush up the deaths of Spalding and Redsall, and they were responsible for Meadows' death, then whatever they were attempting to hide had to be massive. His heart jolted. My God, was it just possible that Ivor Meadows had been right, and that Spalding had discovered something connected with the mysterious death of Buster Crabb? It would explain why the intelligence services were so het up and it might also explain the attempt on his own life last night. It had been a warning to him to lay off, or more than likely the driver had intended to cause him an injury which would necessitate him going off sick for some considerable time. He was tempted to tell Cantelli about the incident but didn't because he knew it would worry him. He also knew that it might put the sergeant's life at risk and Horton would never do that. He cared for him too much.

His voice tight with rage he said, 'The killer has made it look like a mugging and I bet when the unit reports into Meadows' flat they'll find it ransacked with no trace of fingerprints or DNA. This death will be covered up just like the others. It stinks, Barney, and I for one can't accept it.'

'So what did Meadows witness and why kill him?'

Horton willed himself to calm down and think. He watched Clarke photograph and video the ex-Navy man who had made such a pest of himself at the naval museum and in the library. Well, no more. He thought back to his last encounter with Meadows in the dockyard yesterday.

'When I told Meadows about Redsall's death perhaps I jogged a memory. Perhaps Meadows remembered seeing him talking to someone after the lecture or before it on HMS

Victory at the drinks reception, or when Gideon escorted the guests from the *Victory* to the museum, and like an idiot, he confronted this man.'

'There is another option,' Cantelli ventured. 'And it could fit with the missing briefcase or rather its contents and Redsall's empty rucksack. Meadows might have remembered seeing Redsall meeting someone outside the dockyard when he was on his way home.'

Cantelli had a point and a good one. Horton swiftly recalled the times they'd signed out. 'If we can believe the signing-out log then Redsall left at 9.25, five minutes before Meadows, so if Meadows saw him talking to someone out-side it was a longish conversation.'

'Perhaps Redsall had to hang around waiting for this person to show up.'

That was possible. Horton said, 'If Redsall did take Spalding's briefcase, or its contents, and handed it over to this person outside the dockyard that night then why was his rucksack empty when his body was discovered?'

'Perhaps whoever Redsall met wasn't the main man, just a runner and Redsall insisted he would only hand it over to the boss the next day.'

That would certainly fit. He put himself in Meadows' shoes — what would he have done? Having recognized or thought he knew who the killer was would Meadows have gone in for a spot of blackmail? No, that wasn't his style. Horton knew exactly what action he would have taken.

He said, 'Meadows was an ex Royal Navy police officer, and if he knew, or thought he knew, who the killer was he would have questioned him in the hope he could get evidence and solve the case before us. He'd have made notes. He didn't know he was playing in a different league. So either his killer took the notebook along with the wallet and keys to make us think it was a mugging, or the notebook is in Meadows' apartment. Or it was. It might not be there now. But we'll take a look anyway. I'll meet you there; we'll leave this to Dennings.'

Meadows' apartment was less than a quarter of a mile away, tucked behind the Cathedral so Horton didn't have time to consider any further what Cantelli had said about Redsall possibly meeting someone outside the dockyard on Monday night. Together they climbed the stairs to the fifth floor where the door to Meadows' apartment was firmly locked.

'Considerate mugger, locking up after him,' Cantelli said.

'Meadows probably had more sense than to have his address on him along with his house keys.' But if his death was down to the intelligence services they'd have known where he lived.

Horton gave instructions to the uniformed officer to fetch the ramrod so that they could affect an entry. Before he went to do so the officer told them that his colleague was knocking on doors making enquiries. So far they'd learned that the woman next door had seen Meadows walking across the front car park at just after 10.30 last night.

'To meet his killer no doubt,' Horton answered.

Within minutes the door had been forced open. With latex-covered fingers, Horton entered. All was silent. He stepped into the lounge, where everything was in place and exactly as Horton had remembered, cluttered with photographs and navy memorabilia.

He said, 'If the key was taken by the killer, who was not your average scumbag thief but a professional, then he could have searched this flat for anything incriminating and removed it.'

'Someone might have seen him entering or leaving the building.'

'We live in hope.'

Cantelli took the bedroom and bathroom while Horton rapidly studied the photographs of naval officers and crew, ships and the places Meadows had visited while in the Navy. Horton felt sorry for a man who had lived so much in the past. He crossed to the computer on a small desk beside the window overlooking the Wightlink terminal, and beyond that Oyster Quays, and glanced down at the desk. On it were a few handwritten scribbles on loose-leaf sheets of paper. Horton flicked them over. Meadows had jotted down notes about discipline in the Navy during the Seven Years War between 1756 and 1763 and during the French Revolution and Napoleonic Wars 1793 to 1815. There was reference to the source material and notes on more modern-day criminal activity in the Navy with details of a list of courts-martial during both of the World Wars and some sketchy details about studies that had been undertaken by various experts of reviews into the Royal Navy's criminal justice system. There was no diary, and no notebook. Horton hadn't expected to find the latter. There was also nothing to indicate who Meadows had gone out to meet last night unless it was on his computer and Horton doubted that. Meadows would have kept such information close to his chest. And perhaps the killer was banking on that or had extracted that information from Meadows before killing him. Horton found an address book in the top drawer of the desk as Cantelli entered.

'There's a cordless phone in the bedroom. The last call was to his dentist on Friday.'

'See what you can find in the kitchen.'

Horton flicked through the address book and found the details of a solicitor under 'S'. He guessed Meadows would have made a Will and the solicitor would have the name of his next of kin. He would leave that for Trueman's team to investigate because although Uckfield was insisting this wasn't linked to Spalding and Redsall it was nevertheless a very brutal murder and therefore a Major Crime Team remit. There was also a telephone number under 'M' which looked as though it was a mobile number. Horton removed his mobile from his pocket and rang it. There was no corresponding ring in the flat and no signal. It was dead, like Meadows.

He joined Cantelli in the small, clean and tidy kitchen. 'Only a calendar.' Cantelli indicated one hanging on the wall.

'His dental appointment was next week, and he's crossed it through, so obviously rang to cancel it.'

There was nothing here to tell them who Meadows had met. Taking down one of the most recent photographs from the wall of Ivor Meadows standing beside a naval ship taken at one of the Navy Days, Horton extracted the photograph and slipped it into his pocket. In the corridor he rang Trueman and updated him, requesting fingerprints and SOCO. He said they also needed to remove the computer for forensic examination. Uckfield would raise his eyebrows at that, dismissing it as unnecessary because it didn't fit with the mugger theory, but Horton knew Trueman would request it and then tell Uckfield later, after he discovered it had been done most probably. Horton also gave instructions for the residents to be questioned about any strangers seen entering or leaving the building last night.

'What now?' asked Cantelli when they were outside. 'Go back and report to Bliss?'

It's what they should do. And she would instruct them to return to the station, to wait to be assigned their duties in connection with the murder investigation. But Horton was not in the mood to be told what to do or to hang around.

'Interview Matt Newton, Barney, ask him if he remembers what Redsall was carrying when he left the dockyard on Monday night. Also, if he saw him hanging about outside by the waterfront at any time . . .' Horton's words trailed off as another thought occurred to him. He felt his nerve-ends tingling as he quickly continued, 'Meadows told me he walked along the waterfront. I thought he meant the Hard, but he could have entered Oyster Quays and walked along *that* waterfront.'

'It was raining, would he have gone out of his way to do that?'

'But it's not out of his way, Barney; he could have taken a short cut through the Wightlink ferry terminal, then it's across the road and he's here, home. That could be where Meadows saw Redsall talking to someone, at Oyster Quays, and where Redsall insisted that he would only hand over the contents of Spalding's briefcase to the boss the following day.' Horton's mind raced as he followed this through. 'So he left the guest house early the next morning to go to meet him. And as he didn't show up until later that day, and dead, that means this boss was based some distance away.' Horton rubbed his head and frowned as he tried to put it together. Could Redsall have travelled to the Isle of Wight to meet this person? 'There's no sign of Redsall entering the marina on foot, and that means he could have been on board a boat, and the only two that came in that evening were Carl Ashton's and Rupert Crawford's.'

Cantelli looked startled. 'You're not saying that someone on one of those boats killed him?'

Was he? Cantelli hadn't met Agent Ames because he'd been on holiday while she'd worked with Horton on an investigation, but Horton couldn't see her being involved. So that left Ashton, his crew and his clients, one of whom worked for a biomedical company. Could Redsall have met someone from Ashton's yacht on the Isle of Wight and gone on board? Was Ashton lying?

He said, 'I don't know what I'm saying but get Walters to check if the CCTV footage from the Oyster Quays marina for Monday night is still available and if it is to look for any sign of Meadows and Redsall. If Bliss starts nosing around, keep this from her.'

'And you?'

'I'm going to the Isle of Wight.' But first he'd check whether Ashton's yacht or Rupert Crawford's had been moored up at Oyster Quays on Monday night.

CHAPTER SIXTEEN

The answer was disappointingly no in the case of Crawford's yacht, and yet as Horton headed across to the Isle of Wight on the ferry, he also felt relief, certainly where Harriet Ames was concerned. He would have liked it to be Rupert Crawford. Ashton's yacht though had been moored up in Oyster Quays on Monday night, but the manager confirmed that Ashton hadn't been there, only Melanie Jacobs and Steve Drummond, and they'd left before the marina office closed at sunset. So it seemed unlikely that Redsall had met anyone from it as the timing was wrong, unless either of them had returned later or Ashton had shown up. Horton asked for a list of boat owners to be emailed to him and he checked the signing-in log for those visiting the pontoons late Monday afternoon and evening. There were only a few names, none of them Horton recognized connected with the case, but he came away with a copy of the log.

He called Cantelli but got his voicemail. He left a brief message saying what he had discovered. Cantelli must be interviewing Matt Newton. DCI Bliss tried ringing him twice. Both times Horton ignored her call. She was probably fuming and already filling in the papers requesting his immediate transfer. He grabbed something to eat before the ferry docked and as he headed for the waterfront town of Cowes from the Fishbourne ferry port he pushed aside the thought that he'd also be able to keep his appointment with Professor Madeley. He could consider that later. First there was Carl Ashton.

Ashton's surprise swiftly turned to annoyance as Horton was shown into his office at Cowes Yacht Haven. 'What are you doing here?'

'A small matter of murder?'

'Murder? You mean that man found on my boat? But he died of natural causes.'

'Who told you that?'

'No one, I just assumed.'

'Then you assumed wrong.' Horton knew that strictly speaking Ashton was correct, or rather according to the official version he was. Uninvited he took the seat across Ashton's desk.

Ashton glowered at him with impatience. 'Can't this wait? I'm up to my eyes in trying to tie everything up for Cowes Week.'

'No, it can't,' Horton said crossly.

'You can't think that I've got anything to do with it and neither have my crew or clients.'

'I'm glad to hear it but you don't mind if I check.'

'Yes, I damn well do.'

'Well tough,' Horton said angrily as the bloody and beaten body of Ivor Meadows flashed into his mind, and before that, Redsall's crumpled body on Ashton's yacht and Spalding sprawled out in that dock. Tersely he said, 'There's no record of Daniel Redsall having signed into the marina and neither does he show up on the security cameras. So we're left with the question of how he got there and one idea is that he could have come by boat.'

'Not by mine, he didn't,' Ashton declared angrily, immediately catching Horton's drift.

'Are you sure?'

'Course I'm sure! I would have noticed him.'

'Would you?' Horton eyed Carl Ashton closely, adding, 'You checked it over when you met the crew and clients?'

'No. But I think I would have seen a fully grown man who hadn't paid for the ride blundering around on board,' Ashton retorted with heavy sarcasm.

Horton didn't think that Ashton was involved in murder and yet there was that story he'd told him about being threatened. Was it just that — a story, a pack of lies? But why lie? Had he invented it in case he needed something to cover for Redsall's death? But no, that didn't make sense. He said, 'What did you do when you went on board?'

Ashton gave a heavy, irritable sigh. 'I talked to the crew and clients, asked if they had a good day, that sort of thing.'

'Where?'

'In the cockpit.'

'So you didn't go below?'

Ashton shifted, looked bewildered and then annoyed. 'There was no need. The yacht was already made up. We left not long after I arrived to go for a meal, as I've already told you.'

'Did any of the others go below while you were there?'

'Steve did, I seem to remember. Simon Watson and Nigel Denton had their bags on deck. Look, this has nothing to do with me or my clients. Now I've got work to do.' As if on cue his phone rang. He picked it up. Horton grabbed it from his hand and slammed it down. 'How dare you—'

Horton eyed him narrowly. 'You always were a selfish bastard—'

'I don't have to—'

'Yes, you do. Now I want some straight answers to my questions. Clear?'

Ashton threw himself back in his chair and ran a hand over his head. Horton noticed the lines etched around his bloodshot eyes. Ashton was working hard, and Horton suspected playing hard too.

Ashton nodded.

'Where were you Monday night?'

'Monday? But that man died on Tuesday.' Horton said nothing, just held Ashton's bewildered stare, forcing him to add tersely, 'I was here working until 9.30, went for something to eat in the club, which you can check if you don't believe me,' he added sarcastically, 'and then went back to the flat in East Cowes Marina.'

Horton could easily check that. He didn't think Ashton was lying. He stretched across the photograph of Redsall. 'Are you sure you've never seen him before?'

'I saw his body, remember,' Ashton replied caustically.

'Take a closer look,' Horton repeated firmly. 'People look different when they're alive.'

Ashton winced at the phrase, but he sat forward and took the photograph with an expression of distaste as if the dead man might return to haunt him. And maybe he would, thought Horton, if he found a connection between them. He watched Ashton's reaction carefully but there was no flicker of recognition.

'I've never seen him in my life.' Ashton pushed the picture across his wide desk littered with paper.

'And the name Daniel Redsall?'

'Means nothing to me. Now if that's—'

'Tell me your movements for Tuesday.'

'You can't think—'

'Tell me,' Horton said sharply.

Stiffly Ashton replied, 'I was with you at the Bridge Tavern telling you about the threats being made to me, which you've done nothing about except to run some names through a computer,' he added contemptuously.

'Have there been any more?'

'No.' Ashton shifted and glanced away.

'So apart from being with me between one and two o'clock on Tuesday, what else did you do?'

'I drove along the coast to Emsworth where I had a meeting with a marketing client who is also designing a new website for us. I left there about 4.30, made some calls in my car and then returned to Portsmouth.'

'What time?'

'I told you. I arrived at Oyster Quays at 6.30 or thereabouts.'

'So your calls and the drive to Portsmouth took you two hours!' Horton said incredulously, knowing that the drive from Emsworth to Portsmouth would take twenty minutes, half an hour at the most.

'No. I went to Gosport Marina first,' Ashton replied somewhat defensively and hesitantly.

'Out of your way, that.' Ashton would have had to drive past the northern outskirts of Portsmouth and twelve miles further to the south into Gosport.

'I went to look at a boat.'

'For your fleet?'

'No, for me personally. Look it's no big deal. It's just a motor boat. I thought it might make a change from sailing.'

'And did you take it out?'

'Yes.'

'Alone?'

'Yes. Look, what's this got to do with anything?'

'Where did you go?'

'Out in the Solent.'

'So you went past Oyster Quays.'

'You know I did, coming out from Gosport. There's no other way into the Solent.'

'Did you stop there?'

'No.'

If he did stop, he didn't sign in at the marina; perhaps the CCTV cameras had picked him out although Walters hadn't mentioned it. He let it go for now.

'Then you drove back to Oyster Quays?'

'Yes. And you know the rest.'

Ashton's phone rang and he snatched it up with a glare at Horton. This time Horton let him answer it. 'Good to speak to you, Regan, yes everything's fine, the yacht's just being made ready now. Can you just hold on a moment?' Putting his hand over the receiver he said, 'Have we finished?'

'Do you know a man called Ivor Meadows?'

'No.'

'Where were you last night?'

'In the club having a drink and something to eat until ten o'clock, you can check that too. Then I went home.'

'Alone?'

'Yes. Is that it?'

'For now,' Horton said portentously. 'I'll need a full itinerary for Tuesday and I want to talk to Melanie and Steve, where can I find them?'

'They'll tell you in the office and they'll give you a copy of the itinerary. Sorry about that, Regan. Yes, everything's fine. Frantic of course . . .'

Horton collected the itinerary from a flustered-looking young woman in a noisy and busy office, and got directions of where he could find the yacht with Melanie Jacobs and Steve Drummond on board. He headed there mulling over what Ashton had told him. He had been evasive and uneasy but that didn't mean he was Redsall's contact or responsible for his death. His alibis would check out for Monday and last night, so he couldn't be involved in the deaths of Spalding and Ivor Meadows. He was a little uncomfortable about the fact that Ashton had been on board a boat, and not his own on the Tuesday afternoon. There was the possibility that he could have met Redsall at Gosport and dropped him off at Oyster Quays by boat, but the timing was wrong because it would have been early afternoon and that meant that Redsall would have wandered around the pontoons for at least an hour or more before Ashton's arrival, without being seen, which clearly wasn't possible. If he had gone on board someone else's boat, then whose? And if he had left the marina and then returned to it later after dusk, he would certainly have signed out. Or would he? Horton recalled the mistakes made with Spalding not signing out at the dockyard on the night he met his death — was it possible the same thing had happened at Oyster Quays? Or perhaps whoever had been in the office had been on the phone and had either not seen

Redsall or waved him through. Redsall then returned later that evening, slipped into the marina and had met his killer.

And if Redsall had gone on board Ashton's motor boat and been taken back to Gosport Marina then how did he get back to Oyster Quays? Ashton could have given him a lift back in his car, but why should he, and why would Redsall return to Oyster Quays marina? Also, where did this fit with his theory that Spalding and Redsall could be involved in terrorist activity? Or at least Redsall might have been and Spalding was working for the government. Ashton simply wasn't interested in politics except to vote Conservative whenever there was an election. No, Horton thought he could rule him out. And he could probably do the same with Melanie Jacobs and Steve Drummond and the fact that Redsall could have been hiding on board the yacht. It had been a bit of a wild shot anyway. But now that he was here, he would check it out.

Horton located the yacht on the crowded pontoon. A suntanned, shapely and very attractive woman in her late twenties who he took to be Melanie Jacobs was checking the lines. She was certainly Carl Ashton's type. Her straight long blonde hair was carelessly pulled back with strands falling around her heart-shaped face. Her eyes were a remarkable sapphire blue and her teeth white enough to make him glad he was wearing sunglasses, which he removed as he introduced himself. Her smile slipped when he told her he was following up the death of the man found on the yacht. She called out to Drummond at the bow, who nimbly made his way around the deck to join them. Drummond, tall, dark-haired and muscular was also late twenties or possibly early thirties and his smile stayed more or less in place as Melanie made the swift introductions and explanations. Both were wearing shorts, deck shoes and polo shirts bearing the name of Ashton's company, Sail Away Events, and the corporate logo.

Melanie offered him a drink, which he accepted because it afforded him the opportunity to go below decks. As

Melanie crossed to the galley and opened the fridge Horton surveyed the plush interior. Everything was neat and clean. He knew these boats well but decided to play dumb about the layout to see what he could elicit from them.

'Nice yacht, plenty of room,' he said, taking the can of Diet Coke from Melanie Jacobs. 'How many cabins are there?'

'Three, a double in the bow and two double cabins in the stern. And we can sleep another two here in the main cabin, which is usually where Steve and I sleep, when we're really busy.' She tossed Drummond a smile, before adding, 'Making a total of eight on board.'

'Impressive.' Horton swallowed his Coke, watching Drummond's reaction and seeing by his worshipping glance that he liked it best when they were really busy. But he also caught a flicker of pain in the dark brown eyes and a flash of anger in the slight tightening around his jaw. Horton wondered if he had just found Ashton's stalker.

'Did you want to look around?' Melanie asked.

Horton did. He crossed to the bow and peered into the shower room and toilet to his right, spotlessly clean, before entering the double cabin, where the bed was made up and everything was pristine. Turning back, he said, 'Who were the clients you had on board on Tuesday?' Ashton had told him but no harm in asking again.

'Simon Watson from Longman Biomedical and Nigel Denton from an agricultural firm. Simon's a chemist and a good sailor, he's been out with us many times, but it was a first for Nigel.'

A chemist. Interesting. Horton thought of Dr Clayton checking to see if Redsall had been drugged. 'Were the cabins used?' he asked, as he headed back through the galley to the aft where, as Melanie had said, he found two further separate cabins.

Drummond answered. 'Only the one at the bow to put our things in; it's closest to the heads.'

So, thought Horton, these two rear cabins had been left untouched. It was possible that Redsall could have been inside one, but not dead because the time of death was between 7.30 and 9.30 p.m. And according to Ashton they'd already left the yacht by 7.30. A fact that had been confirmed by Agent Ames. He wondered whether he'd bump into her while in Cowes before quickly reminding himself that the town was heaving with holiday makers and sailors and that it was highly unlikely.

'Who locked up on Tuesday?' he asked.

Melanie answered. 'I did.'

'Did you go below?'

'No.' She glanced at Drummond.

'I did. I'd left my phone behind.'

'Where?'

'In the galley. Here.' Drummond indicated the table.

That confirmed what Ashton had told him. Horton addressed Melanie. 'When did Mr Ashton tell you about the body being found on the boat?'

'He called me at home. It must have been about 12.30 a.m.'

Horton eyed her closely. Was that a lie? Horton wouldn't mind betting Ashton had headed for Melanie's flat in Southsea after leaving Rupert Crawford's yacht.

'I phoned Steve in the morning and we went to Oyster Quays to bring the boat back here and clean it up.'

Horton handed her a photograph of Redsall. 'Have either of you seen this man before?'

Melanie glanced at it as Drummond took it.

'Is he the man who was found on board this yacht?' Melanie asked nervously looking up at Horton.

'Yes.'

She peered over Drummond's shoulder. 'I don't know him.'

'Me neither,' said Drummond.

Horton eyed them steadily. They didn't appear to be lying. 'Have either of you heard of Daniel Redsall?'

Drummond answered, 'No.' Melanie shook her head.

Horton drank some Coke. 'Take me through what you did on Tuesday.' He had the itinerary, but he wanted to hear it from them. There was always the possibility they'd deviated from it. He put the photograph back in his trouser pocket.

Drummond said, 'I met Simon Watson and Nigel Denton at the marina office at Oyster Quays at nine a.m.'

'Did they arrive together?'

Melanie answered. 'Yes. They'd come in Simon's car. We had breakfast on board, bacon rolls, pastries, then Steve gave a safety briefing, which took us up to just after 10.15 when we left the harbour. We went out into the Solent and hoisted the sails. The weather could have been better but at least it wasn't raining and there was enough wind to do a fair amount of sailing. We came into Cowes Yacht Haven for lunch, arriving here just after one p.m.'

'You all sat together for lunch?'

'Of course.' She eyed him as though he was daft.

'Did anyone leave the group for any length of time?'

'I had to go out to take a call from Carl, and Simon had a message on his phone when we arrived and had to make a call.'

Drummond said, 'I went for a pee and a cigarette. I don't remember Nigel leaving the club.'

Melanie continued. 'We left the marina shortly after 2.15 and went back into the Solent for more sailing. I set a triangular course. It was good. We had tea on board then returned to Oyster Quays at 5.30, cleaned up and Carl joined us at 6.35. We went for a meal and Simon and Nigel left the restaurant just before eleven o'clock.'

'Did anyone leave during the evening?'

'No,' Drummond answered.

Horton thought that if Redsall had come on board during the day there were two places he could have done so, either here at Cowes during lunchtime, which meant either Melanie Jacobs or Simon Watson had met Redsall at the yacht and let him on board, or he'd gone on board at Oyster Quays on Tuesday morning after leaving the guest house early. But Horton couldn't see how he could have been on board all day without any of the four, or three if one of them was involved, knowing that he was there. He asked what time they left Oyster Quays marina on Monday night. Their times checked out with what the marina manager had told him, and both confirmed that Ashton hadn't been at Oyster Quays on Monday night and that neither of them returned to the yacht. They had a drink together and then went home. Drummond said his flatmate could vouch for that and Melanie said she'd spoken to one of her neighbours at 9.30. Horton thought he could rule them out of being involved. But he had one more thing to check.

He removed another photograph from his pocket, this time of Douglas Spalding, and asked if they knew or recognized him. He drew a blank and got the same result when he showed them a picture of Ivor Meadows.

Climbing back up on deck, Horton surveyed the colourful scene with the yachts decked out with flags flapping in the stiff breeze against the sound of the halyards slapping against the masts. Turning, he said to Melanie, 'Can you tell me where you were last night?'

She flushed and looked away as she answered, 'I was here working most of the evening.'

'And after that? Did you return to Portsmouth?'

'Why do you want to know?' she asked warily.

'We need to check everyone's movements because there's been another death.'

'But it can't have anything to do with us.'

'Where were you last night, Ms Jacobs?' *As if I didn't know.*

'I stayed at Carl's flat in East Cowes Marina.' Her head came up. 'It makes more sense than travelling back to Portsmouth. I'm staying there for Cowes Week.'

So Ashton had lied about that; he said he'd been alone, but perhaps he'd done so to protect Melanie's reputation. But

Horton didn't think Ashton was that chivalrous, he probably didn't want anyone to know of their affair — better that way for when he ditched her and picked up with the next one.

'And you're staying there too?' Horton addressed Drummond, knowing full well he wasn't. He caught the unmistakable flash of fury in Drummond's eyes as he looked at Melanie. It didn't take much to see that he worshipped the ground she walked on and was furious at being rejected in favour of Ashton. Here was Ashton's poisonous letter writer and tyre slasher.

'Wrong gender,' Drummond said cheerfully, but Horton heard the bitterness in his voice. 'I'm staying with some of the other crew in a house Carl's rented for the week.'

'And you were there last night?'

'After twelve thirty; before then we were in the pub and then bought some fish and chips and staggered home.'

And there would be witnesses. Horton climbed off the boat. He waited until Drummond had gone below before turning back and addressing Melanie. 'Was Carl with you last night?'

She flushed, glanced behind her and said quickly, 'Yes. We went for a meal in a pub near the marina and got back to the flat at ten thirty.'

Horton had no reason to doubt her. As he headed out of the marina, he rang Cantelli and this time the sergeant answered. 'Newton claims he didn't see anyone meet Redsall outside the dockyard. He didn't even look and I believe him; the man's in a terrible state and I can't say I blame him with his wife so ill. I had to interview him at the hospice. He remembers Daniel Redsall leaving and the fact that he was carrying a rucksack but other than that he couldn't tell if Redsall's rucksack contained a block of concrete or bugger all. Bliss has been on to me belly-aching about you not answering your phone. I said that I thought there was something wrong with it. Don't think she believed me. She asked me what you were doing and I muttered something about trying to trace Ivor Meadows' last movements after you spoke to him yesterday. I told Bliss I was helping to interview residents in and around the area where Meadows lived.'

'Is there any news on the investigation?'

'Not that I've been told.'

'Contact Gosport Marina and ask them if they remember seeing Carl Ashton there on Tuesday afternoon. He says he was trying out a motor boat he was considering buying. Check the times and see if Walters has found any sign of Ashton mooring up at Oyster Quays on Tuesday afternoon, before his corporate yacht entered the marina. I don't believe he's our killer. I just want to be sure. Try and keep Bliss at bay as long as possible.'

'Might not be too difficult, Walters tells me she's in meetings most of the afternoon.'

Good. That would give them a bit of breathing space unless Uckfield summoned them to assist in the Meadows enquiry. But for now, Uckfield would have to wait and so too would the investigation into the deaths of three men because it was just after three and Horton was already late for his meeting with Professor Thurstan Madeley in the exclusive and elitist Castle Hill Yacht Club. He only hoped he'd still be there.

CHAPTER SEVENTEEN

Horton was shown into the crowded Pavilion Room over-looking the Solent where he found Madeley at a table by the window. Horton recognized him from the photographs on the Bramshill police college website and it seemed Madeley recognized him because he rose as Horton approached. He apologized for being late as they shook hands. Horton knew his scrutiny of Madeley was reciprocated. He saw an intelligent man in his late fifties with a long domed head culminating in thinning grey hair, bright, shrewd and curious hazel eyes, a wide mouth with lips a little too thin and a slightly superior manner behind the smile. He didn't know what Madeley saw.

Horton took the seat opposite him. 'I appreciate your time, Professor Madeley.'

'I couldn't refuse. I'm somewhat intrigued by your request and how it fits with an investigation.'

His voice had traces of a Midlands accent, Staffordshire possibly. 'I'll be brief as time is pressing,' Horton answered crisply, removing from his pocket the photograph that Ballard had left on his boat. 'I want to know if you recognize any of these men.'

Madeley took the picture with a quizzical glance before directing his full attention to the photograph. He studied it carefully in silence and then turned it over. Horton could feel his heart pounding and hoped that Madeley couldn't hear it. The sound of laughter and talk in the room behind him seemed abnormally loud. After what seemed an age but could only have been a minute at the most, Madeley looked up. Eyeing Horton steadily he said, 'No. I'm sorry, they're not known to me.'

Horton felt the disappointment keenly, although he tried desperately not to show it.

Madeley continued, 'The date on the reverse corresponds to the sit-ins at the London School of Economics. They are possibly students.'

Horton had got that far himself. 'You don't remember seeing this photograph before then, while collating the archive project?'

'No. It's obviously from a private collection that wasn't donated to the archives.'

'I'm trying to find out who they are.'

'May I ask why?'

Truth or lie? If he fabricated a case would Madeley bother to check on it? Why should he? But if he did and discovered Horton had lied, would he become even more curious and start to ask questions about him and his credentials as a police officer?

No, Horton saw that it had to be the truth. This man was no fool and he'd spot a lie a mile away. Besides Horton knew that the only way to provoke a reaction — or perhaps he should say another reaction if Zeus was responsible for the incident last night — was to tell the truth and keep asking questions.

He said, 'I believe that either one or more of these men knew my mother, Jennifer Horton, and that by locating and talking to any of them it might help me find out what happened to her.'

'What did happen to her?'

Horton had that prickling feeling between his shoulder blades. Madeley knew. How? He must have checked him out before the meeting. But he wouldn't have access to his personal file and besides there was nothing on it about his mother's disappearance.

Madeley had talked to someone.

'She disappeared on the thirtieth of November 1978.'

Madeley showed no surprise. It could simply be the man's normal demeanour but Horton doubted it. Madeley sipped his drink. Horton had noted that he hadn't been offered one. Madeley said, 'That picture was taken eleven years before she disappeared. Why do you think it's connected?'

'It was given to me by someone who knew something about her and why she vanished, and before you say, "why don't I ask him?", I can't because he's also disappeared.'

'But if you know who this man is can't you run him through the databases and find him?'

Madeley was guessing that he had already done so. It wasn't much of a guess; Madeley would know the system very well. Horton said, 'You compiled an archive project on the student protests and by doing so must have seen hundreds of documents and photographs and conducted considerable research. Is there anyone I can talk to who might be able to help me identify these men?'

'I'm sure it must have occurred to you that the date could be false and have nothing to do with the sit-in.'

'It has.'

Madeley nodded and looked thoughtful. 'These men would be in their mid-sixties by now. Some of them could be dead.'

'They could all be dead for all I know.'

'Your mother's disappearance is still on file; you could have the photograph of each man computer enhanced to show what they might now look like.'

Horton had already considered this. It would mean using police resources and therefore officially requesting the case be investigated. But all he had to do was show this picture to DCS Sawyer of the Intelligence Directorate and that would be enough for Sawyer to use whatever resources he had at his disposal to uncover the men's identities in the hope it might lead him to Zeus. So far Sawyer had not requested that Jennifer's disappearance be reopened officially; instead, he'd tried to enlist Horton's covert help in locating Zeus. Maybe it was time to go public.

Horton said, 'It wouldn't name them though.'

'It might if one of them was recognized.'

Horton put the photograph back in his pocket. There was much that Madeley wasn't saying but equally, Horton thought with growing interest, he was saying a great deal. 'It was a long shot anyway.' He rose.

'What will you do now?' Madeley asked, looking up at him.

Was he surprised Horton had capitulated so quickly and easily? He looked it. Horton felt like saying 'that depends on you' but he said, 'Thank you for your time, sir.' He stretched out his hand. Madeley took it and held onto it for a moment longer than was necessary.

After a brief pause, he said, 'DCI Lorraine Bliss attended my lecture last week at Bramshill.'

Horton was slightly taken aback at the change of topic.

Madeley smiled. 'She's a very ambitious woman. I talked to her for some time after the lecture. She mentioned you.'

And not in glowing terms, he guessed. Horton was relieved he hadn't tried to fob Madeley off by telling him he wasn't a police officer.

Madeley's smile didn't slip as he added, 'I believe she'll go far.'

Unlike me. Horton caught the hint of a warning and he shivered despite the heat. 'I'm sure she will.' Horton turned to leave, wondering why Madeley had changed the subject. Was that to distract him from what he thought he'd picked up on in the subtext? But Horton hadn't even taken a step before Madeley's clear voice said, 'Dr Quentin Amos.' Horton spun back.

'Amos was a lecturer in March 1967 and involved with the students. He was very supportive of them. He's retired now of course, in his mid-seventies. He might be able to help.'

Horton looked at him in puzzlement. 'I didn't see his name in the archive project.'

'No.' The monosyllable was heavy with portent.

'Do you know where I can find him?'

'No, but it shouldn't be difficult, not for you.'

Horton held Madeley's cool stare for a moment. 'Thank you, sir.'

He made his way across the crowded room, his mind so preoccupied with the conversation with Madeley that he almost collided with a blonde woman in the doorway. He stepped back, an apology forming on his lips, when he found himself facing Agent Ames. He should have known she'd be a member of a club that counted Royals and celebrities amongst its clientele. Although pleased to see her he was also dismayed because now he'd have to explain why he was there. She was bound to ask.

'How's the investigation going, sir? Did you want to talk to us?' She'd naturally assumed that was the reason for his visit. 'There's been another death,' he said, quickly trying to think how he could connect it with her and her sailing buddies, but before he could elaborate his name was called and he looked beyond Ames to see former DCI Mike Danby heading towards them.

'What are you doing here?' Danby shook his hand and smiled a greeting.

Horton didn't see that he needed to explain his presence to Danby.

'Thought I might become a member,' he joked. 'Just looking over the place to see if the clientele are respectable.'

'I doubt that, but come and meet some of them.' Danby headed into the Pavilion Room leaving him no option but to re-enter it. Ames flashed him a smile. Horton turned and saw Danby cross to a table where he addressed three men. As Horton made towards them, he could see Madeley at his seat with his back to the room. The three men Danby was talking to must have seen him with Madeley and couldn't have failed to see him leaving the room, and with a groan, he saw that two of them were Rupert Crawford and Ben Otis. Ames would know he hadn't been here to question them and she was bound to be curious as to why he'd been leaving the Pavilion Room.

Danby began to make the introductions but Horton interjected. 'I've met Mr Crawford and Mr Otis.'

In daylight Ben Otis was younger than Horton had first thought, nearer to forty-five than fifty-five. He was dark-haired with very deep brown, almost black eyes, and he looked extremely fit. Otis gave him a friendly smile. Crawford ignored him.

Danby said, 'And this is Lord Ames.'

Horton hid his surprise. Ames rose and proffered his hand. He was in his late sixties, grey-haired, lean and fit, with a keen-featured face, which bore a resemblance to Agent Ames about the eyes. He was casually but smartly dressed and wearing an expression that seemed vaguely familiar to Horton, probably because he'd seen it on Harriet Ames' perfect features. Lord Ames gestured him into the seat and offered him coffee. Horton declined the latter. 'I'm working, sir. Haven't got time.'

Crawford looked up. 'Is it to do with that body on Ashton's boat?'

What did he say now when they must have seen him sitting with Madeley? But then they wouldn't know that Madeley wasn't involved in the investigation, and neither would Harriet Ames.

'Yes.'

Otis said, 'Have you any idea how the body ended up there?'

Danby answered, 'If DI Horton has then he's not going to tell us.'

Otis smiled while Crawford, seemingly bored with the conversation, returned his attention to the message he was sending via his mobile phone.

Horton said, 'His name was Daniel Redsall. He was a marine archaeologist and attended a lecture on Monday night given by Dr Douglas Spalding, who was found dead that night. Sadly, we now have another fatality and a homicide of a man called Ivor Meadows who was also at Dr Spalding's lecture.'

Otis looked shocked. 'That's dreadful. So, you think the deaths are connected?'

'It's possible.' He didn't add *and I'm the only one who believes that*.

'Redsall,' repeated Lord Ames thoughtfully. 'I seem to remember we had a Redsall as a member. A Navy man. Could he be a relation?'

'Daniel Redsall's father was Rear Admiral Jonathan Redsall.'

'Of course, I remember him now. He died some years ago. Nice man, good sailor. He had a house here in Cowes and one on the mainland. His wife didn't like the sea very much so he used to come here with his sister, Beatrice. She was a very good sailor.'

This was useful background information but it didn't get Horton very much further forward, except for one thing. Beatrice Redsall. 'Is she still a member?'

Lord Ames answered, 'I don't know.'

Harriet Ames said, 'I could check.'

Her father looked at Horton and said, 'Is it pertinent to the investigation?'

'We don't know what is at this stage,' he answered vaguely. 'It's a case of gathering as much information as we can.' He caught Danby's knowing glance. OK, so it was the standard answer, but it was true, nevertheless. He added, 'I'd also like to know if Daniel Redsall was a member.' Horton doubted it but no harm in asking and he'd like to know if either Daniel or Beatrice had been here on the Tuesday Daniel had died, but he'd ask Ames to check that out for him when away from the others.

Lord Ames said, 'I'm sure the Club Secretary will be pleased to assist with your investigation.'

Horton removed the photograph of Redsall from his pocket. 'Maybe you recognize him, sir.' He showed it to Lord Ames, who shook his head and handed it across to Danby. With a shake of his head Danby handed it back to Horton.

Horton then showed Otis and Crawford the photograph of Ivor Meadows asking if they'd seen him before. As neither man had been at Oyster Quays on Monday night it seemed unlikely. They both denied knowing him and the same with Douglas Spalding when Horton repeated the routine. He rose, thanking them for their help.

Harriet Ames jumped up. 'I'll show you out.'

Danby said, 'Good luck with the investigation.'

Horton caught his sly glance, Rupert's patronizing one and Otis's amused one, but Lord Ames had already looked away and was pouring himself a coffee as though Horton didn't warrant a farewell — he was nothing, just a mere speck on the carpet to his Lordship.

At the entrance to the club Horton halted. 'What does Ben Otis do for a living?'

'Nothing. He doesn't have to. He made a fortune selling his computer software company years ago.'

She held his gaze. He had been mad even to think he could stand a chance with her. Apart from her job they had nothing in common. She came from and moved in totally different circles to him. An investment banker, a multimillionaire and Daddy, a peer of the realm, while he was just a kid from the back streets of Portsmouth, who'd had very little education, no money, no father, a mother who had walked out on him and a failed marriage behind him.

She said, 'I'll ask the secretary about Beatrice and Daniel Redsall and call you when I have the information.'

She turned and walked away. He got the sense that something in his expression had betrayed his thoughts. What had she seen though? Anger? Resentment? Distaste? He hurried away, glad to get out of the cloying atmosphere of privilege and wealth. He felt irritated that he'd let his thoughts show and that she'd seen them, but what bothered him more as he headed back for the ferry was the fact that the three men had seen him talking to Madeley. Horton doubted if Rupert Crawford would have taken any notice or bothered to question why he was interviewing Madeley but Ben Otis and Lord Ames must be curious and he could see by her expression that Agent Ames had wondered why he'd been leaving the Pavilion Room when clearly, he hadn't been questioning her father and his friends. She'd had more sense than to question him, however.

With annoyance he pushed the thoughts aside and returned his concentration to his conversation with Madeley. He'd asked Madeley if he recognized any of the men in the photograph and Madeley's answer had been 'They're not known to me.' That wasn't quite the same thing. Horton felt sure that he had recognized them or at least one of them but he didn't *know* whoever it was. Why not say though? Madeley had mentioned having the photograph computer enhanced to show the men as they might now look, and when Horton had replied that he couldn't see how that could help Madeley had said, 'It might if one of them was recognized.' The only way that *he* would recognize one of the men was if he was a celebrity, a politician, sportsman or on their files as a criminal.

Horton just made the four o'clock ferry with seconds to spare and while the hills of the Isle of Wight slipped away behind him and the buildings of Portsmouth drew nearer, he again studied the photograph. Could one of these men be Zeus, who had been caught and imprisoned once? Or perhaps one of the men was another criminal, who was inside, and that might give Horton the opportunity to talk to him.

Then there was Quentin Amos. Horton stared at the yachts and pleasure craft on the blue shimmering Solent. Why was Amos's name missing from the archive project? And why wouldn't he have any trouble locating him? The answer clearly was because Amos was on file. And Horton was very keen to know why.

As the grey granite structure of the Round Tower came into view Horton's thoughts veered back to Ivor Meadows' bloodied body lying on the ground of the popular viewpoint. It looked as though it was still sealed off because there was no one on it to wave at the ferry as it slid closer towards its berth. If Meadows had seen Redsall meet someone to tell them he had obtained the contents of Spalding's briefcase then when during the evening of Monday had Redsall taken the contents? If Newton was telling the truth and Redsall had signed out at 9.25 p.m. and couldn't have slipped back inside the dockyard, he couldn't have hung around outside the museum waiting for Spalding. It couldn't have been during the lecture either. The only time it could possibly have been was when the refreshments were being served and when Spalding had been talking to the guests. Several things began to shift into place. Meadows had seen Redsall slip back into the conference room and had only remembered it after Horton had jogged his memory yesterday by showing him Redsall's photograph. Meadows had also recalled he'd seen Redsall outside talking to someone. And that had to be some-one Redsall knew or recognized. Someone he wasn't afraid to confront and someone he was confident enough to meet late at night in a remote location. Horton thought it was time he re-interviewed Julie Preston.

CHAPTER EIGHTEEN

Julie Preston looked up as Horton entered her office. He caught a flicker of fear in her eyes behind the square-framed spectacles and thought she looked paler and more tired than on his first visit.

'I heard about Ivor Meadows' death on the news at lunchtime,' she said tremulously. 'I feel terrible talking about him the way I did.'

'Did you also know that another man who attended Dr Spalding's lecture is dead? Daniel Redsall.'

Her eyes widened and her face paled even further. 'But that's . . . that's dreadful. Was it an accident?'

'We're treating all three as suspicious.' Or at least he was.

'Three? Of course, Dr Spalding.' She glanced down at her desk and picked up a pencil which she began to fiddle with.

Taking out the photograph of Redsall, Horton asked her if she remembered him.

'I saw him talking to Dr Spalding over the refreshments but it wasn't for long before Mr Meadows butted in.'

'Did you see Daniel Redsall during the lecture?'

'I wasn't really noticing.' She shifted and again pushed a hand through her hair. 'It was dark in the lecture room.' Not that dark.

'And I wasn't always in there,' she added hastily, her eyes flicking up to his and away again. 'I had to pop out and make sure everything was all right with caterers.'

'Of course.' Horton left a short pause.

She shifted position and eyed him warily.

After a moment he said, 'How did Dr Spalding seem during the lecture?'

'Fine. He was fine.'

'Are you sure?'

'Yes. But as I said I wasn't always there.'

Horton heard fear in her voice. And he knew why. It was simple. 'Could you show me the Princess Royal Gallery again?'

She scrambled up and led him across the landing, through to the conference room. The chairs were stacked at the sides but the screen and lectern were still in place at the front of the room. She hovered nervously beside him. After a moment he turned to her and said quietly, almost conversationally, 'You weren't in here at any time during the lecture, were you?' He wondered if she'd deny it. She seemed about to then under his steady scrutiny capitulate.

'No.' She stared down at the carpet.

'How long have you and Neil Gideon been having an affair?'

Her head came up and her eyes widened with alarm before he caught a tell-tale flash of relief. 'We're not,' she said confidently.

No. He knew that. There was only one person it could be.

'But you are with Lewis Morden.'

Alarm crossed her face. She opened her mouth as though to refute it but could see by his expression that it was pointless. 'Please don't tell my boss. I'll lose my job.'

'And Lewis Morden will lose his.'

'He only came up for ten minutes.'

'A quick one then,' Horton sneered to get a reaction.

Her eyes flashed with anger. 'It's not like that. We love one another.'

'Yeah, and his wife doesn't understand him,' Horton said cynically.

She looked away.

'How long has it been going on?'

'A few months,' she answered miserably, then adding more defiantly, 'the museum was shut, there wasn't any security risk. No one could get in or out, the audience were in the lecture room, and there was nothing to see on the security monitors.'

'There were the caterers.'

'They've all been security checked at the highest level, and besides they came straight in and were busy setting up the buffet.'

He let that go. 'And this romantic assignation happens every time you and Lewis Morden are in the museum together at night during a function?'

She nodded, looking miserable.

'What time did he return to the control room?'

She shifted.

'Julie, it's important that you tell me the truth.'

'I took him some food and just before the caterers packed away, he slipped down the back stairs and around by the side door into the museum and control room.'

'And he came up to your office when?' She hesitated. 'Don't lie to me, Julie.'

'Ten minutes after the lecture started.'

'So, about 7.45 p.m. And he left the monitors running?'

'I guess so.'

Without anyone watching them, which was a lucky break for Redsall — or did he know about Julie Preston and Lewis Morden's assignations? If he did then someone had told him. Who? Neil Gideon? All Redsall had to do while Spalding was talking to the guests was slip back into the gallery, take the laptop computer from Spalding's briefcase, replace it with something of an equal weight so Spalding wouldn't check inside it, put the laptop in his rucksack and slip back in amongst the guests.

He said, 'What did you and Lewis do after everyone had left?'

'Lewis helped me do a sweep of the museum, as I told you, and then he left. I locked up and Neil Gideon walked me to my car. Will you have to talk to Lewis?'

'What do you think?'

'But you don't have to tell David, my boss.'

'I think that perhaps you had better do that.'

She looked mortified at the thought. Horton added, 'I want a list of all the functions where you and Lewis Morden were together, and I want a copy of the guest list at each one.' He'd cross-check them for anyone who might have been working with Redsall and against all the names he had so far amassed during the investigation. 'I'll be back for it in a moment. Where can I find Morden?'

'In the museum.'

He left her looking very unhappy and worried and made his way downstairs where he found Morden checking over one of the exhibition rooms. After some bluffing and denials, he finally capitulated and confirmed what Julie Preston had told him.

'When I got back to the control room, I looked at the monitors and everything was fine,' Morden said with an air of bravado.

Horton said sharply, 'It would be then. How many times have you and Julie done this before?'

Morden shrugged.

'She means that little to you,' Horton said contemptuously.

'Four times.'

'When exactly?' He'd get the dates from Julie but no harm in asking now.

'Twice in May, June and this last time.'

'And was Dr Spalding lecturing on each of those evenings?'

'Only in May and this last one, the other two talks were from a local historian and someone from the Dockyard Society.'

Horton would check that guest list to see if Redsall had attended any of those other lectures but he didn't think so because he was betting that Redsall had only come over here after Spalding had visited him in Northern Ireland at the beginning of July. He showed Morden a picture of Daniel Redsall.

'Do you remember seeing this man on the monitors at Dr Spalding's lecture?'

Morden studied it. 'No.'

'Have you seen him before?'

'No.'

'How about Ivor Meadows?'

'Yes, I know him. He comes into the museum. He's a bit of pain, thinks he knows more than the curators, always banging on about the Navy and the importance of keeping naval artefacts and security measures. The way he carries on anyone would think he owns the place.' Morden smiled.

Solemnly Horton said, 'Mr Meadows was found brutally murdered this morning.'

Morden started. His eyes widened and then he rubbed a hand over his face. 'Look, I didn't know that. I only meant—'

'Did Ivor Meadows know about your affair with Julie Preston?'

'No!'

'Are you sure?'

Morden shifted. 'How could he? We were always very careful.' But Horton wondered. Had Meadows seen Julie leave the room? Had he caught a glimpse of Morden in the corridor? Was that why he'd collared the curators and gone on about security measures? But if Meadows had known that Morden had left his post then why hadn't he said?

'Where were you last night, Mr Morden?' Horton asked curtly.

'At home. You can't think that I—'

'Can anyone verify that?'

'My wife.'

'All night?'

'Yes. I got home about six thirty and didn't go out again until I came to work this morning.' Morden was looking alarmed. 'My wife, Debbie, will tell you that.'

'I'm glad to hear it. We'll check.'

'You won't have to tell Debbie about me and Julie, will you? I mean that's got nothing to do with anything.'

Horton didn't answer. He collected the lists from Julie wondering what a pretty slim thing like her saw in the cocky overweight Morden, but then DC Walters too had his admirers and Horton could never understand that either. He scanned the list of names. Not surprisingly Ivor Meadows had attended all four public lectures, so too had Marcus Felspur. He also noted that Brenda Crossley, the guest house proprietor, had attended the previous lecture given by Douglas Spalding in May, which interestingly she hadn't mentioned. Redsall's name didn't appear on any of the lists. Horton called in at the security office and asked who had been on duty on the dates Julie had given him. Neither Matt Newton nor Neil Gideon had been. So perhaps Gideon didn't know about Morden and Julie Preston. Perhaps Redsall had just taken a chance. He'd also counted on Spalding not checking the inside of his briefcase, but perhaps he'd known that by the time Spalding would leave the museum he'd be suffering from the effects of a drug, one which the toxicology tests had failed to pick up, or rather the test had been rigged to show a negative result. There was someone on the inside. There had to be. Someone who knew exactly what went on and could time things to perfection and instruct Redsall.

Horton asked the woman on the security desk to check if Ivor Meadows had signed into the library the previous day. He had, shortly after Horton had spoken to him at 11.05 a.m. Meadows had signed out of the security office at 11.35 a.m., so his research that morning hadn't taken him very long. Horton was informed that the library was closed. He hadn't realized the time. It was gone six. Bliss would be baying for his blood.

He tossed up whether to delay his bollocking by re-interviewing Brenda Crossley but he didn't see that she'd be able to add much to the investigation just by having attended one of Spalding's lectures.

Preparing to face the DCI's wrath he returned to the station to be greeted with the news from Cantelli that Bliss was still in a meeting, or to be precise in another meeting. Horton recalled what Madeley had said about her being very ambitious and destined for dizzy heights, which no doubt she'd reach at super speed. He also wondered what Bliss had said about him and why his name had cropped up in their conversation. He should have thought about it before but he'd been preoccupied with other matters. Perhaps she had asked Madeley's advice on how to rid herself of an insubordinate copper who wasn't the world's best team player and who treated paperwork as a contagious disease to be avoided at all costs.

Horton relayed to Cantelli the outcome of his interview with Julie Preston.

Cantelli said, 'Gosport Marina has confirmed that Ashton was there on Tuesday just before four o'clock. He took a motor boat out for a trial; the broker selling it was tied up with another customer so Ashton went out alone.'

Walters looked up from his computer screen. 'There's no sign of Redsall on the pontoons on Monday night or on the boardwalk.'

'And Ivor Meadows?'

'Nothing so far.'

'Keep looking and recheck the footage for Tuesday afternoon to see if Ashton moors up at Oyster Quays. And get hold of any CCTV footage you can along the Hard for Monday night, outside the dockyard and by the road that runs down to the railway station, and check it for sightings of Redsall and Meadows any time from 9.15 to 10.30 p.m.'

'Hope you're going to pay for my laser eye treatment when I go short-sighted,' Walters grumbled, reaching for another Jaffa Cake.

'You already are. And you wear contact lenses, so stop moaning.'

In his office Horton rang through to Trueman. 'Has the autopsy report on Meadows come in?'

'Not yet. But Meadows' next of kin, his sister, is on her way down from Liverpool. We've booked her into the Holiday Inn Express and Marsden's meeting her there in half an hour. I've sent Meadows' computer over to the high-tech unit as instructed.'

'Thanks.'

'There's nothing from SOCO yet on the scene of crime and no murder weapon has been found at the Round Tower. There are also no other sightings of Meadows apart from the one at 10.30. I've got teams asking around the pubs tonight so something might come in later.'

'I take it Uckfield's still insisting on towing the party line and that Meadows' death has nothing to do with Spalding's and Redsall's?'

'Yes. He's in with Dean at the moment so he might return with a change of heart.'

'I won't hold my breath.' Horton rang off and cleared a space on his desk by pushing all the paper to one side. He checked through his messages and emails to see if the police in Coleraine had come up with a sighting of Spalding but there was nothing. Feeling disappointed he pulled up the autopsy report on Spalding, which Dr Clayton had forwarded to him as she had promised, and read it through looking for something that might have been missed. There was nothing. And no report of traces of vomit being found on Spalding's clothing.

His phone rang and he snatched it up, half-expecting it to be Bliss, but he was pleased to find it was Dr Clayton herself.

'I've just emailed the autopsy report on Meadows to DI Dennings, and I'm sending it across to you now, but I thought you might like to hear what I've found.'

'Hang on, I'll get Cantelli.'

He crossed to his door and called him in, leaving the door ajar so that he could see if Bliss hove onto the horizon.

Returning to his phone and gesturing Cantelli into the seat across his desk, Horton said into the receiver, 'I'll put you on loud speaker. Go ahead.'

'The victim, aged sixty-six, suffered from atherosclerosis, a potentially serious condition where the body's medium and large arteries become clogged up by fatty substances, such as cholesterol, so I'd cut out those bacon butties, Sergeant,' she said.

'Got to have some vices.'

'Yes, but too many won't make old bones.' Swiftly she continued, 'This in the victim led to coronary heart disease. He died of myocardial infarction, also no doubt precipitated by the shock of the attack. The blows to the head were severe but the victim was already dead by the time he received the second, third, fourth and fifth blows.' Horton thought that was a blessing.

Gaye Clayton continued. 'He was struck with a cylindrical heavy object, possibly about ten to twelve inches in length. I examined the skin and surface wounds for trace evidence, and found fragments of what looks like metal. I've sent them to the lab for analysis. Tom has also taken photographs and measurements of the wounds to help identify the weapon, and I placed a piece of plastic wrap over the heart of the wound and traced it with a pen and got a small round shape, which I've also emailed to you.'

Horton called up his emails as she was speaking and found it. 'Any ideas what it is?' he asked.

'A piece of lead piping? A metal tube? Something that culminates in a round flat shape as you can see, not a jagged edge. Blood would have spattered over the killer and I saw traces of it on the wall which your scene-of-crime team would also have noted and photographed. The spatter pattern indicates it was a medium-force impact, streaky with drops of blood about two millimetres in size.'

Cantelli said, 'So the killer would have blood on him.'

'Yes.'

Horton said, 'It was dark and so far no one claims to have seen the attack or anyone walking away covered in blood.'

Cantelli said, 'If the killer is living with someone, his or her partner must have seen the bloodstained clothes.'

'Not if he ditched them before returning home,' suggested Horton. 'He could have taken off protective clothing such as a raincoat or jacket, and underneath been wearing shorts and a T-shirt. As the location is not far from the sea, our killer could have run down the steps, through the hole in the wall, and taken a dip in his shorts and T-shirt to get rid of the blood. Then either ditched the coat in the sea, although that's risky because the high tide would have washed it up, or ditched it on his way home. Or he could have taken it home and put it in the washing machine, as if he lives alone, no one would know. Maybe the killer had a rucksack like Redsall and stuffed the coat in there. Are we looking for a man or a woman?'

'Could be either,' Gaye Clayton answered. 'Meadows was five feet eight and by the angle of the blow he was leaning forward when he was struck, as though he was bending over looking at something on the ground. He can't have been doing up his shoe laces because he was wearing slip-ons. He was struck with force but that doesn't rule out it being a woman.'

And the women who featured in this so far were Alvita Baarda, Melanie Jacobs, Jacqueline Spalding, Erica Leyton, Julie Preston, Brenda Crossley, Dr Sandra Menchip and Beatrice Redsall. Horton hadn't met Baarda or Menchip so he couldn't say whether they were capable of carrying out such a violent attack. Out of all of them he could see Beatrice Redsall doing such a thing but only Julie Preston and Alvita Baarda had been at Spalding's lecture. But if Redsall had killed Spalding under someone's instructions by injecting him with a drug then that changed everything.

'Time of death?'

'Between eleven and midnight. There was alcohol in his blood, but not an excessive amount.'

Horton said, 'Anything further on the tests on Redsall?'

'Sorry, didn't get time today but unless you have any new bodies for me tomorrow, I'll be on to it first thing.' He thanked her and rang off.

Cantelli said, 'Interesting what she said about a woman. If Spalding and Redsall were drugged then poison is often a woman's weapon, but bashing Meadows over the head? I'm not so sure.'

'Perhaps she was desperate and had no other choice. Or perhaps she was clever, knowing we'd put it down to a mugging. I can't see Julie Preston involved. Would you say Alvita Baarda was capable of this?'

'No. She couldn't be bothered. It would all be too much trouble for her and I don't think she'd be bright enough to plan it. If she hated Spalding and wanted to destroy him, she's much more likely to disgrace him by going to the newspapers or putting it all over the Internet.'

'And Dr Sandra Menchip?'

'She comes across as a very principled woman. She's clever, but she was travelling home from her holidays in Greece on Monday and didn't get in until one a.m., so she certainly had nothing to do with Spalding's death. I believed her when she said she didn't know Redsall. And I certainly don't see Jacqueline Spalding killing anyone or plotting to kill her husband.'

Horton agreed. He also said they could rule out Melanie Jacobs because she had been with Ashton. 'That leaves Erica Leyton who knew Spalding and could have known Redsall. We both think she's a bit of a tease, so she could have cajoled Redsall into helping her get rid of Spalding, though I've no idea why. Redsall might have become infatuated with her. She's also clever, but I have trouble seeing her bashing Meadows over the head and I can't see how Meadows could have known her or recognized her.'

'Unless he'd previously seen Spalding with her in the museum library.'

Cantelli had a point. Horton said, 'Then there's Brenda Crossley, the guest house owner. She was in the Navy, as was her husband. She attended Spalding's lecture in May, which Ivor Meadows also attended. Spalding could have contacted her about his research. When I mentioned the name Redsall to Meadows he might have made a connection between Brenda Crossley and Rear Admiral Jonathan Redsall. They might have served together on the same ship some years ago.'

Cantelli picked up the theme. 'I guess Spalding could have discovered something that was damaging to Brenda Crossley and connected with Jonathan Redsall.'

'Brenda tracks down Daniel Redsall and invites him over.'

'Why?'

Horton continued, quickly pulling together the strands. 'To get rid of Spalding's research, because it would damage her and Daniel's father, Jonathan. Marcus Felspur told me that Spalding had only presented the brief outline of his research into women in the Royal Navy at the lecture and that he would publish and present the full paper in the new academic year — perhaps that's what Brenda was desperate to stop. And perhaps that's what the intelligence services don't want coming out. We know Spalding flew to Northern Ireland on the fourth of July and in all probability met up with Daniel to tell him what he'd discovered. Daniel doesn't want it exposed, whatever it is; perhaps *he* made contact with Brenda Crossley. He arrives at the guest house and together they plan to get hold of the full research Spalding has conducted and destroy it. We only have the Crossleys' word that Daniel left early that morning. He could have been in the Crossleys' apartment going through the computer and deleting the files. Then he could have taken the laptop out and ditched it in the sea before meeting someone at Oyster Quays. Then there's Beatrice Redsall.'

'But could she have killed her nephew?' Cantelli asked, shocked.

'She didn't like him very much and she certainly didn't forgive him for not following in his father's footsteps.'

'That's not a motive though.'

'No. But if Spalding had discovered something that would denigrate her beloved brother, she might kill to hush it up. Perhaps Daniel Redsall choosing to stay in the Crossleys' guest house has nothing to do with the case and Beatrice Redsall is responsible for all three murders. Or perhaps Brenda Crossley approached Beatrice after Spalding had been to see her, and together they conspired to silence Spalding and Meadows. Brenda might not have wanted Daniel Redsall dead but Beatrice thought otherwise.' Horton recalled Brenda Crossley's reaction when he and Uckfield had called at the guest house late the night Redsall's body had been discovered. She hadn't seemed upset but neither had she appeared worried or guilty. 'Get hold of the Navy records of Ivor Meadows, Jonathan Redsall and Edward and Brenda Crossley. Look for anything that connects them. Also see what background you can get on Beatrice Redsall. We'll re-interview her and Brenda Crossley after Dr Clayton has the toxicology results on Daniel Redsall.'

Cantelli returned to his desk. Horton decided to shelve his thoughts on Meadows' murder for a while but instead of tackling his work he called up the police national computer. With a racing pulse he searched for Quentin Amos and sure enough there he was. Rapidly and eagerly, he read the information. Amos had several convictions going back over the years for violent assault and criminal damage, all linked to protests. The first had been in 1968. He'd also been found guilty of importuning in a public place in 1988 and the address they had for him on record was just fifty miles up the A3 in Woking. Horton sat back, his mind trying to absorb this new information. How had Madeley known Amos's record? OK, so he was a consultant to the police but that didn't make him privy to all their information — or did it? Or had he contacted Amos about the archive project and discovered his criminal record? Possibly. But there was more than that nagging at the back of his mind.

He glanced at the clock. It was almost seven. No one had called him into the incident suite to assist in the investigation into Meadows' murder, which was unlike Uckfield. And Bliss was suspiciously silent. He thought he might know the reason. This entire case was being subdued, whitewashed. Uckfield was going through the motions. They didn't want him stirring things up. So as his presence wasn't needed Horton grabbed his helmet and jacket, told Cantelli and Walters to call it a day and go home, and said that was where he was heading. Instead, he made for Woking and Quentin Amos.

CHAPTER NINETEEN

It was almost nine when Horton turned into the entrance of the six-storey flat-roofed apartment block in a suburb of Woking that had once been select, but was now clearly in the advanced stages of terminal decline. The large Edwardian houses surrounding and opposite from it were across a busy road and had once belonged to professional families. Now they were divided into bedsits and let to tenants who cared little for their shabby and inferior homes and about the same amount for the streets around them, which were littered with takeaway cartons, broken glass and beer cans. The block of flats, which was listed as the last known address they had for Quentin Amos, looked to be in the same sad state of affairs, with overgrown grass verges, weeds sprouting through the concrete and the doors to the entrance scuffed and scratched. Horton hoped that his Harley would still be where he'd left it when he finished interviewing Amos, if he was still living here. He might have moved and if so, Horton had had a wasted journey.

He located the intercom and pressed the buzzer for flat three. As he waited with an accelerated heartbeat for it to be answered, he turned back to the street. There didn't appear to be anyone watching him and there had been no sign of any dark four-wheel-drive vehicle following him intent on eliminating him, or indeed any vehicle. But then perhaps they (whoever they were) didn't need to follow him. Madeley could have told whoever was after Horton that he'd given him the information about Amos. It didn't take a genius to see that Horton wasn't at the station or on his boat and conclude that he was following up that lead. Maybe they'd get him on the way home? Or perhaps Amos was long gone and Madeley had fed him a false trail, either deliberately or accidentally. Horton didn't know, but he sensed one thing, and that was that he didn't trust Madeley as far as he could throw him.

There was no answer. Horton tried again while steeling himself against disappointment. Then came a crackle followed by a sharp voice. 'What do you want?'

On the journey here Horton had had plenty of time to decide his tactics. He'd been delayed by two road traffic accidents. He'd tossed up whether to announce himself as a police officer and use officialdom to get himself admitted, or to tell the truth. Judging by Amos's record though he thought saying he was a police officer was more likely to get him the closed-door treatment and the 'you can't come in without a warrant' response.

'Mr Amos?'

'If you're selling solar panels, double glazing, collecting for orphaned animals or you're homeless, unemployed and selling dusters to rehabilitate yourself into a corrupt and greedy society then you can sod off. I'm broke, hate animals, and I stopped believing in the redemption of mankind a very long time ago.'

Horton couldn't help smiling, then taking a breath he said, 'My name is Andy Horton and I'd like to talk to you about my mother, Jennifer.'

There was silence. Horton heard the wailing of a police siren somewhere. Amos could say, 'Who? Never heard of her.' The silence seemed to stretch for ever but perhaps that was just his taut nerves making him think that. Horton was beginning to wonder if Amos had simply ignored him and returned to his television, but there was another crackle and the sound of laboured breathing, then the buzzer sounded to admit him. With a constricted chest and pounding heart, Horton took a deep breath and stepped inside the grubby and worn tiled lobby, hardly daring to believe he might get one small step closer to finding out something about his mother. He located flat three at the rear of the building and was about to knock on the door when it opened, and bathed in the light from behind it, Horton faced a very thin, balding elderly man, with a prominent, slightly hooked nose, hunched shoulders and yellowing skin. The eyes that studied Horton were sharp but sunk deep in dark-rimmed sockets. It was obvious to Horton that Amos was seriously ill, but equally obvious that his mind was still razor sharp and by allowing him entry it was clear that he remembered Jennifer Horton.

Amos's eyes travelled over Horton greedily, registering and assimilating every small detail without any reaction. He inhaled then stepped back, admitting Horton into a small and none too clean lobby. The flat smelt of urine, stale food and alcohol.

Horton waited while Amos shuffled past him and ahead into a wide lounge with large glass patio doors opening onto an expanse of darkness.

'I back onto the cemetery, so they won't have far to take me when I go, which won't be long. Sit down.'

Horton removed two piles of books from a battered and threadbare chair, placing them on the floor. He sat. The room was crammed with books; they spilled out from the crowded shelves, onto the big oak table and chairs to the right of the patio doors and over the floor. There was a laptop computer squeezed in between the books on the table and paper strewn about it.

'I'm writing my life story,' Amos said, following his glance. 'Though whether I'll be allowed to finish it is a different matter. And I don't mean the cancer will kill me, though there'll be plenty who will be hoping it will. I'd offer you a drink but I can't be bothered to make it, unless you'd like a whisky and that comes ready-made?'

'No thanks. Can I get you one?'

'Already got one.' Amos indicated the amber liquid in a glass on the table beside him.

Horton suddenly found himself unable to speak. He was staring at a man who he knew would tell him about Jennifer and he was incredibly nervous. His heart was knocking against his ribs and his palms felt sweaty. What was he about to learn? Would it be so awful that it would scar him more than he'd already been scarred? But surely that wasn't possible; he'd thought the worse for years. There was still time to cut loose, to decide he'd had enough of the past. But he didn't move. He couldn't. He knew that Amos sensed all this in him. The silence stretched on. Horton could hear a clock ticking and outside the squawking of a startled blackbird which seemed almost as loud as a jumbo jet flying overhead.

Amos lifted his glass and swallowed some whisky. After he had set it down carefully, he said, 'It took you a long time to find me.'

Horton's stomach somersaulted. Was he looking at his father? He didn't know what to say. Explaining why it had taken him years to discover what had happened to his mother would take too long, and he didn't see why he should, not yet.

Amos continued. 'You look like her about the eyes. Hers were as blue as yours.'

The breath caught in Horton's throat. His chest tightened and he willed himself not to clench his fists, not in anger but in pain, and hurt, and emptiness.

'She was a very attractive girl,' Amos continued. 'Full of life. Always laughing. Liked having fun.'

That fitted with what he'd been told by others — the fun bit especially, which those who had spoken about her had implied she liked having with men.

'But then she was only seventeen and why shouldn't she love life, and having a laugh? Christ, if you can't do it then before life kicks the shit out of you and spits you in the eye, when can you?'

The stuffy, smelly room crackled with bitterness. There was enough hatred in the old man in front of him to poison the air. Quietly Horton said, 'When did it start to go wrong?'

Amos eyed him shrewdly, 'For me or for her?'

'For both of you.'

'I'm not your father. Jennifer was never my lover. Wrong gender, duckie, as you no doubt know if you've run me through your computers, which you must have done.'

Horton eyed him with surprise. 'You know that I'm a policeman.'

'A detective inspector, yes. I also know that Jennifer disappeared in 1978 and you were thrown on the mercies of social services, God help you, until one man discovered this and began to put things right, well as right as he could, given the circumstances.'

Horton thought he'd stopped breathing. He could hardly believe it but here, in front of him, was someone who knew about him and his past. Rapidly he forced his mind away from emotional responses to reason, and forced his breathing to remain steady. His body was stiff with tension and emotion.

'Was that man Edward Ballard?'

'If that's the name he gave you.'

Horton had already remembered that Ballard, or whatever his real name was, had given his foster father, Bernard Litchfield, a box containing his birth certificate and photograph of his mother, both of which had since been lost in a fire on his previous boat. But now it seemed that Amos was telling him that Ballard had also been responsible or instrumental in placing him with his final and loving foster parents, police officer Bernard and his wife Eileen. But how did Amos know? Horton doubted he'd tell him if he asked though.

'He also gave me this.' He reached into his pocket and handed across the photograph of the six men and watched Amos closely as those shrewd pain-racked eyes studied it. Amos turned it over.

'The student riots. It got Jennifer the sack. She was a typist then at the London School of Economics but she didn't like towing the line. Keeping silent and being a good little girl wasn't her style. She was too radical, too involved with the students, not that it worried her. Jennifer liked living dangerously.'

Horton sat forward.

Amos continued. 'She was very bright, but like a lot of girls from working-class backgrounds in those days she never got the chance to take any qualifications except secretarial ones, and as for going to university that would have been completely out of the question. I doubt her parents or her school teachers ever thought it remotely possible, even though the new so-called "red-brick" universities were set up in 1963, and for the first time, students could get state support. It was too little too late for Jennifer. Besides, university would have bored her to death. She liked action, which was why she came to London, for the swinging sixties and all that drivel, although it was true to some extent. Jennifer was introduced to me by this chap.' Amos stabbed a bony finger at the man on the far right with long hair touching the collar of his patterned shirt. 'His name was Zachary Benham.'

'Was?' Horton sharply interjected.

'Died in a fire in September 1968.'

Horton felt a stab of disappointment.

'A fire in a mental hospital which killed twenty-four patients. If you check your files, you'll see that no cause was discovered. Could have been arson or carelessness?'

'What was Benham doing there?'

'Good question.' But Amos said no more, leaving Horton to wonder if Benham had started the fire. Or had he been a patient? If he'd been a patient what illness had he been suffering from? And was Zachary Benham his father? But these were clearly questions for another time — if there was to be one, and that might not be so. No, Horton recognized this was his one and only chance.

'What was the relationship between Zachary and Jennifer?'

'Was *he* your father, you mean?' Amos shook his head. 'No. He was keen on her, but then everyone was. Although Jennifer liked to flirt, she was never serious with any of *them*.' He jerked his head at the men in the photograph.

Horton read between the lines. 'Because there was someone else.'

'Yes. I don't know who he was, she never mentioned him and I never saw her with him, but there was definitely someone else. Not that we knew that at the time. Zach tried it on, but she managed to hold him and others in the Radical Student Alliance off, and at a time when everyone was sleeping around that was quite a remarkable feat. There was no easy access to contraception then, or abortion, which was only legalized in 1967, the same time as no doubt you know homosexuality was decriminalized for those over the age of twenty-one, in England and Wales but not in Scotland and Northern Ireland or in the armed forces. That came much later.'

Horton wondered who this other man had been. Ballard? Perhaps. He said, 'So you were a lecturer at the LSE, and that was why she was introduced to you.'

'I was a lecturer, yes, and although Jennifer worked in the same place, I didn't meet her in connection with our jobs. Jennifer worked in a voluntary capacity for the Radical Student Alliance, which I supported.'

'What did she do?' asked Horton keenly.

'Everything short of making public speeches.'

Horton's eyebrows shot up. He grappled with this new slant on the woman he'd remembered for so many years as being a tart who hadn't cared about her child enough to raise him.

Amos swallowed his whisky and continued. 'Apart from organizing the unruly and vociferous group of radical students and producing leaflets and posters, she did the same as the rest of us — she protested against war, apartheid, victimization, the establishment; you name it we rallied against it. This was the sixties and we had a lot to be angry about.

We have a lot to be angry about now — greed, corruption, cruelty, an uncaring and dispassionate government and society — but do we get off our backsides and do anything about it? No, we write to *The Times* and put it on the Internet,' he sneered. 'Not back then. This was the time of the mass anti-Vietnam War rally in Grosvenor Square, which led to the Grosvenor Square riots; the Cold War and double-agent George Blake breaking out of jail masterminded by the Soviet Union; the disturbances in Northern Ireland; the civil rights marches led by Martin Luther King in America. God, there was plenty to occupy us and it was fun.'

Then Amos's face clouded over. 'Then Zach died in a fire in 1968, Timothy Wilson died in a motorbike accident in 1969 — he's the man on the other end of the photograph; James Royston took a drugs overdose in the same year — he's the middle one with the Beatle haircut — and I got arrested for criminal damage, assault and having sex with an underage boy in 1971, a triple hat-trick that saw me serve five years in a not very pleasant place.'

Horton sat back, his mind racing. He and Jennifer had lived in London when he was small, so how old had he been when they'd moved from what he remembered as being a nice place overlooking the river to that smelly little overcrowded house? No more than about five. And then they'd moved to Portsmouth where he'd gone to school, so he must have been about six.

He pushed the thoughts aside and brought his mind back to the photograph. Sitting forward he said, 'That leaves these three men.' Horton indicated the two men sporting beards and untidy long hair wearing the patterned open-necked shirts, and another clean-shaven man with short fair hair.

'The second from the right with a beard is Antony Dormand; next to him again with a beard is Rory Mortimer, and the fair man, I don't know him. He must have come with one of the others. I don't know what happened to them or where they are now but you'll probably be able to find out only . . .' He sat back, grimacing with pain and looking exhausted.

'Can I get you anything?' Horton asked, concerned. Amos managed to shake his head. 'I'm sorry if I've exhausted you and brought back painful memories.'

Amos opened his eyes. 'They weren't all painful. There were good times too and at least I was alive and so were those men, and I don't mean in the physical sense.' He took a breath and Horton could see it was an effort for him to continue. He flapped a hand weakly as though to say, 'give me some time'. Horton did, fearful for him while trying to digest what he'd learned. He knew there was more that Amos could tell him but whether he was too exhausted or didn't want to Horton wasn't sure, though he guessed it was a bit of both. He made to push the photograph back in his pocket when he stalled. Glancing down at it his attention was caught not by the two men Amos had just named but the fair stranger beside them, the man Amos claimed not to know. There was something familiar about him and it wasn't because he'd stared at this picture countless times. No, he'd seen this man or someone very much like him before and recently, but he couldn't place where.

Amos recovered. His expression both sad and serious he said, 'Ballard, or whatever his real name is, left you that photograph but he's not the only one who knows about Jennifer and these men, and I don't mean me. Who told you about me?'

'Professor Thurstan Madeley,' answered Horton putting away the photograph.

A shadow crossed Amos's cavernous face.

'Do you know him?' Horton asked.

'No.'

Horton frowned, puzzled. Clearly that was a lie. 'He oversaw the student protest archive file and that's how he knew of you.' But Horton knew that wasn't the truth, because Madeley had known a great deal more than that, such as Quentin Amos's police record.

211

Amos gave a cynical and pained smile. 'Maybe. But this photograph wasn't in it.'

'No.'

'Have you wondered why?'

'It was the only copy.'

'And one that was given to you by a man you can't trace.'

'Yes.'

'And you've asked yourself why it was held back all these years and why it was kept and not destroyed?'

'Yes.'

'And your answer?'

'Because it's been on file somewhere or kept by someone who thought it might come in useful one day.'

'And the reason for that?'

'Because someone didn't want one or more of these men to be identified as being either involved in the protests or at the protest on that day. He or they were supposed to be somewhere else.'

'And some people are paid to sanitize the past.'

Horton knew he meant Madeley and equally that Madeley was more than just a consultant to the police. But Amos's words also triggered thoughts of the investigation into the deaths of Spalding, Redsall and Meadows, along with something that Marcus Felspur had said to him about people wishing to bury or distort the truth. This was what had happened here and it was happening over the investigation into the deaths of Spalding, Redsall and Meadows.

'But why was I given your name?'

'Think it through,' Amos said sharply, as though addressing one of his former students.

Horton did. 'Because I already had the photograph and they'd know I'd trace you in the end.'

'Yes, but look at me, man. By the time you found me unaided I could already have been dead.'

Horton swiftly reconsidered. 'Then they needed me to find you soon. And they want me to find one or more of these men for them.'

'Maybe.'

Was there something vital he was missing here? His head was thumping and he couldn't think what it was. Then it came to him. They wanted him to find Ballard.

Amos's voice broke through his swirling thoughts. 'Secrets and lies,' he said quietly. 'Someone's kept silent for a long time. They might want it to stay that way. You might think the days of spies and the Cold War are over and that I'm an old man seeing shadows across every ripple of the sea, but they're not over, there is always evil below. Be careful, Andy Horton.'

A chill ran through him. He knew that the next time someone came after him he might be lucky to escape with his life.

Horton could see he'd get no more from Amos, and besides, he didn't know that he had much more to give. He promised to return but Amos brushed it aside. 'I'll be dead by then.'

He left and rode home slowly and carefully in the dark sultry night, his mind only half on the thankfully quiet road, the other half on what Amos had told him trying to make sense of it. But when he reached the yacht, he still didn't have the answers. He was tired beyond belief and thought that if they came for him now, he wouldn't stand a chance.

He drank a long cold glass of water and, throwing off his clothes, showered to wash the smell of illness and deceit from him before lying on his bunk staring into the darkness. Ballard wanted the truth about what had happened to Jennifer to be discovered, by him at least, and perhaps he also wanted to find one of the surviving men in the photograph, but with his resources in intelligence, just like Madeley who also had to be involved with the intelligence services, then why didn't they do it themselves? The simple answer was they didn't want to get their hands dirty; they didn't want to be implicated. He was a scapegoat. If he went around asking questions then one of these men, the one they were after, would be provoked into coming out into the open, making a move, and perhaps last night had been the opening gambit. Then the intelligence services could claim it was nothing to do with them. He was being fed bits of information and they were using him to lead them to this man, whoever he was. He wouldn't show up on any database, in fact Horton was betting neither of the two names he had from Amos would. And the third man?

Again, Horton conjured up the lean youthful face. What would he look like now some forty years later? Why did he strike Horton as being familiar? Then he stiffened as another thought occurred to him. Slowly he shook his head with a sad smile. Quentin Amos had given him what he could, or rather what he'd been permitted to tell him, because the last thought Horton had before sleep overcame exhaustion was that Quentin Amos was also working under instructions from British Intelligence.

CHAPTER TWENTY

Friday, 8.30 a.m.

It was a thought that still held weight in the light of a humid and heavy morning. And he'd been correct; neither of the two names Amos had given him checked out on the police database. He'd arrived at the station early and conducted a search. But he needed a lot more time to research them further and he didn't have that now. He might not have it in the future, he thought grimly, if there were more attempts on his life. He wondered when they might strike again. A thought that made him edgy but which he was more determined than ever wouldn't prevent him from continuing his research and doing his job, which was to find a clever and callous killer.

From his office window he'd watched Uckfield arrive. The Super had looked tired and cross, more so than usual. He must know this was a cover-up and it looked as though it was preying on his mind. Horton was tempted to try and reason with him again, but it would probably be a waste of breath.

He put the finishing touches to CID's performance figures for July and emailed them to Bliss. He didn't think they'd bring a smile to that frozen face. The customer satisfaction survey would have to wait unless Cantelli and Walters felt particularly inventive. His mind drifted back to his interview with Quentin Amos as he shuffled his paperwork round his desk. There were so many questions that he hadn't asked, which had swarmed around his head all night like angry wasps. Amos must have known Jennifer well. So what had she really been like? What had made her laugh, cry, get angry? Who had she liked and hated? What had she done when not protesting? He could remember so little about her; he'd spent years trying to eradicate all memory of her. What views he'd held had been tainted by what others had told him and by his own bitterness. He should return to see Amos and soon. He didn't care for being bait for British Intelligence. Who was it they were trying to flush out? Who wanted the truth stifled at all costs? The similarities of his own situation with those of the case weren't lost on him. He wondered if the key to the first lay in the deaths of those three men in that photograph: Zachary Benham, Timothy Wilson and James Royston. And the key to latter? He wasn't sure and yet a tantalizing idea danced and swayed on the edge of his mind like an out-of-focus image, but before he could adjust the lens, the sound of voices in CID caught his attention. Bliss was talking to Cantelli and Walters, who were researching the Navy careers of Meadows, Redsall and the Crossleys. Not that they'd tell Bliss that — after all they weren't supposed to be investigating Spalding's or Redsall's deaths. If she found out she'd go all frozen Queen of the North on them. But Cantelli would do a nice little whitewash job, of that Horton was certain. He'd had years of practice.

A few seconds later Bliss breezed into Horton's office looking as bright as a laser beam and as fresh as newly laundered money. He eyed her thoughtfully and suspiciously, wondering if she knew he'd seen Madeley yesterday. But why would Madeley tell her about their meeting? And as far as he was aware Bliss knew nothing about his childhood. The thought that she might discover it sent a flutter of panic and fear through him. He had no idea what her reaction might be — perhaps she wouldn't even care, perhaps her own childhood had been as bleak as his, he didn't know and he wasn't interested, but his emotions made him feel vulnerable and that in turn filled him with anger. Then reason asserted itself. Madeley's masters moved in much more exalted and clandestine circles than that of a mere DCI in CID. And perhaps Dr Douglas Spalding had also moved in the same higher echelons.

She didn't sit but paced his office filling it with simmering energy; actions that he felt were designed to make him feel tense, apprehensive and insecure. But perhaps that was just him overreacting. His nerves were on edge because of his lack of sleep. He had to get a grip on himself. He sat back, picked up a pencil and twirled it casually while eyeing her. She stopped pacing and scowled at him. Yes, she'd have to do better than that to intimidate him.

'The mugging by the railway station on the Hard last Thursday night, what have you done about that?' she demanded. Before he could say he'd been on holiday at the time, she continued. 'Any similarities with the attack on Meadows?'

So that was the way her mind was working. She thought she might have a lead and clear up both cases, which would look good on her file. 'None,' he said firmly.

'How do you know that?' she barked.

'Because Meadows' death is linked to Spalding's and Redsall's.'

Her eyes narrowed. 'Spalding committed suicide and Redsall died of sudden death syndrome.'

'If you say so.' Horton threw down his pencil.

'I do. This mugger could have attacked and killed Meadows, it's not a million miles away from where Meadows' body was found, which couldn't have escaped even your attention. The fact that we didn't catch him after the first attack means a man has now lost his life. I want him caught before he does it again, understood?'

'Perfectly, Ma'am.' And before Uckfield's team finds him, which was what Bliss was really saying. How convenient for the intelligence services to have a scumbag mugger put his hands up to it in return for getting off with a short sentence — or worse, a suspended sentence. He wondered if Bliss had been primed to point him in the wrong direction, perhaps that's what one or more of those meetings had been about yesterday. Or perhaps that was just his suspicious mind in overdrive. But it would backfire because she'd just given him permission to continue looking into Meadows' death. Not that he needed it; he would have done so anyway.

'I'll get on to it right away.'

'Keep me fully informed.'

After she marched out, Horton called in Cantelli and waved him into the seat opposite, saying, 'What have we got on a mugging on the Hard last Thursday week?'

'Young man, in his mid-twenties, attacked after leaving the pub opposite the Historic Dockyard on his way to the railway station, phone and wallet taken. Uniform interviewed the publican and the customers on Friday night and we checked the CCTV footage. Caught sight of a slim youth with a hoodie, about twenty, seen running off towards Oyster Quays but we couldn't get a good look at his face unfortunately. The video is being enhanced and uniform are asking around. I've got our informers sniffing around too, but nothing so far.'

'Bliss thinks he's responsible for killing Meadows.'

'He could be, I suppose,' Cantelli reluctantly agreed. 'But there was no weapon used. The victim, who was inebriated, was jumped from behind, knocked to the ground, and kicked. It happened within seconds. From the CCTV footage the suspect is seen earlier outside the pub then moves out of view. I think he was just hanging around waiting to pick out the most likely looking victim.'

'We'll release the CCTV footage to the Major Crime Team and send the file over.'

Cantelli eyed him quizzically and with a worried frown. 'Andy, you look tired. Is anything worrying you, and I don't mean the case?'

Horton found it almost impossible to confide because of the scars of a childhood which had taught him the hard way not to trust, but he was a heartbeat away from doing so now to the one and only person he counted as a friend. He was tempted to tell Cantelli everything. He badly wanted someone to offload the ideas that were crowding his mind concerning his mother's disappearance, but how could he put Cantelli's life at risk? It was unthinkable. Instead, he told him his divorce had come through. Cantelli looked sad. Horton knew the sergeant could tell that wasn't everything troubling him, but Cantelli wouldn't probe any further and neither would he offer up any platitudes about how Horton could make a fresh start and move on with his life or forget what had happened, because they both knew he couldn't.

Briskly Horton said, 'Anything on Meadows or the Crossleys?'

'Walters is still working on it. But I looked up Rear Admiral Jonathan Redsall in Debrett's. The son of Vice Admiral Thomas Redsall. He was educated at Eton, Trinity College, Cambridge and the Royal Naval College Dartmouth. He served on HMS *Hardy* when it was deployed to counter and carry out surveillance of Russian activities in 1967 during the Cold War and on HMS *Neirne* in the Far East, Singapore in 1969, after which he rose rapidly in the promotion stakes until he ended up as a top adviser to NATO. Promoted to Rear Admiral in 2000.'

And died eight years ago, according to Beatrice Redsall, which Cantelli confirmed, adding that Beatrice Redsall had never taken up paid employment which again bore out what she'd said about assisting her father and then her brother in their careers.

Horton's phone rang. He gestured at Cantelli to remain when he heard Dr Clayton's voice.

'I've got the results of the toxicology tests on Redsall and I think you'd better get over here.'

Horton heard the excitement in her voice and his pulse quickened. She'd found something and that could change this case completely. It might even mean Uckfield would have to launch a full-blown investigation. Horton quickly instructed Cantelli to accompany him to the mortuary and Walters to continue with his research. With eager anticipation he speculated silently what she'd discovered — drugs obviously in Redsall's system, but what kind? As Cantelli pulled into a space outside the mortuary Horton's mobile phone rang. It was Agent Harriet Ames.

'Beatrice Redsall is a member of the yacht club,' she announced. 'But Daniel Redsall isn't.'

Horton hadn't thought he would be. But Beatrice Redsall, yes.

Harriet Ames added, 'She last visited here on 20 June.'

So neither she nor her nephew had been there on the day he'd died. Her visit to the yacht club wasn't relevant to the inquiry and neither was the fact she was still a member.

Ames said, 'Do you need me to do anything else?'

'No. Thanks. Enjoy Cowes Week.' He rang off, wondering what she was thinking and how she felt about him, before telling himself that she'd probably already dismissed him from her mind and gone to meet Rupert Crawford.

They found Dr Clayton in her small office behind the mortuary. 'Redsall *was* drugged,' she announced without ceremony. 'The dose was enough to kill him and it is most certainly the cause of death.'

Horton drew some considerable satisfaction that his suspicions had been justified. Now Uckfield would have to listen to him. But would he? He recalled what Trueman had discovered about Redsall's nervous breakdown. With a sinking feeling he knew what the outcome would be. They'd claim that Redsall had taken the drug himself. Suicide.

With a grim expression he took the seat opposite Gaye. Cantelli withdrew his notebook and took the vacant chair beside him.

Gaye continued. 'It isn't one of the poisons we discussed though, Inspector, a fast-acting one such as nicotine, cyanide or aconite, which reassures me that I didn't miss anything so obvious and neither did the pathologist who examined Spalding. On the contrary, this poison is one that can take some hours to take effect.'

Would Redsall have used such a poison to kill himself? Horton sat forward eager to know more.

'It's hyoscine.'

That meant nothing to Horton but Cantelli looked up from his notebook, 'Isn't that what Dr Crippen used to kill his wife?'

'Spot on, Sergeant, he did. Hyoscine can be detected in the body some considerable time after death, even if the body has been buried.'

'But not if it's been cremated,' added Cantelli.

'No, that would be a tad difficult,' Gaye answered dryly. 'It's an alkaloid found in several plants including henbane and thorn apple, both of which grow wild in this part of the country and can also be found in gardens.'

Horton said, 'So anyone can have easy access to it.'

'Yes. But for someone to have used it as a poison means they'd need to know what they were doing.'

'A chemist?' posed Horton, thinking instantly of Simon Watson, the client that had been on board Ashton's yacht on Tuesday.

Gaye said, 'Or someone with medical knowledge: a doctor, nurse, or pharmacist. It could also be someone who has an interest in natural medicine or poisons.'

And that opened up the field. There was Spalding's GP, Dr Deacon, but Horton couldn't see him bashing Ivor Meadows over the head, although Meadows' death had been hastily improvised and not meticulously planned like the others and that meant they were also looking for a planner, someone who was clever and careful. Deacon matched that profile.

He turned his full attention back to Gaye Clayton, who continued. 'It's also sometimes known as scopolamine and is used medicinally in very small doses to relieve depression and anxiety.'

Horton's heart plummeted. That fitted perfectly with Redsall's profile. He could see by Cantelli's expression that he was also following the same line of thinking. 'If Redsall had been suffering from depression, could he have been prescribed a drug containing hyoscine and taken an overdose?'

'There's nothing on his medical records to show that he's recently been prescribed anything that contains hyoscine.'

That was something at least, but Redsall could have got hold of the drug by some other means, the Internet for example, where it was easy to buy drugs, or he could have got it from a friend.

Gaye said, 'It's also prescribed, again in very small doses, to alleviate stomach pains and to overcome travel sickness.'

Now Gaye Clayton was throwing into doubt his theory about Spalding's death. Could he have been wrong all the time? It was beginning to look that way. Despondently he said, 'Spalding went to his GP for a prescription for antidepressants and travel sickness pills.'

'It wouldn't have been a high enough dose to kill him.'

'Unless he'd saved up previous prescriptions.'

'Possibly, or he might have obtained the drug elsewhere and taken an overdose, but his tests came back clear and as his body was released to the undertakers before I could take further organ samples, there's no way of conducting further tests — except,' she held up her hand to silence Horton, 'I managed to track down and purloin the original organ samples. And guess what? Yes, hyoscine shows up. In my opinion it contributed to his cause of death, the fall into the dock. But it doesn't mean that someone drugged him, just as in Redsall's case it could have been self-administered.'

She was voicing Horton's fears. But he wasn't giving up yet. 'Except for the fact that two deaths shortly after one another and by the same method must be construed as suspicious.'

Gaye sat back in her chair and eyed him thoughtfully. After a moment she said, 'It's a strange poison for a killer to choose because it's not terribly reliable and its reaction on the body is not fully understood because it can vary between individuals. As I said before it can take several hours to take effect.'

Horton swiftly considered this, ideas forming in the back of his mind. Eagerly he said, 'What are the symptoms?'

'Headache and vertigo.'

He recalled what Julie Preston and Ivor Meadows had said about Spalding at the lecture. Spalding had been frowning and rubbing his head as though he'd had a headache.

'It also causes extreme thirst, dry sensation of the skin and possible blurred vision,' added Gaye Clayton.

Cantelli interjected. 'Alvita Baarda said Spalding kept asking for drinks.'

'And Meadows confirmed that. He told me Spalding was drinking copious amounts of water. He thought it was because he fancied Alvita Baarda but he must have been reacting against the poison.'

Gaye said, 'Hyoscine also causes hallucinations.'

Horton threw Cantelli a glance. 'That fits with Spalding's death. Spalding, drugged, leaves the naval museum; he's been gradually feeling the effects of the drug after his lecture. Outside he becomes disorientated and, suffering from vertigo, he sees everything revolving around him. Because of this he could have believed he was anywhere — he might even have believed he could fly, hence the climb onto that fence and the leap into the dock. And before that he could have staggered towards the sea, lost hold of his briefcase, which ended up in the sea.'

Gaye said, 'That sounds possible.'

Horton continued. 'And in Redsall's case he stumbled onto the yacht, fell into a coma and died. So when were they drugged?' he asked Gaye eagerly.

'That's the difficult bit because with hyoscine there is no exact time of knowing when it was administered. In Spalding's case it could have been several hours before he died.'

Horton rapidly thought. But before he could speak Gaye added, 'He was probably given the hyoscine in a drink. The leaves and seeds of henbane could have been put in tea.'

'Which, given his time of death at about 9.30 p.m., he could have been given anytime between 1.30 and 3.30 p.m.'

'Best to say from midday until about four to be on the safe side.'

Cantelli said, 'We know that Spalding was at the university until just after twelve noon, but we've no idea where he went from there until he showed up at the Historic Dockyard at six that evening.'

And they had no idea who he met, thought Horton, and the same applied to Daniel Redsall. 'Redsall's time of death was between 7.30 and 9.30 p.m. so he could have drunk this poison between midday and, say, two o'clock on Tuesday afternoon.'

But Gaye was shaking her head. 'No, Redsall's dosage was considerably higher. He was almost certainly given it much later with his symptoms manifesting themselves over a shorter space of time.'

'How short?' asked Horton.

'An hour, possibly slightly longer.'

Horton quickly thought. 'So the earliest would be 6.30 p.m. and the latest 8.30 p.m. if his time of death was nearer to 9.30 p.m.'

'Yes, give or take thirty minutes or so. As I said it's difficult to be absolutely correct.'

To Cantelli, Horton said, 'Simon Watson could have slipped out of the restaurant on Tuesday night to meet Redsall. He's a chemist. He could have poisoned Redsall and returned to the restaurant.'

'But there's no sign of him or anyone else on the CCTV footage.'

'Could Walters have missed it?'

Cantelli shrugged. 'We can check again.'

'Do that and see what you can find on Watson. See if there's any connection between him, Redsall and Spalding.'

Cantelli nodded. Horton continued. 'If Redsall wasn't poisoned in the marina though, where was he given the drug and why did he go to the marina?'

'To meet someone?' suggested Gaye.

'Yes, but who?'

Cantelli said, 'Perhaps he was told to go there but whoever he thought was going to show didn't because they'd
already been told he would be dead by then.'

'But why was he told to go there?'

'To throw you off the scent,' suggested Gaye. 'I said this
is a clever poison and therefore a clever poisoner. Your killer
administers the drug knowing that by the time his victim is
dead, he'll be a long way from where it was administered,
therefore making it far more difficult to determine who he
or she is.'

Horton rapidly assimilated this. 'That means Spalding's
killer wasn't at the lecture at all. And Redsall's killer is
unlikely to be Simon Watson because he wouldn't have
wanted Redsall ending up dead on Ashton's boat. But still
run a check on him, Barney, just to be certain.'

'Do we tell Uckfield this?' asked Cantelli.

'No.' Horton saw Gaye raise her eyebrows. To her he
said, 'Send your report across as usual, then it's up to Uckfield
what he does about it. I have a feeling though that he might
be pushed into drawing the conclusion that the poison was
self-administered.'

Gaye said she would do so and let Horton know if she
came up with anything else relevant to the inquiry. On the
way back to the car Horton ran through what Gaye had given
them.

'Excluding the possibility of the killer being this Simon
Watson, we've got three possible suspects: Brenda Crossley,
Beatrice Redsall and Erica Leyton, four if we throw in Dr
Deacon.'

'And five if Ted Crossley was in it with his wife.'

'And the motive for each of them?' Horton posed, then
proceeded to answer his own question. 'Ted and Brenda
Crossley killed because of something Spalding had uncovered
during his research into women in the Royal Navy which
would harm Brenda Crossley. The same motive applies to

Beatrice Redsall except that Spalding's research would harm the memory of her dead brother.'

Cantelli zapped open the car looking confused. 'But why would Erica Leyton kill Spalding? If she did it because he refused her attentions, it's a bit weak, and where does Redsall fit into it?'

'You're right. I can't see why she would kill them or Meadows.'

'And what would be Dr Deacon's motive?' asked Cantelli, climbing in. 'Unless he was a doctor in the Navy before becoming a GP and Spalding's research revealed something dodgy about him. Yeah I know, we'll add him to the list to check.'

Horton stretched the seat belt around him. 'It has to be connected with Spalding's research because why else would Redsall need the contents of Spalding's briefcase?'

'We don't know that he took it for certain.'

No, thought Horton dejectedly. But *if* he did then why was it so important? *Why?* It worried away at his brain as Cantelli reversed out of the space and headed down into Portsmouth. He stared at the big fat raindrops splattering on the windscreen. The research was the key, he was now certain of it, but there was something else gnawing at the back of his mind. Something he was missing. What the devil was it? *Think.* Why had Spalding lied about his current research, or rather why had he told three people he was researching into three different areas? Maybe it was the truth. Maybe he said it to disguise what he was really researching, which had thrown the intelligence services into panic. Which had made it essential to steal Spalding's laptop. His mind flashed through what he'd seen in Spalding's office in his home. Then it struck him. My God, it was so astonishingly and devastatingly simple. It had been staring him in the face and he hadn't seen it. And he knew exactly why Redsall hadn't been killed immediately after Spalding.

Eagerly he said, 'Redsall took that computer all right, and I know why, because on it was access not only to Spalding's research but also to his backup files.'

'Eh?'

Excitedly Horton explained, 'Spalding was a naval historian. His research was important, it was how he made his living, so he wouldn't risk having all his research on a computer that might crash or be stolen. There was no sign of an external backup hard drive in his study at his home and no report of a break-in to indicate anyone had taken it. So if he did have one and if it was taken then it was by an expert intruder, which smacks of the intelligence service. Alternatively, Jacqueline Spalding or her father-in-law, Ronald, allowed someone in, someone they knew and trusted.'

'Dr Deacon. He called on them and he has the medical knowledge to know about poisons.'

'Yes, but I don't think anyone broke in or stole any external backup hard drive because Spalding didn't use one. I'm betting he used an online backup service and the killer, with Spalding's computer in his possession, would be able to discover who that provider was. All he had to do was interrogate the computer, locate the provider, claim he'd forgotten his password, get a new one and gain access to all Spalding's research material.'

'So we're looking for someone who knew his way around computers?'

'Yes, but not necessarily a geek or an expert. Just someone fairly competent and comfortable around them.'

'Probably rules out Beatrice Redsall.'

Horton thought it likely, except he knew they shouldn't make prejudgements. She could be extremely familiar with modern technology and he said as much, adding, 'And she could be in league with someone who knows a great deal about computers.' He recalled Ted Crossley proudly boasting they had Wi-Fi in all rooms and remembered silently admiring the Crossleys' rear garden with its trees and shrubs. Perhaps Ted Crossley had worked with computers in the Navy, or Brenda Crossley might have done and they'd kept at the forefront of technological developments. Dr Deacon would also be up on technology. Then another thought occurred to Horton. 'Redsall might have been the computer expert and once he'd obtained the information, he was killed. We need to follow Spalding's research trail.'

'That could take months.'

'There might be a short cut.' Horton rang Marcus Felspur.

CHAPTER TWENTY-ONE

'He's off sick.'

Horton silently cursed. 'Nothing serious, I hope.'

'No, just a stomach bug. Something he ate, he thinks.'

But Horton didn't need Felspur in particular; maybe the library assistant could help. He asked if she was able to pull together the list of research material Douglas Spalding had consulted over the last year.

'I'll do my best, but I'm on my own today so it depends on how busy we are. I'll email it over as soon as I have it.'

Horton knew from his previous conversation with Felspur that it would only present a snapshot of what Spalding might have been researching, but at least it was a start. Back at the station Cantelli began the laborious process of approaching local naval associations and historical societies to find out if Spalding had contacted them. He'd also contact the university library. But as he'd said in the car that would all take time and Horton was growing increasingly frustrated by the delay and by the fact that he didn't have the resources. In addition, Walters was making heavy weather of crosschecking the naval careers of the Crossleys, Meadows, Jonathan Redsall and Spalding because the Admiralty were dragging their heels over giving him access to the records.

Horton thought he knew why, though there was a niggling doubt that he might be getting a little paranoid and obsessed. The deaths could have nothing to do with an intelligence service cover-up. The motive could be far simpler: greed, love, lust, revenge, fear. Or the deaths, excluding Meadows, could be suicide in both Spalding's case and Redsall's, said the small voice at the back of his mind. They had enough crime that wasn't in any doubt to keep them going for a century, so why waste time on this? Because it was murder. He couldn't let it drop, not yet.

He told Walters to add Dr Deacon to his list for checking. The fat detective went into shock and sought comfort in another packet of sandwiches and an extra bar of chocolate. At the rate he was going, Horton thought they'd have to lift him out of his seat with a crane. He wished he had Trueman working on it because he was a genius when it came to research, but that meant Uckfield knowing what Horton was doing and Trueman had told him that on receipt of Dr Clayton's findings, Uckfield had indeed declared the drugs to have been self-administered and he was sticking to that until, and if, the coroner found any differently. Horton knew he wouldn't. Trueman had said there was no fresh evidence on Meadows' murder. No one had come forward to say they'd seen him or his killer.

Horton paced his office; it was raining heavily and his brain felt sluggish. He was finding it hard to concentrate. At the back of his mind Quentin Amos's words nagged away at him and he itched to get on with his enquiries into Jennifer's disappearance, but that would distract him from the murders of Meadows, Redsall and Spalding. If they didn't find some evidence soon, evidence that Uckfield and ACC Dean couldn't sweep under the carpet, then the deaths would be neatly filed away and forgotten in the case of Redsall and Spalding. He doubted if Beatrice Redsall cared very much about the outcome of her nephew's death. She was certainly near the top of the list as far as suspects were concerned. But Jacqueline Spalding, her children and Douglas Spalding's father deserved better than that. Those children shouldn't have to go through life feeling guilty, hurt and angry, believing their father had killed himself.

And Meadows' murder? Horton knew they'd find someone to pin that on. Into his mind came the image of that battered and bloody body. He stopped pacing and stared out of the window without seeing the rain bouncing off the roofs of the cars in the car park, or the police officers escorting villains from patrol vehicles into the rear of the station. Instead, he saw the ancient fortifications in Old Portsmouth guarding the entrance to Portsmouth Harbour where Meadows' body had been discovered. He couldn't stay here. He couldn't think. He picked up his jacket and helmet and made his way through CID, telling Cantelli on the way that he needed some air. He felt Cantelli's worried eyes follow him out.

Fifteen minutes later he was parking the Harley in front of the ancient stone walls. The area was no longer sealed off but the heavy rain was deterring the usual walkers and tourists. He had the place to himself which suited him fine. Alone on the top of the Round Tower he stared at the choppy, swirling dark grey sea. The tide was racing in and he could see a couple of optimistic and bedraggled fishermen at the end of the short pier down to his left and further along the beach. He watched the Wightlink ferry sail out on its way to the Isle of Wight, thinking of Agent Ames and her father Lord Ames in the yacht club where he'd met Professor Madeley. Madeley had to be a member otherwise he wouldn't have suggested meeting there. Or was he? Perhaps he had been the guest of someone who was a member.

His thoughts returned to Ivor Meadows. Why had Meadows chosen this as a meeting place for his rendezvous with the killer? And even if he hadn't chosen it, why had he agreed to come here at the killer's request? OK, so Meadows had been pompous and cockily confident that he could handle himself, but it was a risk meeting someone in such a dark and deserted place at that time of night. But what if he didn't know this person was a killer. Perhaps this person had told Meadows they had some highly sensitive information they wanted to give him which could expose a major crime and no one must know his identity. But actually, it was a lie to lure Meadows here and kill him because this person was afraid he knew something damaging. Yes, Meadows would have fallen for that. And recalling his first conversation with Meadows, when he'd made known his very strong views about women, Horton knew that Meadows would firmly believe he could handle anything a woman could throw at him. So, he thought, gazing across the harbour, if this woman had approached Meadows and was afraid he knew too much and thought he had to be silenced, then she had known how and where to get hold of him.

He considered this fact. Think, he urged his weary brain; put this into some kind of order. Brenda Crossley had attended Spalding's previous lecture in May and Meadows had been there. He might have recognized her but had thought nothing of it until Horton had mentioned the name Redsall. Then Meadows had made the connection between her and Jonathan Redsall. Maybe they'd had an affair. Meadows had approached her. Brenda, afraid that he might expose her affair or some more serious misdemeanour that Jonathan Redsall and others had covered up, had agreed to meet Meadows here and had killed him.

Then there was Beatrice Redsall. Equally Meadows could have agreed to meet her here. Beatrice Redsall had told Horton she'd assisted her brother in his career after his wife had died; perhaps she knew something about her brother that she was desperate to hush up. Desperate enough to kill three men for?

Horton wiped a hand across his wet face as he considered this and continued with his theories. He'd earlier dismissed Erica Leyton but perhaps he shouldn't have done. Cantelli had suggested she might have used the naval museum library for her research into HMS *Challenger*; perhaps she'd met Ivor Meadows there. He could check if she'd signed in there and when. He consulted his watch; the museum library would still be open. He hurried down to his Harley. His phone rang on the way. It was Walters.

'Dr Deacon didn't serve in the Navy. He came from a practice in Devon to Portsmouth four years ago.'

So that ruled him out, but Horton knew it hadn't been Deacon.

'And Simon Watson has never been in the Navy and he didn't go to the same university or school as Spalding or Redsall or live in the same area.'

No, Watson had been just a vague possibility. Horton said, 'Has Cantelli got the list of research material Spalding requested from the naval museum library?'

'I'll put him on.'

Cantelli came on the line. 'I was just going to call you. The librarian phoned a few minutes ago. Guess what? She can't find the file that contains the slips of paper requesting the various research materials. She's looked everywhere but it's missing.'

'I bet it is. Don't they have any record of it online or has that been erased?' Horton said sarcastically.

'They don't have an online system. That is, they did, but it was worse than useless she says and they disbanded it. A new one is under design.'

'How convenient.' Horton quickly thought. 'Go back to her and ask her if Erica Leyton has ever used the library and if so when. If she doesn't know or can't find a record of it, check with the security office. She would have needed to sign in. Give me Felspur's address. I'll see if he can remember what material Spalding accessed. He might also remember seeing Erica Leyton.'

'Hope he's recovered from his stomach bug.'

Horton hoped so too. And that it had been caused by something he'd eaten rather than being anything contagious.

Felspur's flat, it transpired, was only three minutes away on the Harley, just off the seafront in a narrow road of tall Victorian terraced houses that had once been the homes of the wealthy and were now popular with students and housing benefit occupants. Felspur lived in the basement flat in one of the shabbier houses. Horton knew that librarians didn't earn a fortune but he'd have thought that Felspur could have done better than this. Perhaps he was divorced and had a high-maintenance ex-wife and children.

He stepped around the rusting old bicycle, tattered looking pushchair and two wheelie dustbins with carrier bags of discarded food sticking out of their lids and pressed his finger on a bell on the scratched and weather-worn wooden door. There was no immediate answer so Horton tried again, wondering if Felspur had thrown a sickie and gone out. But no, he heard footsteps. The door stuck as Felspur wrenched it open. He started visibly at the sight of Horton, his pale eyes widened with alarm and then clouded with fear. Horton rapidly began to revise his opinion of Felspur. He'd thought of him as being calm, logical, in control, confident — and maybe he was at work — but here he looked weak, vulnerable, sick and terrified.

'I'm sorry to disturb you, Mr Felspur, but it is important. I wondered if I could come in.'

Felspur swallowed and shuffled his feet. 'I'm not feeling well.'

'This won't take a moment.' Horton was beginning to get more curious about the slight, nervous man in front of him, who did look rather ill. 'There's something I need your help on,' Horton insisted, gently pushing Felspur aside and stepping inside. He got no further than two paces. He'd seen places like this before. The narrow hallway was crammed with old newspapers and books; they lined either side of the passageway making it almost impossible to negotiate. Felspur was behind him and that suited Horton fine. 'This is the lounge, I take it,' he said, turning into a room on his right and halted just inside it. The high-ceilinged room smelt of damp, old books, dust and decay. It was also crammed full of clutter. In a glance Horton took in more old newspapers, stacked everywhere. God knew how far back they dated. Plastic bags, the kind that the supermarket used, had been flattened and laid out in piles around the room. Surrounding

234

the three armchairs were empty cans of baked beans, peas, curry, and more which had been washed out and were heaped on the floor. There were even empty pots of yogurt and foil trays, again washed out, piled on top of each other. And either side of the fireplace on shelves in the alcoves were ornaments, old tools, and nautical memorabilia. Felspur was clearly no ordinary hoarder. The man had a mental illness. He couldn't bear to see anything discarded.

'I don't know how I can help you, Inspector,' Felspur said anxiously.

Horton picked his way across to the shelves. 'Fine collection you have here, Mr Felspur.' There were flags, ship models, bits of naval uniforms, a couple of daggers.

'Yes, well I pick these things up in junk shops.' Felspur licked his lips nervously.

'Very specialist junk shops.' Horton picked up a piece of very old blue fabric. 'Why keep this?'

It was a pointless question to ask a hoarder who would keep anything, but Horton was rapidly remembering what Julie Preston had told him about some of the items kept in the attics when she'd demonstrated how she and Morden swept the museum after the functions. Several things clicked into place. Julie Preston and Lewis Morden's assignations; Ivor Meadows' bleats about museum security; the fact that Felspur had attended every evening lecture in the last four months; Meadows' short visit to the library after Horton had seen him on Wednesday morning and Meadows' willingness to meet his killer alone, in a dark isolated place at night.

Felspur shifted position. 'It's . . . er . . . just a piece of fabric from an old dress.'

'A very important old dress, I suspect.'

Felspur looked down and then back at Horton with pleading in his eyes.

'Did it belong to Lady Hamilton?' asked Horton gently.

Felspur swallowed and nodded.

Horton picked up another item. This time a brooch. 'And this?'

'It was hers too.'

'You stole them from the naval museum.'

'No!' Felspur looked horrified. 'I just borrowed them.'

Horton cast his eye over several of the nautical items. No doubt they'd all been stolen from the museum. Conversationally he said, 'When did Ivor Meadows discover that you were slipping away during the lectures and stealing these artefacts?'

'He didn't.' Felspur shifted nervously.

'You knew that Lewis Morden sneaked upstairs for his assignations with Julie Preston when there was an evening function and that no one would be watching the security monitors. That gave you the perfect opportunity to slip away from the lecture, climb to the attic rooms and help yourself. If the caterers saw you, they'd think nothing of it because you were staff.' He saw he was correct by Felspur's pained expression. 'You would just take small things like this fabric, jewellery, pieces of naval uniform, possibly these ship's bottles which you could put in the pockets of a larger jacket and you'd slip back into the lecture.'

'I wasn't doing any harm.'

'You were stealing,' Horton said more harshly, drawing a flush of indignation from Felspur.

'No,' he protested. 'I was preserving and exhibiting. I haven't sold anything. I wouldn't. I just like to look at them. They're shut away in that museum in drawers and cases. That's not right.'

Horton eyed Felspur severely. 'And neither is bludgeoning a man to death,' he said harshly.

Felspur flinched. 'I didn't do that.'

Horton didn't believe him but instead of pressing Felspur, he left a short pause and, changing his approach, said in a quieter, almost casual tone, 'Where were you on Wednesday night, Mr Felspur?'

'Here.'

Horton eyed him interrogatively. 'Alone?'

'Yes.'

Horton smiled. 'Of course. We have to ask these questions. I'm sorry for disturbing you.'

Relief flooded Felspur's pallid face. 'You won't tell the museum about the artefacts, will you? I'd lose my job.'

'I think you had better return them.'

'I will. I promise.'

Horton didn't believe that for one minute. Felspur went ahead to show Horton out, but in the passage, Horton turned right instead of left. He heard Felspur protest behind him. Ahead was a kitchen and next to it a bedroom. Horton stepped inside, ignoring Felspur's wailing. There was barely space for the bed and wardrobe. The room once again was crammed with stuff; this time there were old bicycle parts, old bits of metal, and an assortment of tools, some of them clearly ancient, and amongst them Horton's eyes caught sight of a long cylindrical metal tube rounded off at one end and with a flat oblong shape on the other end. He'd seen something like it before in a drawing that had been emailed him.

'What's that?' he asked, pointing to it as it lay on the floor by the bed.

Felspur shuffled his feet. 'It's a Dolly. It was used by riveters in the dockyard for ship building. Drillers used to drill the holes for rivets then the riveters would drive the rivets in by hand using light hammers on long handles.'

Horton said almost conversationally, 'And is that what you did to Ivor Meadows' head?'

'No!'

'Did Meadows threaten to expose your pilfering? Is that why you had to kill him?'

'No. I . . .' Felspur's body sagged. Horton knew he wouldn't be able to keep up his denials for long. Felspur wasn't off sick with food poisoning or a stomach bug; he was sickened by what he'd done. 'He didn't understand.'

'You told him this at the Round Tower, why there?'

'It was the first place that came to mind. I'd been reading about Henry VIII's ships sailing through the harbour. He came into the library that morning, Wednesday, after he'd seen you. He was so loud; I was scared the customers and my colleagues would hear. I told him I couldn't talk there but I'd tell him everything if he agreed to meet me away from the library that night, at 10.30 p.m. I didn't think he would but he agreed and he came even though he was a little late. I got anxious waiting for him. I was upset; I didn't know what I was doing.'

Not upset enough to go prepared with a murder weapon though. And Meadows would cockily have agreed because he thought he could handle a weakling like Felspur.

'I was going to reason with him. Promise not to do it again and to put the items back, then he started to say that he knew I'd killed Dr Spalding and Daniel Redsall because they'd both seen me stealing. I didn't. It was lies. You'd believe him. I'd be arrested for murder. He wouldn't shut up; he kept saying it over and over again. I said OK, I'd go with him to the police. Anything to shut him up. He turned but stumbled. I picked up the Dolly where I'd left it on one of the seats and hit him.' Felspur sank down onto the bed. He looked up at Horton pleadingly and sorrowfully. 'I love my job and I love that museum. Meadows was going to ruin everything for me. I couldn't allow that.'

No. Horton eyed the broken man slumped on the bed. There was no need for the handcuffs. He reached for his phone and called Uckfield.

CHAPTER TWENTY-TWO

They found traces of blood on the Dolly and Horton had no doubts that it would match Meadows' blood. Bliss was cock-a-hoop that her team had solved a major murder case. Rumour had it that she had even smiled, a rare enough sight to cause many in the station to stumble around like blinded extras in the filming of *The Day of the Triffids*.

There was no evidence to show that Felspur had poisoned Spalding and Redsall; the team was still going through Felspur's flat and that would take days given the rubbish that was in it. He denied it strenuously during the interview and Horton believed him, but give it time, he thought cynically, and if the coroner did rule unlawful killing on Spalding and Redsall then the intelligence services had a ready-made scapegoat to pin both murders on along with a nice neat little motive; Spalding and Redsall had both witnessed Felspur's jaunts to the attics and, scared he'd be exposed, Felspur had drugged them. They might even say that Felspur had approached Redsall with the aim of trying to sell some of the stolen artefacts, which would explain why Redsall had come to Portsmouth. And if they needed to explain Spalding's trip to Northern Ireland then the story could be altered. Spalding had traced stolen items to the Centre for Maritime

Archaeology at Ulster University and together with Redsall they'd decided to expose Felspur. So Felspur had to dispose of Redsall. Felspur knew the security code for the pontoons at Oyster Quays because of his interest in naval history and his connection with the 1942 MGB 81 motor gun boat moored there. He'd suggested to Redsall that they meet there that night. And the empty rucksack? Redsall had merely carried his food and drink in it, which he'd consumed. Spalding's briefcase and its contents were in the sea, after Spalding, disorientated from being drugged, had staggered there before falling into the dock. Whichever way Horton looked at it, the intelligence services would have it neatly wrapped up. They'd fit the facts to suit the circumstances.

Horton had asked Felspur about Erica Leyton. He said he didn't recognize the name but it was possible she had used the naval museum. Did it matter now, Horton thought, heading for home? She hadn't killed Meadows. And Felspur hadn't killed Spalding and Redsall — but someone had. And it had nothing to do with stolen naval artefacts. Tomorrow he'd ask the museum library to check their records to see if Erica Leyton had accessed material there. For now, he needed sleep. But despite his fatigue, instead of turning into the marina car park he continued along the road, where he pulled over opposite the Institute of Marine Sciences building. Climbing off his Harley and removing his helmet he stepped down onto the pebbled beach and began to throw stones into the sea, letting his mind wander where it wished. It roamed first to Spalding's body in Number One Dock in the Historic Dockyard, then to Redsall's body at Oyster Quays near the MGB 81. Neither had been killed where their bodies had been found. Dr Clayton's words drifted back to him . . . *this is a clever poison and therefore a clever poisoner*. What else had she said? Yes, something about the killer administering the drug knowing that he or she would be a long way from where the victim would be found dead.

Both men had died at the furthermost western edge of Portsmouth, and here, where he was standing, was the furthermost eastern edge of the city. This was about as far away from the bodies as you could get if you measured the city limits from east to west. Horton let the stone fall from his hand as thoughts assailed him. Was it possible?

He spun round and stared at the building across the road. Then his gaze swivelled to his right, to the refreshment stall beside the Lifeboat Station. It was perfect and so very clever. Now he saw what must have happened. Spalding had met Erica Leyton here on Monday after he'd left the university. They'd had lunch at the refreshment stall where during the day tables and chairs were set up overlooking the sea. And she had poisoned him. She was a marine biologist, an expert on sea plants, so equally she could be an expert on land-based plants. And she had access to laboratories where she could manufacture the poison. She'd know exactly what she was doing and how much hyoscine to administer. Spalding must then have walked along the seafront to the dockyard, reaching it in time to prepare for his lecture. And Redsall?

Horton crossed the road. No lights were showing inside the Marine Sciences building, the steel gate was locked and the car park was empty. But in his mind, he saw beyond it to the shore where two days ago a small, high-speed boat had headed towards him and Cantelli with Erica Leyton on board. A boat that could have taken Redsall out on Tuesday, and on which, towards the end of the day, she had poisoned him. She must have dropped him off close to Oyster Quays marina, possibly at the Town Camber. She could also have given him the code to get on to the pontoons; she'd know it, as having use of the university boat she must have moored up there before and recently. Perhaps she told Redsall that someone would meet him there. That was a weak point in his theory and so too was why Redsall had agreed to take Spalding's computer, but she was attractive and perhaps Redsall had fallen for her. Perhaps they had known one another when Redsall had worked at the Southampton Institute for Marine Archaeology; their professional paths could have crossed. That didn't explain why Spalding had gone to Northern Ireland though. But if Erica Leyton *had* killed Douglas Spalding and Daniel Redsall, then she had a motive for doing so and that brought him right back to that question of research.

If Douglas Spalding had lied about his research to Felspur and Meadows, then either he had also lied to Erica Leyton, or Erica had lied to them. Perhaps they'd used the *Challenger* research as an excuse to see one another as Cantelli had suggested. So had there been something incriminating on Spalding's computer that Erica needed? Possibly. But there was still also the possibility that her job had been to lure Spalding to his death, obtain his research and then silence Redsall, and if that was the case, then the connection between the two men was the Navy and in particular Rear Admiral Jonathan Redsall. Whatever the reasons he needed to talk to Erica Leyton.

He whipped out his phone and called the number she had given him. There was no answer. Damn. It was only just ten, but she might have gone out for the evening and would return soon. He called the station and asked for her address. Impatiently, he held on while someone called up the various databases that they had access to. It was late. He could follow this up tomorrow. And he'd have to do it alone, or at least with Cantelli, because neither Uckfield nor Bliss would sanction it. But he couldn't wait until tomorrow. He needed to know now. At last, he had the address. She lived about ten minutes away. He could wait for her outside her house. He returned to the Harley and was about to alight when the sound of a motorbike approaching halted him. He recognized its engine. He could swear it was the same bike that had appeared out of nowhere when the black Ranger had been intent on running him over. He tensed. Could this be someone from the intelligence services trying again? But how would they know he was here? No one had followed him.

The bike drew closer. Horton waited. He saw it pull up outside the Marine Sciences building. The figure alighted. For a moment he wondered if it was Erica Leyton who'd returned to work late, but the build was too stocky. The rider turned at the sound of Horton's footsteps as he hurried across the road. Removing his helmet Horton recognized Dr Bradley Marshall.

'Inspector, what are you doing here?' Marshall asked, surprised.

'Hoping to speak to Erica Leyton, but she's not answering her phone. I wondered if she might be working late.'

'I've been trying her for about the last hour without getting an answer, but the signal's not always great inside the building so I thought I'd better check. She's an epileptic and . . . well I was concerned.' While he'd been speaking Marshall had taken out his pass and swiped it across the electronic release; the steel gate slowly swung open to admit them. 'I'll meet you at the main entrance.'

Horton walked to it while Marshall parked his Honda, his words causing Horton to wonder. Could Erica Leyton have taken off for fear of being discovered? Then a chilling thought struck him. Had the intelligence services got to her and silenced her permanently for whatever Spalding's research had revealed? Or was Erica inside the building destroying the evidence that she'd killed two men?

Within minutes Marshall had the main door open and had disabled the alarm system.

Horton said, 'She can't be here, otherwise she'd have switched off the alarm.'

'She might have reset it and left by the rear. We often do that when we're working late. She could be on the raft.'

'At this time of night?' Horton said surprised.

'You don't know Erica, she's fanatical. Dark, cold, wind, whatever the weather and time of day, if the job demanded it, she'll be out there.' He was clearly worried as they crossed the reception area to another door where Marshall entered a number on a security pad. 'But if she is on the raft then I'd have thought she'd have answered her phone.'

Horton followed Marshall into a dimly lit corridor either side of which were closed doors. There was no sign of a light shining from any of the rooms.

Marshall said, 'This is the lab she uses.' He pushed open the door and flicked on the bright lights. Wherever Erica was it wasn't in here, thought Horton quickly, surveying the pristine, clinical well-equipped room.

'I'll try her number again.' Horton turned away, and let it ring, but there was still no answer.

Concerned, Marshall said, 'I'm going to check the raft.'

'I'll come with you.' Horton wondered if he should call in. Stepping from the building onto the shore he said, 'She can't be on the raft, the boat is still here.'

'She might have taken the RIB. It's got better lights on it.' He climbed on board the small motor boat. Horton followed suit stifling his growing unease. Marshall said, 'There are a couple of torches in the locker.'

Horton found them, but didn't switch them on. It was only a short distance and now a calm night. Within two minutes, Marshall had pulled alongside the raft silhouetted in the moonlight. Horton couldn't see any evidence of anyone on board and neither could he see the RIB moored up, although it could be on the other side, hidden by the square shed-like structure in the right-hand corner. It was possible Erica Leyton was there too, but if so, then why hadn't she stepped out from behind it at the sound of them approaching?

Marshall tied off and took the larger torch, leaving Horton with a smaller one, which he stuffed in his pocket as he nimbly climbed over the railing and followed Marshall on board. On the deck he played the beam of light over the raft. The centre of the deck had been hollowed out and filled with water and across it in sections were ladder-like structures. There was a narrow walkway around the edge of the raft roped off from the hollowed-out section and in the far right-hand corner a platform, again roped off, in front of the square shed-like structure.

There was no sign of Erica Leyton. Across the water on Hayling, Horton could see lights from the Ferry Boat Inn but the harbour appeared as deserted as the raft. Snatches of a conversation flashed into Horton's mind like the lights on the distant buoys: *we have five aquarium rooms for studying fish biology and non-native organisms; the latter's my area of specialism . . . seaweeds and phytoplankton.* Marshall's pet topic. Horton had asked Marshall if he'd known Dr Spalding, and now those pinpricks of light exploded in blinding illumination; *I recommended Erica to him and I used to see him when he visited Erica here.*

Evenly, Horton said, 'How long have you known Spalding's research involved Daniel Redsall's father, Rear Admiral Jonathan Redsall?'

He saw Marshall quickly weigh this up, the truth or more lies. Even before he spoke though, Horton knew what his decision would be. The truth, because as far as Marshall was concerned there was no risk in him knowing now. Marshall was confident he could eliminate him just as he'd eliminated Spalding and Redsall. And Erica Leyton? Horton looked down at the water. A cold chill ran through him.

'Since May,' Marshall said with simplicity.

'How did you find out?' Horton wondered exactly what piece of research Spalding had requested that had triggered the alert to the intelligence services.

'He came to ask me about it.'

Horton was confused. Why would Spalding approach someone from the intelligence services if his research was highly sensitive? He must have known they'd want it hushed up. And how would he know that Bradley Marshall worked for them? Surely it was the other way around? Marshall would have made himself known to Spalding in order to silence him. But if Marshall was telling the truth and had no connection with the intelligence services then Spalding must have uncovered something that involved or implicated someone from Bradley Marshall's past and which was connected with Redsall. Something neither man wanted exposed. And something that had led the intelligence services to give orders at the highest level that the deaths of Douglas Spalding and Daniel Redsall were not to be investigated.

Horton's brain raced through what he had learned and heard over the last few days, desperately trying to connect the threads. Whatever it was that had happened must have been either when Jonathan Redsall was a Rear Admiral or when he was climbing the ranks to the top. What had he done to provoke Marshall into murdering three people and stir up the intelligence services to protect the reputation of someone long since dead? Quentin Amos's voice suddenly broke through Horton's swirling thoughts. *Someone's kept silent for a long time. They might want it to stay that way. You might think the days of spies and the Cold War are over . . . but they're not . . .* And with that came the memory of Cantelli's report on Rear Admiral Redsall: *He served on HMS Hardy when it was deployed to counter and carry out surveillance of Russian activities in 1967 during the Cold War . . .* and Jonathan Redsall had served in the Far East, Singapore, after which he had risen rapidly in the promotion stakes. This had nothing to do with terrorism in Northern Ireland, that connection had distracted him for a moment. No, the heart of this lay much further away.

Into Horton's mind came the deaths of three other men: Zachary Benham, Timothy Wilson and James Royston and with it more of his conversation with Amos. He was beginning to see why Jonathan Redsall's past could not be allowed to be exposed.

Marshall's hand came out of his pocket and in it, Horton saw a syringe. He must have palmed it when he entered the laboratory ahead of him.

'Hyoscine?'

'No. Nicotine. You won't suffer long.'

'Unlike Spalding and Redsall.'

'Redsall's death was pretty quick.'

Horton tensed but forced his voice to remain even as he said, 'Seeing as you're intent on killing me, no harm in telling me why Spalding and Redsall had to die.' Horton waited, eager to hear the truth while rapidly trying to fathom a way out of this.

After a moment Marshall nodded, as though to himself. 'In the late 1960s the Royal Navy suffered from a severe bout of homosexuality. Admirals believed that at least half the fleet had committed homosexual acts.'

Horton swiftly recalled what Amos had said about homosexuality being decriminalized for those over the age of twenty-one in England and Wales in 1967 but Amos had added, *not in Scotland and Northern Ireland or in the armed forces, that came much later.*

Marshall was saying, 'It was not only illegal but it was also considered disgusting, and worse, a security risk.'

'Because of the Cold War.' Horton's mind flicked to Quentin Amos and quickly back to the man in front of him who was intent on sticking a syringe into him.

'Yes. It was in the good old days when anyone who didn't conform was considered either a Commie bastard or a secret agent. Hard to believe now, isn't it?' Marshall sneered.

And Horton was beginning to see exactly why Jonathan Redsall was still being protected by the intelligence services. 'Redsall had a homosexual affair.'

'Yes. With my father.'

So that was the connection. 'What happened to him?' Horton asked quietly.

'He was expendable. Redsall was an officer with a public school education and a privileged upbringing. His father was a Vice Admiral. My father was a rating, just a medical orderly. He was dismissed from the Navy and six months later he killed himself and left my mother to bring up a two-year-old child without a pension, without a home and with no money.'

'But it was more than sex,' Horton said. And Spalding had unearthed it.

Marshall narrowed his eyes. 'Yes. Spalding had discovered that a commander on-board the ship on which my father was serving while stationed in Singapore in 1969 was selling vital information to the Russians. This commander had been blackmailed into it because of his escapades in a male brothel. Pictures had been taken and my father, Adrian

Goring, had been given copies of these along with the information about the commander by the woman running the brothel because he gave her some drugs which helped to save her life. Adrian probably didn't care about the commander's sexual preferences, but he might have baulked at the betrayal of his country, or perhaps he thought the information might give him a leg up in the promotion stakes. I don't know. He went to the captain and handed over the photographs believing the matter would be dealt with and it was.'

'But not in the way your father anticipated.'

'No. Nothing was done or said about it for some time. Adrian started a homosexual relationship with Jonathan Redsall and MI6 had the perfect scapegoat. My father. They must have been watching him for some time, waiting to get something on him so that they could clear him out of the Navy and make him forget his allegations against the commander who was still serving on-board.'

'Because the intelligence services were now feeding this commander the wrong information. So he was quite useful to them.'

'Yes.'

Horton eyed the syringe in Marshall's hand. If he got closer, he might be able to dislodge it, or better still knock the heavy torch from Marshall's hand and make him react. In that instance he could grab his wrist, force the syringe from his hand and twist his bloody arm up his back. He edged a little closer.

He said, 'So Adrian was confronted about his relationship with Redsall. When he threatened to tell about the commander selling naval secrets, MI6 said they'd expose his affair with Redsall.' Horton knew how these things worked. 'But that was a lie. MI6 could now use Redsall to help feed information to the Communists and dispose of this commander who was a security risk. Redsall was sound in terms of his loyalty to his country, it was just he made a mistake with his choice of sexual partner. He probably claimed it was just the once, it would never happen again, and that he was led astray by your father.' Horton took another small step closer. 'How did Spalding uncover all this?'

'Documents had been released by the Public Records Office that revealed that many commanders had buried a series of sex scandals in Singapore including homosexual affairs, transsexual prostitutes and male brothels. Spalding researched and cross-checked the records of the officers and enlisted men who had been dismissed, and those who had died shortly after 1969, at the height of the scandal. He was very thorough and meticulous. He found an unusually high number of fatalities on board one ship and a young officer who had been rapidly promoted. Spalding sensed he was onto something. He interviewed those he could find who had served on board HMS *Neirne*. Some had kept private diaries; some had been close to Adrian. Others who felt they no longer had anything to lose by speaking out told him what they'd seen and heard. Gradually Spalding's facts began to back up what had been rumours and supposition. It took him a long time to pull it all together and he had to keep his research very close to his chest.'

And that was why he had lied about what he was really researching. But the intelligence services had been alerted by someone or by something Spalding had requested.

Marshall said, 'Eventually he tracked me down even though my mother had remarried. He asked me if my father had left any diaries or letters. He hadn't. If he did at the time then they were almost certainly taken by the security services and destroyed.'

And Horton knew that must have been what had happened to his mother's diaries. On the day she'd vanished, while he'd been at school, someone had slipped in and cleaned out anything incriminating from their flat, including photographs. Had that man been Ballard? Had he kept two photographs, the one of Jennifer which had been in the tin he'd given his foster father, and the one of those six men? Horton knew he was correct. But time to think about that later — at least he hoped he'd be alive to do so — which meant bringing his full attention back to Marshall. He eased another step closer.

'Presumably Spalding asked Daniel Redsall the same question when he visited him in Northern Ireland in July.'

Marshall nodded. Horton wondered if Beatrice Redsall knew about her brother's shady past. And the answer came back immediately that of course she did. It was why she had travelled to the Isle of Wight and the Castle Hill Yacht Club on 20 June. Spalding had also visited her, or perhaps her nephew had telephoned her.

Marshall said, 'Jonathan Redsall probably said he'd do anything to cooperate with the intelligence services and keep it silent.'

'So your father was dismissed on a trumped-up charge and not for homosexuality.'

'Supplying drugs from the medical unit to the locals who all swore they'd got them from him, well they would, wouldn't they, if they didn't want to be imprisoned. The woman who ran the brothel was too scared to stand up for my father. Redsall was recruited to feed false information to the Russians and the commander died of a heart attack, three months later.'

Very convenient, and that incident must have triggered many questions in Spalding's sharp analytical mind. But which side had induced it? The Russians or the British?

'Who was this commander?'

'Spalding didn't say and it wasn't in his research. He just used the initial "C" when referring to him.'

Horton's mind was spinning. Had MI6 always known that Adrian Goring's son was Bradley Marshall and had kept tabs on him? Spalding had found him so it was likely that the intelligence services had. And perhaps they'd sat back and watched to see whether Marshall or Daniel Redsall would do their dirty work for them, eliminate Spalding and destroy his research.

He thought back to what Beatrice Spalding had told him about her nephew. 'Spalding told Daniel Redsall this.

He wanted it all to come out. His father and his family had made his life a misery. He was angry at the lies they'd told him. Spalding thought he had the two of you on his side; you would want it exposed for the sake of justice and revenge, but that wasn't how it worked out.'

'No. Redsall contacted me. He said it was the last thing he wanted. He hated his father but he'd made a new life for himself and one he enjoyed. He was well respected. It was the past and he wanted it buried. I did too. My father means nothing to me. My mother changed her surname by deed poll and then remarried. I went to university, thanks to my stepfather, and I have an excellent job and one I'm passionate about. Redsall and I joined forces to silence Spalding.'

'But you killed Daniel Redsall.'

'I had to. I needed his help to get the material from Spalding but I couldn't risk him telling anyone that I'd killed him. He might have stayed silent, but I couldn't chance it.'

'So Daniel Redsall came over from Northern Ireland and attended Spalding's lecture. You had poisoned Spalding earlier in the day; you'd arranged to meet him over at the refreshment stall opposite where you added the hyoscine you made in the lab to his tea.'

'His coffee.'

'Daniel took the contents of Spalding's briefcase, including his laptop computer and memory stick, from the Princess Royal Gallery while everyone was having their refreshments and he stuffed them in his empty rucksack, replacing the computer with a couple of heavy books he'd carried in.'

'Wood, actually.'

'Then Redsall walked out carrying his rucksack. What happened to the briefcase?'

'Spalding must have dropped it in the sea.'

But Horton wasn't so sure about that. 'Did you know there were security cameras in the Princess Royal Gallery?'

'No.'

And Marshall wouldn't have cared if Morden had been looking at the monitors because he had made sure that

Redsall's trail wouldn't lead back to him. Keeping his eyes firmly fixed on Marshall, Horton said, 'And the next day Redsall met you at the shore somewhere near here and you went out on the boat. I presume you moored up somewhere and reviewed what Spalding had put on his computer.'

'Yes, a quiet spot in Thorney Channel off Thorney Island. Spalding's research was all there. It made interesting reading and it gave me access to his backup files.'

Horton had been correct about that then. 'But you didn't poison Redsall then.' He recalled what Dr Clayton had said. 'You left that until later in the day before dropping him back to Oyster Quays. How did you moor up without being seen?'

Marshall smiled. 'I didn't. I dropped him at the Camber.' Horton had been right about that too.

'The poison would take about two hours to work. I had no idea where he'd end up, just as long as it was nowhere near me.'

'Did he say he was meeting someone?'

'No.'

Soon Horton would take his chance but there were a couple more things he wanted to know first. He steeled himself for action. 'Where's Erica?'

Marshall's eyes flicked downwards towards the water in the raft. Horton's blood ran cold. The bastard. He'd killed her while she'd been working here. She'd had to die because she might have worked out or could inadvertently reveal that every time Spalding consulted her, he also saw Bradley Marshall. The *Challenger* research project had merely been a cover so that Spalding could see Marshall.

'Did she see you with Spalding at the cafe? Were you afraid she'd put that together with the fact that Spalding always saw you when he came to visit her at the institute? Had she become suspicious?' Horton steeled himself for action.

'It had to be done.'

And Marshall had returned tonight to move her body and dump it out at sea. 'Which section is she in, Marshall?'

Horton snarled, preparing himself; he had a split second to act. 'Which one?' he shouted. 'Where have you put her?'

'That one.' Marshall jerked his head to his left. Horton sprang forward, dealt a violent blow to Marshall's right hand and knocked the torch from it. As Marshall cried out, taken by surprise, he twisted to stab the syringe into Horton's side but Horton was quicker and fitter. With a karate chop he dislodged the syringe, grabbed Marshall's arm and twisted it behind his back. Marshall screamed in pain. Horton rammed Marshall's body against the railings, looking around for something to tie him there, but there was nothing to hand. He needed to call in but his phone was in his right-hand pocket. Still with a fierce grip on Marshall, Horton caught sight of a length of rope to their right.

'Move,' he shouted, wrenching Marshall up and pushing him along the narrow deck to the right past the half railing where they'd climbed on-board.

The surface was wet and slippery. The moon suddenly disappeared behind a bank of cloud. Marshall lost his footing and slipped. Horton went down with him, in the process loosening his grip. It was enough for Marshall to twist and squirm his way out, and within seconds he'd slid through the lower gap in the railings and into the sea.

'Shit!' Horton scrambled up and played his torch on the black swirling mass in front of him. He thought he saw the dark shape of Marshall trying to swim to the shore — the man was an idiot, he wouldn't make it. The current was lethal in the harbour.

Clambering around the edge of the raft, holding the railing to guide him, Horton reached where they'd come on board and slipped down into the boat. He might be able to get to Marshall and throw him a line. Where the hell was he though? The wretched boat wouldn't start. He tried again. The third time it spluttered into life. Horton released the line and pointed the rudder towards the shore, but there was no sign of Marshall.

He needed light, the pathetic little torch had petered out and it was no bloody use anyway. He threw it down in disgust. He needed to alert the Lifeboat. With his hand on the tiller, he could feel the tide sweeping him out of the harbour much faster than he cared for. He turned, flicked open the seat behind him and grappled blindly into it for a flare. His hand curved around something as the coast of Hayling on his left and Eastney on his right raced past him with alarming speed. Releasing his hand from the tiller and letting the tide take him further out he let off the flare. It shot into the sky, bright orange, and lit up the dark pool of water ahead. Yes, he thought he could see something, but was it Marshall? He needed another distress flare. He reached for one. Again, orange lit the night sky, but already he wondered if he was too late. The current was taking him out into the Solent and there was no sign of Marshall. He reached for yet another flare, praying that someone would see it and call the Lifeboat. His prayers were answered some minutes later when, heading towards him from Eastney, was a high-speed RIB.

Horton bellowed across the engine noise as it drew alongside him, mouthing and pointing at the sea. 'Man in the water.' He indicated ahead.

A member of the crew nodded, put his thumb up, and relayed it to the others. They were used to this notorious stretch of water and he watched as they made a circuit ahead as Horton tried to steer the small craft to the shore. He couldn't, the current was too strong. Then ahead he saw another rescue boat making towards him. This time Horton took the line that was thrown to him and allowed his craft to be escorted out to the comparative safety of Southsea Bay. He looked back. The first rescue boat was still searching, but he knew they wouldn't find Marshall.

CHAPTER TWENTY-THREE

Saturday

Horton had called Uckfield and told him where he could find Erica Leyton's body. He relayed what had happened.

Uckfield had listened in silence before saying, 'I'll call Dean.'

'Yes, do that,' Horton had snapped and rung off. He'd returned to his boat and made it ready for sailing. Then he had switched off his mobile and set the alarm for 4 a.m. The sill to the marina would be open by then and at 4.30 a.m. he was motoring into Langstone Harbour in the breezy dark morning, passing close to the raft where arc lights had been set up but were no longer switched on. Everything was quiet. Erica Leyton's body had been brought up. She had done nothing to deserve death, and neither had Spalding and Redsall.

He sailed across to the Isle of Wight, letting the sea and the wind soothe his troubled mind, and watched as the dawn came up. It worked to some extent, but not completely because he knew what lay ahead. He thought it doubtful he'd find a berth in Cowes at the start of Cowes Week so he called Carl Ashton, woke him from his beauty sleep and, cutting off his angry protests, got him to give him the berth he wasn't using that went with his marina flat in East Cowes. Horton said nothing about his suspicions of Steve Drummond being Ashton's vandal. That would lead to Drummond being given the sack. When this was over, he'd have a quiet word with Drummond and persuade him to move on to another job and to hope that Melanie would tire of Ashton. If she didn't, it was certain that Ashton would tire of her and then maybe Melanie would look for a comforting shoulder to cry on. But for now, there was some unfinished business. He knew it would probably remain that way, but after considering what Marshall had told him, Horton couldn't let it rest.

He reached Cowes just after seven thirty, showered, changed and took the chain ferry across to West Cowes where he ate breakfast in the Yacht Haven and watched the throng of visitors on the pontoons making their yachts ready for a day's sailing.

The weather looked set to be fair with a wind strong enough to please most. He thought of Catherine and Emma and wondered if they'd be on-board his former father-in-law's yacht. And would Agent Harriet Ames be on another with Rupert Crawford and Ben Otis? Maybe even with her father, Lord Ames, but he hoped not the latter. And he hoped, as he made his way to Castle Hill Yacht Club, that he'd find Lord Ames there.

On showing his warrant card he was escorted into the Morning Room where Lord Ames was sitting, thankfully alone. Horton saw immediately that he knew why he'd come. Of course he'd know. He'd have been told about the events of the previous night.

'Coffee?'

Horton refused. His stomach was like a tight hard ball. He'd played out this conversation several times in his head throughout the morning but no matter how many times he'd rehearsed it he knew it wouldn't pan out as he expected because he couldn't write Ames' side of the script. He took the seat that Lord Ames offered him across the low coffee table. The room was deserted. Somehow Horton thought Ames must have arranged it that way.

He began. 'Did you know that Bradley Marshall was Adrian Goring's son?'

'Who?'

'And that Bradley Marshall killed Spalding and Daniel Redsall?'

Would Ames continue to deny his involvement? Would he continue to look blankly at him, and feign incomprehension at Horton's meaning?

'I don't know what you mean,' Ames declared politely, with a slightly bemused expression.

So that was the way it was going to be. It was good, but it didn't fool Horton. 'You'd lost track of Goring's son, is that why you allowed me to continue blundering around after nearly trying to kill me, to find him for you?'

'I have no idea what you're talking about, Inspector.'

But Ames did. He knew it all. Horton wasn't going to leave it there.

'Who was Daniel Redsall supposed to meet on the pontoon at Oyster Quays?' Horton asked. He hoped to God it wasn't Agent Harriet Ames, but it could be. Her father looked amused as though he could read his mind. It didn't take much to see that Lord Ames had guessed at Horton's liking for his daughter. If she hadn't been off limits before, she certainly was now. Horton badly wanted Redsall's rendezvous to have been with Rupert Crawford and then he might just vent a bit of anger on the smooth, good-looking supercilious banker or find a way of booking him for something; anything would do, sneezing in public would be enough. But Horton knew it wasn't Crawford.

'Was it Ben Otis?' he said, watching Ames carefully, not expecting the man to betray himself, and he didn't. Neither did he reply, which was an admission in itself. Horton continued. 'Was it Otis who entered the Historic Dockyard from the naval-base entrance on Monday night in order to kill Spalding as he was leaving the museum and take the briefcase containing the research?' Horton knew that Otis's name wouldn't appear on any signing-in log. He'd have top-level security clearance.

'You really do have a remarkable imagination, Inspector.'

'Imagination enough to believe that when Otis arrived outside the museum, he saw Dr Spalding staggering about clutching the briefcase. He grabbed it and then helped push him into Number One Dock, then left by the naval-base entrance. Or perhaps he didn't push him; perhaps Spalding, drugged by Marshall, thought he could fly and jumped. You must have been really pissed off when you discovered the briefcase was empty.'

Ames made no reply. He lifted his coffee cup and took a sip, looking at Horton over the rim.

'From that you knew that Daniel Redsall was working in league with Spalding. Would he reveal that his father was bisexual and had worked as a spy for the British Government?'

'Spy is such a melodramatic word, don't you think? It smacks too much of fiction and James Bond.'

Horton's eyes narrowed. His stomach was clenched hard as iron. 'Beatrice Redsall came here on 20 June to tell you that Spalding had contacted her about his research. He had to be stopped. She couldn't allow it to come out, and neither could you because it would spark too many questions. More dirty secrets and lies would be exposed, damaging some very highly influential people, those still alive and in government and top jobs. When you knew that Daniel must have taken Spalding's laptop you told Beatrice to call her nephew and ask him to meet her on the pontoons at Oyster Quays on Tuesday night. She gave him the security number, which you had relayed to her.'

Again, Horton didn't know this for certain but Daniel's mobile phone records would show him receiving a call from his aunt. Nothing wrong with that, and yes, when questioned she would admit she'd called him. She'd just forgotten she had or she hadn't thought it was relevant. The intelligence services must have given her Daniel's mobile phone number because Horton had believed her when she said she hadn't had any contact with her nephew for years.

'But Beatrice Redsall, who knew all about her brother's past and not from Spalding, had no intention of showing up at Oyster Quays. And Daniel had no intention of giving his aunt the research material, but he was curious to see how desperate she was for it and how much she knew about her beloved brother, so he agreed to meet her there. And even when drugged his agreed rendezvous had stuck in his mind. But instead of Beatrice showing up you had arranged for Ben Otis to meet Daniel and take the laptop computer from him. Otis was to linger on Crawford's yacht and follow the others to the restaurant, putting a sophisticated electronic device on the bridgehead security camera that made everyone think it was recording the pontoon live when it was in fact relaying a completely different image taken on a different day. Then Otis popped out of the restaurant, probably saying he was going to the gents, only he returned to the pontoon to meet Daniel Redsall.' Horton wondered if Harriet Ames would confirm this or whether she'd been told to keep silent. He didn't like to think so.

Horton continued. 'But when Otis got there, he found Redsall dead on Carl Ashton's yacht and no sign of the computer. He could see that the rucksack was empty. He quickly returned to his friends and your daughter in the restaurant, removing the masking device on the security camera on his way.'

'Like I said, Inspector, a remarkable imagination.'

'And with Redsall dead that meant someone else knew the secret and that was dangerous. That's when you realized the killer had to be Adrian Goring's son, and you had to find him and quick. Maybe you had found him. Perhaps you didn't care about him killing Erica Leyton. And now conveniently he's dead. Did you hope that I'd drown too?' Horton said angrily. 'Because you, or whoever you work for, don't like people asking too many questions, but I'll tell you this.' Horton leaned forward and lowered his voice. 'You will have to kill me, because I'm not going to stop asking questions about the disappearance of my mother. I'm going to find the two remaining men in this photograph.' He removed it from his jacket pocket and slapped it down on the table between them. He watched Ames' eyes flick down to it. He wanted to see surprise and fear but he saw only confusion. He couldn't be wrong. He was certain he wasn't.

It was confirmed when Ames said, 'Two?'

'Three of them are dead.'

'That leaves one.'

'Yes . . .' Horton held Ames' eyes . . . 'What happened to Jennifer, Ames?'

He caught a flicker of something but couldn't interpret what it was. Shock? Irritation?

'Where did you get this?' Ames said almost mockingly and yet Horton sensed his anger.

'From a friend.'

Ames didn't ask which friend. He knew Horton wouldn't tell him. But would he continue to deny that the remaining man was him?

'It's a long time since I've seen it. I hardly recognized myself.'

Stiffly, with his gut churning, Horton repeated his question. 'What happened to her?'

For a moment there was silence. Horton could hear his heart thumping against his chest and made every effort not to betray his fury and his fear.

'I don't know.'

Horton didn't believe him. 'She took this picture.'

'Did she? I remember she was friendly with one of the men. James Royston, I think his name was.'

The one that Amos had told him had died of a drugs overdose.

'She was Royston's girlfriend?' Amos had said not. Who did Horton believe? Neither of them.

'Possibly. It was a long time ago. I was only at the London School of Economics because I'd been visiting a friend. I was at Cambridge. I came down because I thought it would be fun. Tragically Tim died in a motorbike accident, couldn't have been very long after that picture was taken.'

'Was Jennifer working for you?'

Ames raised his eyebrows. 'I was a student.'

'Why did she disappear?'

'I didn't know she had.'

Horton's fists balled. This man had fucked up his childhood. He'd like to beat the shit out of him because he doubted he'd ever get the truth from those supercilious lips. He half rose when a voice hailed him.

'I didn't realize you were here, sir.'

Horton spun round to find Agent Harriet Ames behind him. She recoiled at the expression on his face. Her anxious eyes flicked to her father and back to him.

'I'm sorry,' she stammered. 'I'm interrupting something.'

Horton rose and stuffed the photograph in his pocket. Tightly he said, 'No. We've finished. For now.' He threw a final glance at Lord Ames and left.

Outside he stepped across to the promenade and watched the yachts in the breeze with their white and coloured sails. He took a deep breath and unfurled his fists. Would she follow him out here? Did he want her to? Would her father tell her who he worked for? Would he tell her about Jennifer Horton and how the security services had used her and then allowed her to die? But maybe Agent Harriet Ames already knew it, or at least part of the sordid tale.

Had the security services left his mother to the ministrations of an evil man they'd been watching and who they wanted to do their dirty work for them, Zeus, just as they had done with Bradley Marshall? Had Jennifer been killed by Zeus because she knew too much, just as Erica Leyton had been killed by Bradley Marshall, both casualties of their sick machinations?

And where did DCS Sawyer of the Intelligence Directorate and his mission to find the master criminal Zeus fit into all this? Did Sawyer know as much as he, Horton, now did, which wasn't very much? Did Sawyer know about Lord Ames' involvement? Should he pool resources with him?

Horton turned and began walking through the crowds of people, not seeing their faces or hearing their chatter. His head was spinning; his body ached with tension and frustration. Thoughts swirled around his mind like the tide around the chain ferry as it trundled its way across the narrow stretch of the Medina. He thought over what he'd learned and what there was still to learn about Jennifer's disappearance.

He walked through the streets of East Cowes to the marina, seeing nothing, trying to feel nothing, his mind rapidly working. Discounting Professor Thurstan Madeley and Quentin Amos, because they'd been instructed what to tell him, there were four men who knew what had happened to Jennifer Horton: the remaining two men in the photograph, plus Edward Ballard, who had given him the photograph, and Lord Ames. And if they wouldn't tell him then he'd find someone who would. He'd also find the truth behind the deaths of three of those men in the photograph. And he didn't think he'd be given a great deal of time to do so.

As he drew level with his yacht, he reached a decision. There was, after all, only one to make, and it was one that he knew would please DCI Bliss. With his mind made up, he climbed on his boat and made ready to sail.

THE END

ACKNOWLEDGEMENTS

With grateful thanks to Portsmouth Historic Dockyard and the National Museum of the Royal Navy (Portsmouth) and in particular to Rowannah Martin-Cottee and Heather Johnson for their patience and willingness to answer my numerous questions. Also my thanks to Dr Gordon Watson of the Institute of Marine Sciences, School of Biological Sciences, University of Portsmouth for his invaluable help.